THE MAN
WHO FELL FROM
THE SKY

THE MAN
WHO FELL FROM
THE SKY

MARGARET COEL

BERKLEY PRIME CRIME, NEW YORK

An imprint of Penguin Random House LLC
375 Hudson Street, New York, New York 10014

This book is an original publication of the Berkley Publishing Group.

Library of Congress Cataloging-in-Publication Data

Coel, Margaret, 1937–
The man who fell from the sky / Margaret Coel.—First edition.
pages ; cm
ISBN 978-0-425-28030-0
1. O'Malley, John (Fictitious character)—Fiction.   2. Holden, Vicky (Fictitious character)—Fiction.
3. Wind River Indian Reservation (Wyo.)—Fiction.   I. Title.
PS3553.O347M36   2015
813'.54—dc23   2015012397

FIRST EDITION: September 2015

PRINTED IN THE UNITED STATES OF AMERICA

10 9 8 7 6 5 4 3 2 1

Cover illustration by Tony Greco & Associates Inc.
Cover design by Lesley Worrell.

Penguin
Random
House

*For Carl Schneider, my longtime friend and
fount of useful information, suggestions,
wit, wisdom, and encouragement.*

ACKNOWLEDGMENTS

My deep gratitude to all those who were willing to help me with various aspects of this book and who took the time to read all or parts of the manuscript and make suggestions that greatly improved the story: In Fremont County, Mark Stratmoen, coroner; Ed McAuslan, former coroner; Virginia and Jim Sutter, members of the Arapaho Tribe; and Todd Dawson, special agent, FBI. In Boulder, Sheila Carrigan, Beverly Carrigan, Karen Gilleland, Carl Schneider, John Tracy, and, as always, my husband, George Coel. Any errors that may have crept into this novel are mine, and certainly not theirs.

We shall surely be put again with our friends. E'yahe'eye!

*—The Ghost-Dance Religion and the Sioux
Outbreak of 1890, James Mooney*

THE MAN
WHO FELL FROM
THE SKY

1

THE NARROW DIRT road clung to the mountainside between the granite peaks jutting overhead and the drop-off into the valley. Ponderosas, scrub brush, and scruffy undergrowth looked fat and green after the spring rain, greener than Alan Fergus remembered the Wind River range ever looking. It was the fourth Friday in May. The foliage wouldn't turn gray and dusty until the summer heat set in. Tommy had been locked down in a classroom about as long as any twelve-year-old boy could stand, and since Tommy had a day off from school, they had made plans for a fishing trip. He and the boy rose early, the blue-black sky striped in red and pink and white, ate what Alan called a hearty breakfast, oatmeal that would stick to their ribs, and spent an hour in the garage packing up the fishing gear. *Quiet, quiet*, he had reminded the boy. *Don't wake Mom. Let her sleep in for once.* Usually Sarah was the first one up. A good hot breakfast on the kitchen table before she and Alan drove to the body shop and Tommy ran the half block to catch the school bus.

It had taken some work to convince Eton to come in early and handle the front counter until Sarah arrived. All the cajoling and promises of extra time off next week had been worth it. A perfect day to escape, father and son, man-to-man. Tommy, almost grown now, getting so tall. They hadn't taken enough special times together, and before he knew it, Tommy would be gone. Off to some college, most likely. Maybe Laramie. He was a good student. A little restless, but what boy wasn't restless? He had been restless, and his father had taken him to Frye Lake to fish, and it had made all the difference. Sucked the restless, fidgety parts right out of him. Alan had backed out of the driveway this morning as the white-hot sun burst like the afterglow of fireworks in the eastern sky.

Tommy seemed pleased with the change in routine. Bouncing on the seat to whatever music blasted in his earphones, gawking this way and that, pointing out a hawk that lay flat out in the sky, guessing how many trout they would bag today. A dozen, two dozen. *Our limit, for sure.*

Yeah, our limit, Alan agreed.

The road narrowed as it started into a curve. Alan kept the pickup as close to the middle as he dared. The edge could be moist and soft. Theirs wouldn't be the first pickup to slide down the mountainside. He drove slowly, in and out of wide stripes of shadows, and listened for an oncoming vehicle. If he listened hard, his dad had taught him, he would hear a vehicle before he saw it. Although he wasn't sure what he would do. Slam on the brake and back up, search frantically for a wider place in the road in which to pull over.

"Keep your fingers crossed," he said as he plunged into the curve.

"Keep my fingers crossed?"

"That the fish are biting. Should be hungry with the rain. Seen the lake yet?"

Tommy leaned toward the windshield and stared past the drop-off, eager eyes searching for a glimpse of shimmering blue water. The wide curve straightened into a narrow brown road that glowed in the sunlight.

"There it is." The boy's excitement was contagious. First sight of the fishing hole was always exciting, filled with expectations and promises. Tommy tapped the windshield. "Down there. We're getting close."

Alan stole a sideways look. Bull Lake spread below, meandering through the valley, reflections of ponderosas dancing on the blue surface. Another couple of curves, and the road would empty into a long straight shot down to the lake. They'd be there in ten minutes.

"Looks like another fisherman."

"Really? So early in the season?" Alan had been counting on having the lake all to themselves. Nobody else to worry about, no thumping music and portable grills, makeshift picnic tables, lawn chairs, and kids running around, hollering and scaring off the fish. Through an alley between the trees, he spotted the truck parked close to the narrow strip of land where he was planning to stop. He swallowed back the disappointment. There was a good shelf there they could wade onto and cast into deep water where the fish were usually biting. The shelf disappeared on either side of the truck, but if he drove past, he might be able to pick it up again. Part of the fun of fishing for Tommy was the wading, the walking into the water, as if he were walking on the water.

Alan took the last couple of curves, listening for an oncoming vehicle, and headed down onto the straight road that cut through willows and tangled brush along the lakefront. He could see the truck parked ahead, a grayish monster with an extended cab and a metal box in the back. It was nosed toward the lake, water lapping the shore a few feet away. The tailgate stuck out into the road, and Alan had to slow to a crawl to get around it without slipping into the willows.

"Dad! He's in the water."

Alan worked his way around the truck before looking back. My God! A large body—a man's body—bobbing in the water on the far side of the truck. He let the pickup roll a little farther ahead, wanting to spare Tommy another view of the dead man. "I'll go have a look." The pickup jerked to a stop. "Stay here, you understand?"

The boy looked scared, as if he might start crying. He nodded slowly, but he didn't say anything.

Alan got out and slammed the door. The sound reverberated in the crisp, clear air. He glanced back as he made his way through the marshy undergrowth toward the body. Tommy was up on his knees, looking out the rear window, eyes as big as black marbles. He couldn't save the boy from everything. Not from this view of death.

The body rolled and swayed facedown in the water, the back of a dark blue padded vest bulging, arms outstretched, as if the dead man might be attempting to float. The blue jeans looked like heavy weights pulling the legs down. There was an odd feeling of acceptance that clung to the body, as if the man had walked onto the shelf, stumbled, and been unable to get up, so he had settled in and waited for death. Clumps of black hair lifted off a pinkish scalp dotted with black freckles and moles. Alan reached down, then pulled his hand away. What sense did it make to turn the body over? The man was dead, and the look of his face would only burn itself into Alan's retinas. Besides, whatever might have happened, no investigator would appreciate his tampering with the body. He looked around, realizing he may have already interfered by walking over here.

He hurried back to the pickup, punching at his cell, willing it to come to life. No service. No service. The boy was still on his knees, looking out the back window, when Alan slid behind the steering wheel. He turned the ignition and drove forward. There were camping spaces on the other side of the road ahead where he could turn around.

"We're leaving him?"

"I'm afraid he's dead, son. There's nothing we can do for him. We have to report this."

"You think he came up here to fish and fell into the water?"

"I don't know." Alan was thinking he hadn't seen any fishing poles or tackle box in the truck bed.

He took a right toward a camping space and maneuvered the pickup through several tight turns until they were headed back toward the body and the truck hanging over the road. No telling how far he would have to drive up the mountain before the cell phone tapped into a tower somewhere. He looked sideways at Tommy, who was still fighting back tears.

"I'll make it up to you, son."

"I don't ever want to come here again," the boy said.

2

RUTH WALKING BEAR might have been hosting a party. Darting among the Arapahos in the living room, hoisting a metal coffeepot, pulling orange-red lips into a smile around tiny teeth, searching with dark eyes for the next empty mug. "More coffee? Cake? Cookies? Casseroles. Eat up. Eat up." The silver embroidery on her red, Western-style blouse flashed as she moved about. Her flip-flops squished on the vinyl floor. She had curly black hair tinted red, and the curls sprang free from beaded clips like feathers in a headdress. Odors of fried meat, strong coffee, and warm cookies wafted from the kitchen, where women were arranging trays of food and setting out stacks of paper plates. Ruth stopped before one of the elders. "Why, Grandfather, your cup is empty."

Vicky Holden kept an eye on the woman. Something forced and terrified about her. In another life, she and Ruth had attended St. Francis School together. Kids, climbing onto the school bus and crossing the reservation in blizzards and wind and rolling dust.

Ruth had exuded confidence, as if she were driving the bus, in control of the weather, but Vicky had suspected even then that the confidence was a mask, like the party face she wore now. During the years Vicky had been married to Ben Holden, she often ran into Ruth at the powwows and ceremonies. They would chat and gossip—two women together. But Vicky had left Ben and that old life, gone to Denver, and become a lawyer. Everything was different when she returned, or was it just that she was different? It seemed that Ruth and the other women had gone away, set their moccasins on the traditional path, as the grandmothers said, and she had been unable to follow.

Vicky tried to excuse herself from a short, gray-haired woman who claimed she had also gone to St. Francis School, although Vicky had no memory of her. The woman had been peppering her with questions. What had she heard about Robert's death? "People don't fall into a lake and die. Must've been pushed, right? Who might have done it? What does the coroner say?" For some reason, the woman—what was her name? Cathy?— assumed that because Vicky practiced law in Lander, she was part of the conversations in the legal corridors of the white world.

Vicky had dodged the questions. She didn't know the answers, but Cathy, like every other woman on the rez, probably knew quite a lot or thought she did. The women never missed a gathering. They looked after the elders, cared for one another's kids. They lived by the moccasin telegraph and took pride in staying con- nected. What Cathy wanted from her was news to pass on. But the questions had only reinforced Vicky's feeling of being an outsider among her own people. Woman Alone, the grandmothers called her. The Indian lawyer their relatives or friends went to when they got into trouble, but not one of them.

It took several tries before Vicky managed to break free. She made her way through the conversations buzzing about the room and stopped next to Ruth, who was refilling another cup of coffee. "Wouldn't you like to rest awhile?" Vicky nodded toward the hallway that led to the bedrooms. Most of the houses on the rez were the same Federal style with living room and kitchen on one side, a couple of bedrooms and a bath on the other.

"I don't need to rest, and I certainly don't need a lawyer." Ruth struggled to keep the orange-red smile in place. "Robert's dead and I have to go on the way he would expect me to, so that's what I'm doing. You need some coffee?" She started to turn toward the kitchen and the stack of Styrofoam cups visible at the end of the counter.

"No, thank you." Vicky set her hand on the woman's arm. She could feel the tremors rising from somewhere deep inside. "Won't you at least sit down. I can pour the refills." She stretched out her hand to take the coffeepot, but Ruth stood motionless, her eyes on the man coming through the front door.

"Ah, Father John," she said, as if she were expecting someone else. Then she handed the coffeepot to Vicky and started across the room. Conversations started to dissolve, like the wind dying down.

Vicky watched the little crowd surge around the tall, redheaded man inside the door, reach for his hand, pat his arm. He had on blue jeans and a blue plaid shirt. The brim of a tan cowboy hat was curled in his fist against his thigh. It had been a long while since she had seen John O'Malley, the mission priest at St. Francis. She thought of the intervals between their meetings not in days or weeks or months, but in seasons. The fall, the holidays and winter, the spring. He looked fit, strong and straight, yet different somehow. A few more gray hairs at his temples, more fine lines around his eyes. He reached for Ruth and drew her toward him. In the quiet that engulfed the living room, Vicky heard him say how sorry he was. She was thinking that everyone on the rez had come to love this white man who, one day, had shown up among them.

Ruth was leaning against his chest, her red blouse with the shiny embroidery stretched across her spine, shoulders rising and falling as she gulped for air. Vicky walked over and placed a hand on the woman's back, conscious of John O'Malley's eyes on her. Finally she looked up and met his gaze. "She's been holding it in. It's a terrible blow, losing your husband like that."

The room remained quiet, as if a show were going on that held the audience spellbound. Vicky could feel the eyes boring into them, three people huddled together. And the calmness that emanated from John O'Malley, a man accustomed to such situations. So many people he had comforted on the rez, so many inexplicable deaths. They had worked together since he came to the mission almost ten years ago. Trying to help her people: the alcohol and drug addicts, the abused women and neglected children, the scared and lonely warriors facing charges for crimes they hadn't committed.

"I need fresh air." Ruth lifted her head and dabbed at her eyes with a handkerchief that, Vicky suspected, he had handed to her.

"I set up some lawn chairs out back." Dallas Spotted Deer stepped over. Related to the Walking Bear family, one of Robert's cousins, if Vicky remembered correctly. Everyone on the rez was related somehow, distant cousins of distant cousins, in-laws two or three times removed. Dallas had been at St. Francis School when she and Ruth were there. A middle-aged man now with red and blue ribbons woven into black braids that hung down the front of his yellow shirt, and a serious, pockmarked face.

John O'Malley nodded a thank-you to the man as they started across the living room. Past the sympathy-filled faces, past the

kitchen counters piled with food, past the women drawing themselves back to make room. A grandmother darted ahead and opened
the door. They stepped out onto the stoop and down the three
wooden steps, John O'Malley holding on to Ruth's arm, guiding
her toward a pair of lawn chairs. He handed her into one and motioned Vicky into the other. Then he found another chair stacked
against the house and shook it open as he brought it over. He sat
down across from them.

"I'm sorry for breaking down like that, Father." Ruth looked
sideways. A barbed-wire fence ran between the bare-dirt yard and
the pasture where two horses grazed on clumps of grass. The
brown hills traced with green rose in the distance against a blue-
white sky. She slipped off the flip-flops, tucked her feet under her,
and kneaded at the fabric of her jeans skirt as if it were dough.

"You don't always have to be strong," John O'Malley told her.

Vicky looked away. She tried not to smile. There were times in
the past when he had told her the same thing.

"I wasn't expecting Robert to die," Ruth said. "When the fed
knocked on the door and told me Robert had been found in the
lake, I told him there must be some mistake. He said that Alan
Fergus, runs a body shop in Lander, found Robert's body." She
lifted her shoulders and dropped them in a defeated shrug. "The
moccasin telegraph must've gotten the news before I did. Before I
knew it, all kinds of people were at my door."

Mostly related to Robert, Vicky was thinking. A few distant
relatives of Ruth's, but everyone close to her had died or moved
away years ago. And now—a new thought breaking through—
with Robert gone, Ruth would be almost as alone as she was.

"All the women brought food," Ruth was saying. "It's like they
make a lot of food and wait for something terrible to happen." She

dabbed the wadded handkerchief at her eyes again. "The worst part is what they're saying."

"What do you mean?" Vicky said.

"If they aren't saying it, they're thinking it." A stream of tears and black mascara ran down the woman's cheeks. She pulled at the handkerchief in her hands without making an effort to wipe away the moisture. "Stories go around faster than lightning."

"What stories, Ruth?" John O'Malley leaned toward her. "Tell us."

"The fed started it, asking stupid questions. Made me sick to my stomach." John O'Malley was quiet. Patient, Vicky thought, unbelievably patient. He had once told her he had learned patience from the Arapahos, learned to sit and wait while people ordered their thoughts and decided whether he was trustworthy enough to give their thoughts to him. She, on the other hand, had learned impatience from years in the white world, college, law school, the years in a big law firm followed by her own small firm. Learned to jump up, be quick, be alert, never let down her guard. Pace the floor to order her own thoughts; rise in the courtroom: *Objection!*

Ruth unfolded her legs, wiggled her feet into the flip-flops, and shifted forward on her chair, pulling at the handkerchief in her hands. A pair of reddish curls hung loosely along her neck. She was struggling to say something, lips forming and reforming the words. Finally she said, "The fed wanted to know if Robert was depressed. Did he ever talk about taking his life? Had he ever tried to take his life? If he did decide to take his life, how do I think he might have gone about it? What was he saying? Robert walked into the lake, laid down, and died?"

She squeezed her eyes shut, as if she might squeeze out more tears. Then she tossed her head toward the pasture. "He had the ranch. Meant the world to him. Maybe it's a nothing ranch, but we had meat on the table and Robert picked up jobs with the highway department every summer, and I got my job at the dental office. The Creator never saw fit to give us children, but Robert said we'd be okay, just the two of us." She was staring out at the pasture. The breeze riffled the manes of the horses. "I'd say, anybody depressed around here, it was me. Same old, same old every day. No way out. Nothing ever changing. But I never thought he'd leave me like this."

Vicky caught John O'Malley's eye for a second. All she knew about Robert's death had come over the moccasin telegraph. First, to Annie, her secretary. Then Annie had brought it to her. But maybe there was more, facts the telegraph hadn't yet picked up. She could read the same thought in John's face.

He took one of Ruth's hands in his own and waited until she turned back to him. "Nobody knows yet what happened."

"The coroner will order an autopsy and issue a report." Vicky tried to match John O'Malley's calm, assuring tone. "We'll know the truth then." She was thinking the report could take several weeks.

"That's not all the questions the fed asked. Robert have any enemies? Altercations with friends or strangers? Anybody like to see him dead?"

"The fed has to look at every possibility." Vicky was thinking that the local FBI agent, Ted Gianelli, was a thorough investigator. No stone would be left unturned. Eventually Ruth would appreciate his thoroughness.

"Nothing would have happened if Cutter had been with him." Ruth turned toward Vicky. "You remember Jimmy Walking Bear? He went to St. Francis School with us. Got the name Cutter on a

Texas ranch, where he was the best at cutting out cattle during roundup."

Vicky tried for the third time this afternoon to reach back to the years at St. Francis School, all the brown-faced, black-haired kids bent over papers and books at desks arranged in perfect rows, and a nun—Sister Mary Rita, perhaps—or one of the priests explaining a mathematical problem, writing assignments on the blackboard, rapping a ruler on the desk to stop the giggling in the back of the classroom. There were several priests at the mission who taught classes then. Good teachers, the Jesuits. She tried to picture a boy named Jimmy Walking Bear, but all the gangly, pimply boys blurred in her mind.

"I'm afraid I don't remember him," she said.

Ruth waved one hand, as if she were shooing off a mosquito. "Robert's cousin. Two or three times removed, but still a relative. Anyway when Cutter was about eleven, his father packed up the family and moved to Oklahoma. So Cutter grew up not knowing his own people, where he came from. He came back to the rez a couple months ago looking for family. First thing he did was find Robert. They formed a real tight bond. I wish Robert had taken him hunting, but Robert never took anybody hunting . . ."

"Hunting?"

Ruth gave a small smile of memory, unlike the fake, plastered smile she had worn earlier. "Treasure. Robert was hunting treasure. Long as I've known him, he talked about finding the treasure Butch Cassidy buried up in the mountains around Bull Lake when he was hiding out here after a robbery. Robert heard the stories when he was a kid and they clamped on to him, wouldn't let him go. It was his hobby, hunting for that treasure. He worked all week on the highway, laying down asphalt in the hot sun, and on Friday he'd head up into the mountains where it was cool and he could relax and hunt for treasure. He liked to go alone, be by himself for a few days. I never knew for certain when he would come home. If he was onto something, he'd camp up there and keep working all weekend. So I wasn't worried when he didn't come home last night. I figured he thought he found something."

She stopped and bit at her lip a moment. "I never expected him to find treasure. If you want to know the truth, neither did Robert. It was the looking that was fun. Until . . ." She left off again and squinted into space, trying to fix a memory. "When his grandfather Luther died, Robert found a leather case in the old man's barn. Inside was a map. Well, Robert got real excited. Said Butch Cassidy left a map behind, just like Luther always said. With all those movie people on the rez making a documentary about Butch Cassidy, Robert figured there'd be a stampede of people hunting for Butch's treasure. So he took time off his job and went up into the mountains every day. Said he was getting close." She shook her head and rolled her eyes. "He was always getting close."

The screened door opened and people began to flow onto the stoop, down the steps, and across the yard, heading for the lone cottonwood tree and the shade splashed over the dirt. Several women hovered over Ruth, wanting to know how she was doing. Was there anything they could get her?

"I should see about the coffee." Ruth jumped to her feet.

"We'll take care of it." The women wheeled about and started back up the steps. The screened door slammed behind them.

"I have to check on the elders." The lawn chair toppled over as Ruth started past.

Father John stood up. "We'll come with you."

He was so tall, Vicky was thinking as she stood next to him.

She barely reached the top of his shoulder. He looked slim and fit, yet he filled so much space.

"I must be strong," Ruth was muttering under her breath as she started for the house. "I must show them I am strong."

Vicky followed Ruth up the steps and into the kitchen, conscious of the sound of John O'Malley's footsteps behind her.

3

TRAFFIC HAD COME to a dead stop on Ethete Road. The asphalt glowed in the afternoon sun, and dust whirled about the line of vehicles ahead. Father John pulled in behind a white SUV. The minute he stopped, the heat started to accumulate inside the cab of the old Toyota pickup. The prologue to *Pagliacci* blared from the CD player on the seat beside him. It was the last week in May, the Moon When the Ponies Shed Their Shaggy Hair, as the Arapahos marked the passing time. The weather already turning warm. He shuddered to think of how far up the thermometer the temperature might crawl in July.

He got out and tried to see past the SUV. What looked like a bunch of cowboys came galloping across the prairie on the right, raising great billows of dust that hung like brown clouds against the sky. Arranged alongside the riders were cameras on black tripods and, behind the cameras, groups of men and women. Other cameramen in Jeeps followed the horses, holding out cameras. A row of pickups stood at the edge of the road. Beyond the pickups, what looked like a village sprang out of the prairie: a circle of campers, RVs, more pickups.

He got back inside the Toyota, turned up the CD player, and tapped his fingers on the steering wheel. So this was where the Butch Cassidy documentary was being filmed today. Cowboys galloping at full speed, probably portraying the getaway after Butch Cassidy and the Sundance Kid and the rest of the Wild Bunch had robbed a bank or a train. Now the cowboys rode back the way they had come, moving at a slower trot, which, he suspected, meant they would film the scene again. He drummed his fingers harder and wished he had paid attention to the list of filming sites in the *Gazette.* He considered turning around and taking the long way back to Seventeen-Mile Road and the mission, but he had pulled in close to the SUV and a blue pickup had pulled in behind him. It would take some maneuvering to turn around. He decided to wait. One more getaway and maybe the road would open up. The prologue of the opera came to a crashing end. He opened the door to let in more air, but it was hot air, all of it.

He thought of Ruth. She would need to summon strength for the days and months ahead, maybe the years. He had counseled so many people who had lost their life partners, trying to help them find the way forward. But what did he know? He tried to imagine what it would be like to lose someone who was a part of yourself. Like losing an arm. Sometimes, when he was going on about trusting in God, taking one day at a time, and all the other platitudes, he wondered how any of it could ever help.

For an instant, he let the thoughts of Vicky circling the edges of his mind come into focus. There had been times when she had been close to death, and he remembered the icy grip that had taken hold of him. He wondered how he would have managed if, in fact, she were no longer part of the world. He pushed the thought away. Seeing her today had been reassuring and comforting, even in a house of grief.

He got out again and stretched. The cowboys were galloping over the prairie, but this time other cowboys galloped behind, brandishing guns. A series of pops split the air. Lawmen after Cassidy and his gang. But did they ever catch up with him? He tried to remember the bits and pieces he had read about the Wild Bunch, the movie he had watched years ago. Who knew if the stories were based on historical fact? He realized another cowboy was coming along the line of vehicles, talking to the drivers. He waited as the man stepped back from the SUV and started toward him.

"Sorry for the inconvenience." The cowboy had pale blue eyes and sun-reddened skin. "Director wants one more shot." He gestured toward the prairie and the riders reining horses into a line. "Always a danger the horses might break away and run across the road, so tribal police say we have to keep the roads clear. Give us a few more minutes."

The man had started for the pickup behind when he turned back. "Say, you wouldn't be that mission priest we've heard about."

"I don't know what you may have heard, but I'm Father John O'Malley, pastor at St. Francis."

"The director would like a word with you." He glanced over at the horses again. "Todd Paxton. Looks like he'll be tied up the rest of the day. Could he give you a call?"

Father John pulled out the little notebook and pen he kept in his shirt pocket, wrote on the top page both the mission telephone number and that of his cell phone, and handed it to the cowboy.

"Todd thinks you might be able to help us out." He gave a nod of appreciation and walked back to the driver's window of the blue pickup.

Father John slid behind the steering wheel. He wondered how much help he could be to the director of a documentary film on Butch Cassidy. About as much help as he had been to Ruth.

ANOTHER TWENTY MINUTES passed, the opera well into Act I, *Don, din, don, din,* and the vehicles ahead started forward. Father John pressed lightly on the accelerator as the old pickup growled and shook and finally settled into twenty miles an hour. Ahead actors in cowboy hats milled about; horses grazed on sparse outcroppings of grass. Like a giant machine, the crowd started rolling in the direction of a blue and white truck with a metal curtain raised on one side, revealing what looked like a counter in a diner.

Finally he was past the movie site, the pickup shuddering as it picked up speed, the SUV already far ahead, glinting in the sun. He turned onto Blue Sky Highway and picked up Seventeen-Mile Road heading east, thinking about Butch Cassidy and the Wild Bunch and what the reservation must have looked like more than a hundred years ago. The same endless stretch of prairie, the same brown foothills stretched low on the western horizon, probably some of the same log cabins around the rez. The same feeling, he suspected, of openness, expansion and—what was it? Freedom.

The blue billboard with St. Francis Mission in large, white letters loomed over the road ahead. He slowed past the billboard and turned into the tunnel of cottonwoods. Branches scraped the top of the pickup; white downy fluff painted the road. He could feel the rear tires slipping, and he slowed down. He had been trying to forget that the tires were bald. No money this month for replacements. He would have to remember to drive carefully.

He turned onto Circle Drive, the mission all around him. On the west, the redbrick residence; at the far end of the circle, the gray stone school building he had turned into the Arapaho Museum; and lined up to the east, the white stucco church decorated with bright red, yellow, and blue geometric symbols of the Arapaho—lines for the path of life, triangles for the buffalo, tipis for the people—the dirt road that led to Eagle Hall and the guesthouse, and on the other side of the road, the large two-story yellow stucco administration building sheltering among the cottonwoods that crept away from the tunnel. Bishop Harry stood at the foot of the concrete steps tossing a Frisbee to Walks-On. The dog leapt on his three legs through the tall grass in the center of Circle Drive, then paddled back like a swimmer pushing through the waves. He started for the bishop, pivoted on his single hind leg, and came at a full run toward the pickup. Father John stepped on the brakes. A spray of gravel and dirt peppered the pickup's rear end. He leaned across the CD player, opened the passenger door, and helped the dog crawl onto the seat, the Frisbee still clenched in his jaws. He closed the door and, running his hand over the dog's soft coat, drove to the front of the administration building, and pulled in next to the bishop.

Bishop Harry Coughlin, gray hair going white, pale blue eyes, a permanent band of sunburn across his nose and cheeks, walked over to the pickup and opened the door. "You interrupted a good game of Frisbee just when I was winning."

"Against Walks-On?" Father John turned off the opera, got out of the pickup, and waited for the dog to lumber across the seat and jump down. He closed the door. He was thinking that this old man—this competitive Frisbee player—had to be close to eighty years old, but he had never asked the bishop's age. The bishop seemed healthy and strong despite the two heart attacks and surgeries that had sent him to St. Francis, supposedly to rest. Another subject Father John never brought up. The bishop had spent thirty years looking after thousands of Catholics in Patna, India, and on the first day he arrived at the mission he had made it clear he did not know how to rest and would die if he tried. As simple as that. Father John had cleared out the back office, occupied at various times by various assistants. A parishioner donated a used laptop, and Father John found one of the kids on the Eagles, the baseball team he coached, to set it up. The bishop had settled in.

"You missed a visitor," the bishop said as he led the way up the concrete steps. "Maris Reynolds. I told her to check back later." He turned toward the muffled sound of an engine in the cottonwood tunnel, and Father John followed his gaze. "I believe your visitor may be returning."

Father John walked back down the steps to where Walks-On stood shaking the Frisbee, eyes lit with expectation. He waited until the pink Cadillac sedan that looked as if it had materialized out of a retrospective film on American cultural icons pulled in next to the Toyota. Then he threw the Frisbee into the grass and watched Walks-On bound past the elderly woman emerging from behind the steering wheel. He walked over and held the door as Maris Reynolds straightened herself to her full six-foot height and patted her blue-flowered dress around her hips. A large red bag hung off one arm.

"Always nice to see you," Father John said.

"Likewise, I'm sure. Is there somewhere quiet we can talk?"

"It's pretty quiet everywhere." The mission, the entire reservation—

the quiet of open spaces. From his first day at St. Francis, he had been drawn into the immense solitude.

"I like the shade on a warm day like this. If it is all the same to you . . ." The woman gestured with the red bag toward the picnic table and benches under a cottonwood in front of the church, then walked around the car and started along the gravel road.

Father John fell in beside her. "How about something cool to drink? Iced tea? Lemonade?" He was pretty sure he'd seen Elena place pitchers of both in the refrigerator this morning.

"No, thank you. I am perfectly comfortable." The woman stepped into a circle of shade and sat down on the bench facing the table, as if she were positioning herself to play a piano concerto.

Father John sat across from her. "What can I do for you?"

"For once, you are wrong, Father." She fixed him with a hard gaze, but she was smiling. "The question is, what might I do for you? I am going to come straight to the point," she said, opening her bag and slipping out a white, letter-sized envelope. "I've never gone for circling the point with a lot of trivia about the weather and the kids' health and everything else the Arapahos use to take up time. My philosophy is: state your business and get on with it."

"A useful philosophy." Father John smiled. He was accustomed to the polite preliminaries that ensued before any conversation with an Arapaho, the way of connecting with another human being. Maris Reynolds lived on a ranch near Dubois, surrounded by other ranches, all owned by whites.

She opened the envelope and tipped out a smaller envelope, which she pushed across the table. "I have brought you a gift," she said. "I believe the Arapahos would call this a double gift. I had the first pleasure of receiving these tickets to the Central City Opera from my son in Denver. Since I have no intention of spending two days driving to and from Denver to attend an opera, I have the second pleasure of giving this gift to you."

"That's very kind." Father John opened the small envelope and glanced at the tickets. *Rigoletto*. August. Orchestra seats. It had been years since he had seen an opera. Years since he had listened to a live orchestra, to voices that soared like the voices of angels. Years since he had lost himself in the music, the elaborate costumes, the settings. All of it bigger than life, magical.

"I imagine your son might have a couple of friends who would like the tickets."

"Poppycock." Maris thumped her knuckles on the table.

"Poppycock?"

"Yes. A very good word. Derisive and dismissive. I believe our culture is much diminished by forgetting such useful and exacting words. I have made it my business to use such words at every opportunity in order to bring them back into general usage. Now that you've been reminded of *poppycock*, I hope you will pass it on to others who will also pass it on. Within a short time, it will be heard everywhere."

Father John smiled. "I wish you luck."

"Thank you." The woman looked as serious as if he had just wished her luck on a long journey. "I believe you are avoiding the tickets."

"It's very generous of you." Father John slid the small envelope inside his shirt pocket. He could imagine the orchestra playing the prelude and the opening notes of "Questa o quella," and the hush falling over the theater as the curtains parted. "I'd like very much to go to the opera . . ."

"That settles it. You will go."

"I wish it were that easy."

"Of course it is. You must find a way." She swung her legs around the end of the bench and pulled herself upright. "I must be going. I'll have to take a roundabout way home to avoid that foolish film crew that has been closing roads everywhere."

Father John stood up and walked the woman along the graveled road to the pink Cadillac. She stopped at the driver's door and waited for him to open it. "He was a good man, Butch Cassidy. Never killed anybody in his years of outlawing. I hope the documentary will reflect the truth."

Gathering the blue flowery skirt around her, she folded herself behind the steering wheel. "George Cassidy is how he was known in these parts. He was a good friend to my grandfather."

"How did your grandfather know him?" Father John leaned against the edge of the door, reluctant to shut it and send her on her way.

"Cassidy owned the ranch next to ours. About 1890, I believe, during a time when he tried to leave the outlaw life behind. When my grandfather fell off a horse and broke his leg, Cassidy jumped in and worked both ranches, Grandfather's and his own. Kept Grandfather from losing everything to the no-good banks, vultures waiting for ranchers to fail so they could snap up the land. Well, Cassidy made sure that didn't happen. Strange things did happen though, if the stories in my family are to be believed. Cassidy was a genius with horses. He could talk to them and they talked back to him, told him all kinds of things about the approaching storms, the condition of the trails in the county, the best pastures. My father said that his father told him how Cassidy's ranch always had a fresh supply of fine, healthy horses. Naturally Grandfather assumed he bought them or traded for them." She gave a little gurgling noise that erupted in her throat in imitation of laughter. "He found out later Cassidy also had a genius for rustling horses. He could lasso a horse and lead it away right past the owner. Next thing Grandfather knew, his neighbor wasn't around anymore. The ranch house and all the buildings were vacant. He heard Cassidy had been convicted of stealing a horse and was on his way to prison in Laramie." She turned and blinked up at him. "I guess in the end he couldn't stop going down the outlaw path. Doesn't mean he was a bad man. He shared his loot with the less fortunate."

Maris glanced at the door, and Father John shut it. He leaned into the open window. "Did you ever hear that he buried treasure in the mountains?"

"Hah!" She gave a bark of laughter. "Stories of buried loot have been floating around for decades. More than one fool has lost his life clumping around the mountains, falling off ridges, sliding down steep, rocky slopes . . ." She stopped and turned sideways, still staring up at him, eyes wide in comprehension. "Don't tell me that's what happened to Robert Walking Bear. Is that why he was in the mountains alone and managed to wade into the lake and drown? Thought he'd find Cassidy's buried loot in the lake, did he?"

"I don't know."

"Cassidy himself couldn't find the loot." She shook her head and smiled to herself. "Oh, he came back to look for it, all right, despite all that poppycock about him getting killed in a shoot-out in Bolivia. In 1934, he was right here, visiting friends on the rez and ranchers hereabouts. Took a camping trip with friends into the mountains to search for the box of gold coins he had buried. My father was a young man. He went along as a guide. He never forgot Butch Cassidy." She shrugged and let out a long sigh of surrender. "I don't expect film people to get it right. They never do. I really must be going." She jammed the key into the ignition and jiggled it back and forth until the engine sputtered into life. Then she backed into Circle Drive and gave a little wave. "Enjoy the opera," she called as the Cadillac shot forward into the cotton-wood tunnel, gravel and white fluff dancing behind the wheels.

4

June 2, 1899

JESSE HEARD THE beat of horses' hooves before she did, but his hearing had always been keener than hers. He could hear a bird fall from its nest. They had just sat down to the stew she had prepared for dinner. Steam rose out of the pottery bowls; the smells of hot meat and broth filling the log cabin. Anthony, the hired hand Jesse had taken on a month ago, eyed the bowls with anticipation after helping Jesse mend fences all day.

"We have visitors." Jesse rose out of his chair in a quick, fluid motion, as if he were sliding off the back of a bronco. He went over to the rack of guns by the front door, pulled out the Springfield, and handed it to Mary. Then he took the Winchester for himself. Glancing over one shoulder, he told Anthony to watch the back door. A holstered revolver bumped against the man's hip as he headed to the kitchen. They had been through this before. Out on a ranch in the middle of the Wyoming prairie with nothing but the infernal wind, blizzards that whitened the earth in winter, sun that seared and dried the hay and left the cattle and horses desperate for water in the summer, and the nearest neighbors a good ten miles away. Strangers were sometimes welcome. Different faces, good stories, news from the outside world. It depended on the strangers who happened to find the dirt road to the cabin.

Jesse stepped outside and crossed the porch, his boots quiet as moccasins. He moved into the shadows away from the dim beam of light from the front window. Mary stepped into the shadows on the other side. The horses' hooves were beating hard, coming closer. A million stars overhead made her feel small and insignificant, as if what was happening now were nothing. In the light of the stars and the moon that hung in the east, she could make out two figures riding toward them. Big men in hats, hunched over the saddle as if they had ridden a long distance. Spurs jangled over the sounds of the hooves.

"Stop where you are!" Jesse's voice was firm, a man not to be trifled with. "Any closer and you will be dead men. My woman here can plug a rabbit between the eyes."

"Jesse? That you?" The riders pulled up. The horses snorted, pawed at the ground, and swung their heads.

Across the beam of light, Mary could see that Jesse held the rifle ready. She heard the click as he pushed the lever up and down. "State your name," he called. But she had recognized the voice and so had Jesse, she was certain. A voice from the past. She would never forget it. Still she gripped the rifle until Jesse had made certain that the man was who they thought he was and not an impostor.

"George Cassidy." The rider shouted his name. "This here is Harry Longabaugh, my partner. Folks call him Sundance."

Jesse stood in place, the rifle pointing to the ground now. "Dismount and let me see you."

The riders slid off the horses. "Been a long time, Jesse." The rider came forward, holding out his hand. The other man took the reins.

In the starlight, Mary could make out the familiar face, older-looking, a little tired, with a red scar on his cheek, but the same merry eyes, the mouth ready to break into a loud, bellowing laugh. He wore dark-colored corduroy trousers and jacket. The black, soft-brimmed hat that he always liked sat on his head. He walked the same, shoulders back, head high, as if he owned the world. Eight years ago he had owned her world. A man she had never expected to see again, and here he was, as if he had fallen out of the sky.

"Good heavens, man." Jesse stepped off the porch and started pumping Cassidy's hand. "We gave up on you. Decided you'd ridden off into the sunset."

"I'm still around." Cassidy was smiling, those big teeth gleaming in the light. "I was hoping you'd remember an old friend."

"How would we ever forget. Isn't that right, Mary?" Jesse glanced at the end of the porch where Mary stood rooted to the ground, as if she had been planted there.

"Mary?" Cassidy jumped onto the porch. "Well, I'll be dog-goned. Mary Boyd! How you been getting on, Mary?" He looked around, eyes bright with surprise and comprehension. "Don't tell me you married this old scoundrel. I'll be doggoned," he said again. "Never would have figured it."

Jesse let out a bark of laughter. "Almost five years now," he said. "We got ourselves a good ranch here and a hired hand to keep everything humming. We take care of what's ours."

"Glad to hear it." Cassidy kept his gaze on Mary, then swung around and walked down the steps to Jesse. "It's good to see old friends getting on."

"What brought you here, George? You been up to your old ways?"

George was shaking his head. "No more rustling for me. Sundance and I"—he motioned toward the man holding the reins—"moved on to bigger payoffs."

"I thought you wanted to live an honest life." Mary heard her own voice, sharp and doubtful, piercing the quiet.

"I tried, Mary." Cassidy looked back at her. "God knows I tried. But it seems like once you start down a road of crime, nobody lets you get off. I'm not going to give up trying, but meanwhile a man's got to eat. And Sundance here and the rest of our outfit . . ."

"I hear they call you the Wild Bunch."

Cassidy laughed at that. "We're not as wild as those posses they send after us. But we're pretty good at what we do. We'd like to stay here a little while, Jesse, if that fits into your plans."

"We don't have plans." Jesse bunched a fist and hit at Cassidy's arm. "The blizzards and dust storms, they have plans. The bank, it has plans. We just try to keep on."

"What do you have here?"

"Hundred head of cattle to herd into the high pasture, two dozen horses, three of them wild and needing to be broken."

"We're good with horses, and Sundance here can herd cattle to the moon, if you like."

"Can't pay you."

"All we need is a place to bunk, some grub, and we'll help you out."

"Deal." Jesse pumped George's hand again, then stepped back to the porch. "Get out here, Anthony."

The man stepped past the screened door, and Mary realized he had been standing just inside. He was skinny and tall with the humped nose and black hair of the Arapaho.

"This here is George, an old friend," Jesse said. "You can learn a lot from him. Isn't anything he doesn't know about horses."

"Some folks call me Butch." George made a big point of shaking the man's hand. "Name I picked up working in a butcher shop. Over there is the Sundance Kid. Picked up his name in the Sundance jail."

"Jail!" Mary heard the anxiety in her voice. Who was this man George Cassidy had brought to their ranch?

"Didn't do anything wrong. Went to jail for what some other cowboy did. Never mind. He's a real fine fellow."

"You can bunk in the barn," Jesse said. "There's a water pump and good hay for your horses. Anthony will show you around. When you're ready, come to the house for some of Mary's fine stew."

"Thanks, friend." George gave a salute off the rim of his cowboy hat. "It won't be forgotten."

"We're in your debt," said the Sundance Kid, the first words he had spoken. He seemed closed up and dark, Mary thought, sunk inside his own thoughts, not like George—she could never call him Butch—who moved with the starlight. He liked people. That was the difference between these two men leading the horses around the cabin toward the barn in back. George liked people.

Thirty minutes later George and Sundance were seated at the table over bowls of stew, steam rising like feathers. Draped over the back of George's chair was a brown saddlebag worn almost yellow and packed solid, the flaps straining against the metal buckles. Anthony took his place on the other side of the table, head down, spooning chunks of stew into his mouth. Mary sat at one end, Jesse at the other. She passed the plate of warm bread she had taken from the oven to George. Nothing ever planned here, she was thinking. Everything falling from the sky.

They made polite small talk. She smiled, thinking back on how George had learned the polite preliminaries from her people. How hard it had been! George, seated on a log stump in front of Grandfather's tipi, which Grandfather had always preferred to the wooden boxes the government had built when the Shoshones and Arapahos went to the rez. George would squirm and clamp his lips together until finally he couldn't hold the words back any longer and they had burst forth with a stream of laughter. Grandfather had taken to George Cassidy like a son.

After the men had wiped their bowls clean with pieces of bread, Mary went over to the sideboard and carried a tray to the table with a bottle of whiskey and four glasses. George wasn't much of a drinker, she remembered, and neither was Jesse. She didn't know about Sundance. A small toast, she was thinking, to the success of whatever caper her visitors had just pulled off.

Jesse poured a finger of whiskey into each glass and passed them around the table to the men. "May you live long and free," he said, holding his own glass toward George and Sundance.

Mary took her seat again as the men downed the whiskey. She hated the taste of whiskey, hated the smell, hated the ways it had changed her friends, drove them off their lands, turned them into whores and bums that hung around the agency on the reservation, looking for handouts. She considered making herself a cup of tea, but she didn't want to leave the table and miss the conversation.

"What was it this time?" Jesse set his glass down. Most of the brown whiskey remained, shimmering in the candlelight. "Horses? Bank?"

"Nah." George shook his head. "Never was much for rustling horses. Not enough money in it."

"You used to like it well enough." Mary felt all four pairs of eyes turn to her. "You went to prison in Laramie for stealing a horse."

George threw his head back and laughed. "Stole a few horses in my time, but I never stole *that* horse."

"Strikes me banks are more dangerous," Jesse said.

Sundance had turned toward George, staring at his profile. "Better leave it at that."

"Tomorrow morning everybody in these parts will hear the news. Moccasin telegraph is better than the real thing. What difference if our friends hear it first?" George dropped his chin and chuckled. "Let's just say the Union Pacific Overland Flyer Limited had to make a sudden stop down around Wilcox."

"Train?" Jesse was partway to his feet. "You saying you robbed a train? Nobody can get away with that."

Mary could feel the muscles in her stomach tightening. Robbed the Union Pacific! George had stepped into another world, gone to a place from which he could never return. The railroad company would never forget. They would run him and Sundance and the rest of the gang into the ground.

"Somebody flagged the train down. Naturally the engineer stopped, thinking the bridge ahead was out. Well, it was about to be out, but not until the gang ordered the conductor to cut off the passenger cars behind the baggage car. After that the engineer obligingly pulled the baggage, express, and mail cars across the bridge before the whole thing blew to smithereens. Two miles up track, the engineer stopped again. It's a wonder the baggage car didn't blow sky-high when that fool express messenger refused to open the door. The gang had to set off another blast of dynamite. Blew off the roof and flattened that fool against the back wall. They blew the safe when he refused to open it. The man is crazy! The gang filled up the bags with him limping around, crying, saying the railroad was gonna fire him and how was he supposed to feed his kids? I ask you, how was his kids supposed to eat if he'd been blown to pieces?"

"They're going to come for you with a posse the size of an army," Jesse said.

"They'll have to find us first."

"You used the old method?" Mary said. George had told her once that he planned the robberies and the rustling. Everything thought out ahead of time, every possibility taken into account. The gang would stash horses, water, and food along the getaway route, so they could cover a hundred miles, two hundred miles, on fresh horses, while the posse's horses would run out of strength.

George was grinning. "We rode all day before we stopped to split up the takings. Then we took different directions. Me and Sundance kept going north until we reached friends."

"How many days you got before they're onto you?" Jesse had finished his whiskey and was refilling the glasses.

"We got forever. Don't we, Sundance?" He glanced at the man next to him.

"I figure we work here for a while," Sundance said. "Keep our noses clean and stay away from the bars in Lander until things quiet down. Then we'll be on our way."

George took another sip of whiskey and pushed the glass away. He started to his feet. "Let's face it, Jesse. Posses don't want us, anyway."

"Except to kill us," Sundance said.

"Well, maybe they want that. But they'll be chasing their shadows across Wyoming looking for this." George patted the saddlebag. "You can do what you want with your share," he said to Sundance, who gulped the rest of his whiskey and stood up next to him. "I'm putting my share where they're never going to find it."

5

FROM THE PARKING lot Vicky could hear the drums beating and the high-pitched voices of the singers. She wedged the Ford Escape into a narrow space between two campers and threaded her way around the haphazard rows of pickups toward the powwow grounds. License plates from all over the West: Montana, South Dakota, North Dakota, Colorado, New Mexico, Arizona. The Wind River Reservation was on the powwow highway, and the top prizes large enough that the winners could spend the rest of the summer driving across the empty, sweltering plains to the next powwow. Dancers spilled across the parking lot, regalia jangling and glistening in the sun, feathered headgear waving against the blue-white sky like dried stalks of wheat. All ages: grandfathers and grandmothers, teenagers, toddlers scuffing along in beaded moccasins. The dancing would begin at ten o'clock, twenty minutes from now. Most of the dancers would be lining up, ready to dance into the arena, shawls and blankets swirling about their shoulders. These were the latecomers, and she was one of them.

She had planned to drive to the powwow grounds early, have coffee with the elders, visit with people she used to be friends with. Reconnect. Take every opportunity to be among her people. Instead of the Arapaho lawyer in the white world, she would be an Arapaho woman in her own world. But she had worked late last night. Lander was ghostlike when she left the office, circles of light from the streetlamps flaring over the darkened houses and buildings. She had taken home a briefcase filled with papers she intended to read and had fallen asleep on the sofa, paper trailing off the cushions and onto the floor. It was after midnight when she crawled into bed. She had slept restlessly. Half-aware of the empty side of the bed where Adam had slept, wondering where he had gone when the realization had hit her like an arrow out of the darkness. Adam had left. They were no longer together.

The grounds were packed. People milling about and crowding the food booths, dancers jostling one another, the honor guard forming at the edge of the arena. Rows of lawn chairs had been set up around the arena, and the elders were settling in under umbrellas fastened to the armrests to create little patches of shade. Red and white coolers stood next to the chairs. Vicky spotted Annie walking toward her, Roger not more than a foot behind. They had found each other in her office. Annie Bosey, the secretary she had hired when she wasn't sure she needed a secretary, because she had seen herself in Annie, divorced, two kids, trying to make her way. And Roger Hurst, the lawyer she and Adam had hired when the firm was Holden and Lone Eagle. She and Adam would handle the big cases. Natural resources on Indian lands. Oil. Gas. Water. Timber. Roger would handle the little cases that, as Adam had put it, didn't matter to anybody. Except people charged with DUIs, assault, public inebriation. People getting divorced, desperately trying to get their children back from social services, wanting to make a will to protect what little property they had managed to accumulate. Ironic how the number of little cases had kept increasing. Finally she and Adam had decided to dissolve the firm, and he had started his own natural resources firm, which he merged into a large firm in Denver last fall. Adam was good at natural resources; he was the best. The little cases now took up all of their time, hers and Roger's.

Annie handed her a Styrofoam cup. "Saw you drive in." The aroma of hot coffee made Vicky blink. She could feel Annie's eyes on her. "You all right?"

"I can use the coffee." Vicky sipped at the plain, black liquid, hot and strong the way she liked it. God, Annie knew her so well! Answering the phone, working on the computer, making appointments, ushering clients into her office. Studying her. Studying her. There was no one on the rez she was closer to than Annie.

"Lot of people looking forward to seeing you," Roger said. "Grandmother Nitti." He gestured with his head toward the grandmothers in the first row of lawn chairs. "The grandfathers over there." Another gesture toward the old men seated together, apart from the women. Easier for all of them to gossip. "Some of your old school friends."

Vicky smiled over the rim of the coffee cup. This white man, more at home on the rez than she was, but then, he spent more time here. With Annie's big, sprawling family and her kids and all their friends. He had changed everything for Annie. He was security, safety, certainty. Vicky had grown fond of the man for all he had given to Annie. And he was a good lawyer, smart and tenacious. He cared about the small cases. So different from Adam, she thought. So busy caring for the big cases, he couldn't see the small.

"Ladies and gentlemen." The announcer's voice boomed over the loudspeakers strung overhead. Heads turned in unison toward the man in the cowboy hat, fringed leather vest and blue jeans with the mike in his hand. He stood next to the table where six women were still registering dancers. "Welcome to the second day of the Arapaho powwow. We want to extend a special welcome to our tribal friends from all over Indian country." A loud whoop went up among the crowd; people clapped and shouted *Hou!* "We wish all the dancers luck and hope you have a fine day. We're going to start with the intertribal dances and move on to the contests. Morning Star drum group will accompany the dancers."

The drums started pounding. Vicky could feel the tiny vibrations running through the ground. People lumbered out of the lawn chairs, the old women standing crookedly and uncertain, holding on to the backs of chairs, craning their necks to see the first dancers dance into the arena. She was sorry she had missed the Grand Entry March last night. It was always a thrill to see the men standing tall and straight, saluting the flags as the honor guard marched in: Long rows of men and women in uniform—army, navy, air force, marines. Warriors who had served in every war in the last seventy-five years. Europe. Japan. Vietnam. Kuwait. Iraq. Afghanistan. Dressed in old uniforms, carrying the flags of the United States, Wyoming, and the Arapaho Nation—citizens of all three, her people.

The announcer led the pledge of allegiance, his voice booming across the grounds, nearly drowning out the low voices of the crowd. The sound of the drums burst through the air.

Now she watched the dancers from different tribes, a kaleidoscope of colors whirling about the arena, the drums as steady as the beating of her own heart. This was home, where she belonged.

The drumming and the dancers stopped at the same instant, and the dancers started to file out. It was then that Vicky saw the movie cameras pointed toward the arena. Other cameras scanned the crowd. Still another camera turned on the dancers starting to line up for the contests.

Roger must have followed her gaze because he said, "They're making a documentary film about Butch Cassidy. We talked to one of the producers over at the coffee booth. They want to get the flavor of the rez, put things in context, convey a sense of the life here."

"Butch Cassidy was here a long time ago."

"He said there were powwows then."

"Ladies and gentlemen." The announcer's voice erupted over the grounds. "Now for the first contest. The traditional dancers."

Again the arena burst into color and motion, like fireworks on the Fourth of July, as the dancers came dancing out. Voices of singers rose over the thud of drums like the call of birds in a storm.

"Not like this," Vicky said. For a minute, the dancers in beaded leggings and bone breastplates and feathered headdresses, dipping and stamping out dance steps, faded into the black-and-white photos in books about the early days on the reservation. Dark shadows of tipis intermixed with log cabins that sloped toward the bare dirt ground, ragged horses with sagging backs in the corrals, and the people—her people—in dusty overalls and calico dresses that hung on thin, bent frames. The men wore cowboy hats, pulled low against the sun. The women with braids wrapped around their heads, holding small children in their arms. Stopped in time, all of them. The photos of powwows had always surprised her. A break from the everyday hardness. The old dances, passed down through time, a memory of life on the plains. In the photos the dancers wore the same overalls and calico dresses. No fancy, jangling regalia and headdresses. All of that had been traded to the white traders for food.

She gripped the coffee cup and stared at the cameramen, trying to swallow back the anger sparking in her throat. What did they know of the past, these white people looking to fill in the story of Butch Cassidy? What would they show the outside world? The bright, shiny life in Indian country? She wanted to yell: *It wasn't like this a hundred years ago!*

"You sure you're all right?" A worried note drummed in Annie's voice. The traditional dance ended and the dancers were heading back to the sidelines. The grass dancers would dance next, an ancient dance that mimicked the warriors stalking game in the tall prairie grasses.

"If they want to portray the rez a hundred years ago, they have to show more than this." The drummers beat out a new song as the grass dancers tapped into the arena, bent over, peering at the ground, hands shielding the brightness from their eyes. The regalia jangled and swayed, feet stomped in rhythm to the drumbeats.

"But this is nice, isn't it? All the people together?" A man's voice, from behind. Vicky glanced around. Behind her was an Indian, tall and slim in a white cowboy shirt that clung to muscular shoulders and chest. Handsome, like a warrior in the old photos, with shoulder-length black hair parted in the middle and black eyes that reflected the sunlight.

"Sorry. I didn't mean to butt into your conversation. Some of my best memories are the powwows. You're Vicky Holden, right?"

"I don't believe we've met."

"Fifth grade, St. Francis School. I sat behind you and pulled your braids. Jimmy Walking Bear. Go by the name Cutter now." He stuck out his hand. Brown with long, slim fingers. Vicky hesitated a moment before she shook hands. His palm was rougher than she had expected. He had the confident manner of someone used to giving orders rather than doing the work himself.

"Annie Bosey and Roger Hurst," Vicky said, nodding from one to the other.

"St. Francis?" The man called Cutter was looking at Annie. "I must have been gone by the time you started kindergarten. Good to meet you both." He turned back to Vicky. "The Indian lawyer in Lander. I hear you divorced Ben Holden and got yourself a law degree. I didn't think anybody could ever stand up to Ben. I'm impressed."

"It was a long time ago." She felt a shudder, as if this stranger had yanked back the veil of her life. She couldn't place him. One of the dark faces from the past that swirled around her. So many people had come and gone in her life. He was Robert Walking Bear's cousin. A distant cousin, Ruth had said, but still a relative.

The jingle dancers filled the arena now with a cacophony of sounds, like the noise of a thousand ringing bells. She watched them sway and tap their feet in rhythm with the drums, then turned back to the stranger. "Ruth mentioned you."

"Oh yes," Annie joined in. "Welcome home."

He nodded. "Dad took us off to Oklahoma when I was eleven. I decided it was time to come back. Get to know the relatives. Find out where I came from." He listed toward the arena then took in the crowd. "I can't get over Robert dying like that," he said. "Keep thinking it wouldn't have happened if I had been there. We'd gone into the mountains a few times. He liked looking for Butch

Cassidy's treasure, not that he believed it existed. It was more like he wanted to believe. So I went along. I wanted to get to know my cousin, cook a couple steaks on the campfire, throw back a beer. I was supposed to go with him the day he died, but I had to go to Casper for a job interview." He drew in a breath and looked around again. "Jobs are few and far between around here. I keep thinking I shouldn't have gone."

"What do you think happened to Robert?" Something off-kilter, Vicky was thinking. Ruth said that Robert always went treasure hunting alone.

"Nobody knows. Spoke to Ruth this morning. She's waiting for the coroner to release Robert's body so she can get him buried."

"Poor Ruth," Annie said. "Everything on hold. She's going to need her relatives." She hesitated, then plunged on. "She doesn't have any close family of her own, just Robert's people."

"I been thinking, maybe that's why I got the urge to come home. Maybe my relatives need me."

Vicky tried for a smile. It was a comforting thought somehow, that people were drawn to those who needed them. "Nice to meet you," she said. Then she added, "Again." She nodded at Annie and Roger, who stood holding hands, then started toward the grandmothers, feeling as if an envelope of loneliness had swallowed her. The cameras scanned the dancers, lingered on the drummers, and swept across the crowd. She could be in the film, she was thinking. Modern Arapaho woman. Woman Alone.

6

A TAN PICKUP backed out of the driveway, skidded to a stop, and shot forward. Vicky waited until the cloud of dust had rolled past before she turned into the driveway and stopped in front of the small, white frame house. Red buds sprouted on the geranium plants next to the stoop. Ruth stood in the doorway. She gave a little wave that resembled a hand gesture blocking the sun. "Thanks for coming," she called as Vicky got out of the Ford.

There was a frazzled look about her, Vicky thought. The same red blouse she'd had on two days ago, the same wrinkled jeans skirt. She had replaced the flip-flops for scuffed-looking sandals. Hair mussed, black shadows under her eyes, a tremor in her hands. As if she hadn't slept for a long time and was living on caffeine. "Folks keep calling and coming over. Dallas Spotted Deer was here. Wanted to know how he can help me. Help me with what? A new life?" Ruth threw the comments over one shoulder and motioned Vicky through the living room into the kitchen "Coffee?"

"No, thanks." Vicky felt as if she might jump out of her skin with another cup of coffee. Someone had handed her coffee while she visited with Grandmother Nitti and the other grandmothers. Polite pleasantries, the weather, the dancers twirling about, the regalia flashing in the sun. When the polite pleasantries had worn themselves out, there had been nothing to discuss. Vicky had seen the questions in Grandmother Nitti's eyes. Where had Vicky Holden gone? Who was this lawyer from the white town? They had sat in silence a long moment and watched the dancers. Emmy Many Horses from Wind River High School had placed third in the jingle dance, a purse of about one hundred dollars. Could be a fortune to the girl.

Vicky had clasped the old woman's hand in an effort to reconnect, she supposed, and smiled at the other grandmothers before taking her leave. She walked among the grandfathers, paying her respect, and moved through the crowd, searching for familiar faces. Smiling, nodding. Making small talk against the thumping drums, the swish of moccasins on the hard-packed dirt. She was walking back through the parking lot when she heard the footsteps behind her. She slid into the Ford as Cutter took hold of the door and leaned toward her. "Leaving so soon?" He was grinning, eyes shining. "I was hoping we could talk. Catch up."

"Maybe some other time." She tried to pull the door shut.

"How about dinner?"

"I'm pretty busy."

"I hear the Lakota that's been hanging around took off."

"You can't always believe the moccasin telegraph."

"What about it?"

"The moccasin telegraph?"

He tossed his head and gave out a bark of laughter. "Dinner."

Vicky hesitated. Something about Cutter drew her in: Trying to reconnect, trying to find himself in his people. Struggling with the kind of emptiness that she recognized in herself.

"I'll be in touch," he said, pushing the door shut. She caught a glimpse of him in the rearview mirror, staring after her, as she drove away.

Now Ruth poured a cup of coffee and sat down at the table. "Cutter called this morning." She motioned Vicky into the chair across from her. "He offered to come over, but I told him, 'Go to the powwow. Enjoy yourself. We don't all have to be dead.'"

"Any word from the fed?"

"It was an accidental death by drowning, but he won't say so." Ruth tilted her chin and stared at the ceiling. "They're still waiting on autopsy results. Maybe they think Robert got drunk and fell into the lake."

"Did the fed say that?"

"He didn't have to." She slurped the coffee. "Wanted to know if Robert had been camping. Did he have a tent? 'Tent?' I said. 'Are you kidding?' He always took a cooler with sandwiches and a thermos. But he slept in the bed of the pickup under the stars. He would never wrap himself inside a tent. It would be like crawling inside a coffin." She shrugged and set the mug down hard on the table. "At least the fed's no longer hammering about suicide. I been thinking I need to go to the lake, see where Robert died."

"We can do that."

THE ROAD CLIMBED into the mountains. Every time the Ford took another turn, Vicky had a sense of the earth dropping away. The reservation shimmered in the far distances below, and vehicles crawled along Highway 26, sunlight flashing off chrome. The Ford punched deeper into the sky. Ruth was saying something about how Robert loved going to the mountains. An Arapaho of the plains, where the sky dropped all around, in love with the mountains! "We are blue-sky people," she said. "We came from the blue sky, the way I heard the story. You ask me, it wasn't the mountains Robert loved. It was the hunt for treasure."

Vicky gripped the wheel tighter as they started down into the valley. Around and around until Bull Lake came into view, a silvery mirror reflecting the sunlight. Patches of wildflowers glowed red, blue, and yellow among the pines. "Did he come here often?"

"I never asked."

Vicky drove around another curve and pulled the visor down against the sun. They were dropping fast, the lake coming up to meet them now. Another couple of turns and the road flattened out and ran straight ahead like a racetrack. She pressed down slightly on the accelerator and gave the Ford its head as it bounced and skidded over the ridges of tire tracks. A phalanx of investigators and coroner's officers had been here. Ahead was a strip of land that jutted into the lake, a half circle of yellow tape arched from the shore. She nudged the Ford to a stop. "Looks like this is the place."

Ruth stared straight ahead, past the yellow tape swinging in the breeze, to some point in the lake. She was silent.

"We don't have to go over there." Vicky had started to open the door. The sweet smells of wild brush and wildflowers and the lake invaded the Ford.

Ruth pushed her door open, swung out, and slammed the door behind her. Before Vicky caught up, Ruth was closing in on the tape. She stopped for a moment, as if she had encountered a wall, then pushed the tape down with one hand and climbed over. "I have the right," she said.

Vicky stepped over the tape and followed Ruth around the clumps of grass and willows, the purple flares of pasqueflowers. The water made a swishing noise as it washed onto the narrow band of sandy shore. A fish was jumping out in the lake.

"So this is where Robert died." Ruth kept walking until the water lapped around her sandals. She turned away from the lake. "I can feel him here. He didn't want to die. He was surprised." She spoke slowly, parsing the words. "Do you think I'm crazy?"

Vicky shook her head. She could hear her grandmother's voice: *What happens in a place stays in a place, changes the place forever.*

The breeze riffled Ruth's hair, plucked at her blouse. She came forward and dropped onto a boulder. "I want to sit here awhile."

Vicky backed away to give the woman solitude and space. The yellow tape snapped and danced. All of this—a life—for a treasure hunt? It seemed ridiculous, a cruel joke. She had heard rumors of buried treasure since she was a kid. Butch Cassidy himself had buried his loot in the mountains and left behind a map, but no one she knew had ever seen it. Still the story persisted, along with a thousand other stories and rumors and what-ifs that drifted across time and kept the present a prisoner to the past.

Except for the tire tracks, the ground looked undisturbed. A little to the right of where Ruth was sitting was a deeper set of tracks. Robert could have parked there, and the fed had impounded the pickup. Mute testimony to what had happened.

She stepped back over the tape and started walking along the road, past the spot where Robert's truck had sat, taking in the stretch of rocky, gray mountains around her. Looking for what? Some sign, something unusual. What had Robert done? Driven to the lake, parked, and then what? Decided to spend the night? Sitting on the shore, maybe on the rock where Ruth sat now, eating sandwiches, washing down each bite with a sip of warm coffee? Walking into the lake—the freezing water from the snow running off the high peaks—stumbling, falling. Giving up? Lying down and drowning? Incredible. She had known Ruth and Robert since they were kids. Strong as oxen, both of them. Like the people in Old Time, unbowed by the hardships that came their way.

She realized she had walked a good half mile. She glanced back. Her Ford looked solitary, out of place, parked at the side of the road, the mountains rising above, and on the other side, the strip of land stretching into the lake. Ruth, a small, quiet figure on the rock. She started off again, and that is when she saw it: a campsite in the brush across the road from the lake. Tire tracks ran off the road toward the site. She followed the tracks, picking her way around the brush and boulders. Activity here, but when? A week ago? A month ago? She could hear Grandmother's voice in her head: *Tracks remain forever.* Tracks of the wagon trains plowing across Indian lands were still here. Tracks of mules and wagons hauling gold out of the mountains were still here. In the most pristine places with no one else about, the past was here.

Someone had camped here around a fire pit. Ashes and blackened pieces of wood chips littered the pit. A vehicle had been parked on the far side, depressions of the wheels far enough apart to suggest a truck. Bigger than a pickup.

What happened? She heard the demand in her own voice. As if the campsite, the fire pit, the tire tracks, the mountain itself could provide an answer.

The brush crunched behind her, and she swung around. Ruth was coming toward her. Cross-country, through the prickly pears and rocks and scrub brush. Yellow paintbrush lay trampled behind her. She gestured toward the fire pit. "Campsite?"

"Looks like it."

"So that's why the fed wanted to know if Robert had a tent."

"There's no telling how old this campsite is."

"Could be recent," Ruth said. "Could have been here days ago. Could have been here when Robert died."

"I'm sure the fed is looking . . ."

"Looking for what? A truck or SUV with people who watched my husband die in the lake and drove out of here? Didn't try to help him?" Ruth's voice rose into the mountain quiet. Moisture glinted in her eyes. "Drove onto the road and away from here. South Dakota. Montana. Not caring what happened?"

"Ruth, we don't know . . ."

"Don't tell me I don't know! The truth is everywhere. In the lake, the shore, the rocks. He didn't want to die, Vicky. Robert did not want to die."

7

THE STAINED GLASS windows glowed red, yellow, and blue in the morning sun. Technicolor patches of light lay over the pews and the brown faces of the parishioners. A low undercurrent of prayer, like the hum of electricity, ran through the small church. "Our Father who art in Heaven. Hallowed be thy name."

Father John looked around at the parishioners scattered about the pews. He knew everyone by name. His own family seemed remote, far away, another time and place. The people here were his family now. The elders and grandmothers, the mothers poking kids to their feet, the squealing babies, the bored, stone-faced teenagers. A big, unwieldy, imperfect, and beautiful family. Odd how it always came as a surprise to find himself at a mission in the middle of Wyoming. He had never imagined himself a priest. Then something had started happening to him. A nudging, a calling. Unspoken questions that left him twisting and turning in the night, demanding an answer. *Whom shall I send?* Finally he had answered: *Send me, Lord. Send me.*

After Mass he stood outside with the sun bouncing off the white stucco church and shook hands, wishing his parishioners a good day, a happy day, telling the elders he would stop at the senior center for a cup of coffee this week, promising Mary Louise White Bonnet he would visit her mother in the hospital. At some point he noticed the white man hanging back, shifting from one foot to the other on the patch of grass that lay between the church and Circle Drive. His parishioners ignored the man. After they had filed past on their way to coffee in Eagle Hall, the white man walked over and extended a fleshy, bearlike hand. "Father O'Malley?" He hurried on, not waiting for an answer. "Todd Paxton. We're making a documentary about Butch Cassidy. I'm the director. Would you have a few minutes?"

He had it then, the reason his parishioners had given the man a wide berth. Probably wasn't anyone on the rez who hadn't been inconvenienced by the filming, stuck in long lines while the actors rode across the prairie.

The man had the smooth hand of someone who worked with cameras or computers, not horses or cattle. Like the hands of his parishioners, hardworking, outdoor hands. "Give me a few minutes," Father John said. He wanted to walk back through the church, check the pews for keys and glasses and baby bottles, hang up his chasuble and alb in the sacristy closet, fold away his cincture, put the Mass books in the cabinet. "Go on over to Eagle Hall and get yourself a cup of coffee. I'll meet you there."

Father John made his way past the tables and groups of people. Shaking hands again, smiling, patting the old people's shoulders. The air in the hall was a fug of fresh coffee smells. Outbursts of laughter punctuated the low roar of conversations. Elena, the mission housekeeper, blocked his way and handed him a mug of coffee. "A little cream, the way you like it," she said. She knew everything about him, this elderly woman with gnarled, arthritic hands and hair the color of steel cropped around her head. She was probably in her seventies, although she might have crossed into her eighties. The subject never came up, since it made no difference. She ran the residence, ordered the bishop and him around the way she had been ordering the priests around at St. Francis for decades. She was a living archive of memories. He thanked her and took the coffee. So like his mother sometimes, he thought, it was uncanny. Running the kitchen and the house and everything beyond. Praying for one of her sons to become a priest, like all Irish mothers of her generation. Give a son to God and he will be yours the rest of your life. No other woman to take him away.

Todd Paxton sat alone at a table in the far corner. Dark hair falling over his forehead, narrowed, observant eyes glancing about the room. Arapahos flowed around him, coffee cups and doughnuts in hand, eyeing the white man in their midst—the stranger—and moving on. Father John pulled out a chair across from the director, sat down, and took a sip of coffee.

"Hope this isn't an imposition." Paxton occupied himself pushing a half-filled cup in a little circle about the table. "Lot of people here to see you."

"It's not an imposition. What can I do for you?"

The man stopped pushing the cup and leaned forward. "We've been filming on the rez for a week now. Next week we intend to film at the Hole in the Wall up in the Bighorns where Butch and his gang hung out, then move on to Brown's Canyon on the Wyoming-Utah border. My research suggests Butch spent a lot of time there. The place was desolate; deputies and posses avoided it. Would've been like riding into an ambush." He laughed softly. "I am definitely getting the vibe that Butch was a smart man. The reason he and Sundance didn't get caught was because Butch outsmarted the law. Except for that one time, of course, when he went to the Wyoming prison for stealing a horse. We've been filming all the places he knew around here. Lander. Dubois. The Wind River. The Little Wind River. Ethete. Arapahoe. The powwow. You name it, we have footage."

"Powwow?"

"And farmers' markets. Provides context, gives a sense of life on the rez today. I understand it was different a hundred and thirty years ago, but it's the same people. Arapahos and Shoshone. People don't change that much. I found a book with photographs of life on the rez in the early days. They had powwows and get-togethers." He took a quick drink of coffee, set the cup down, and pushed it away. "But we need more. We need to talk to people with stories about Butch handed down in their families. People whose ancestors knew him, hid him on their ranches. I'm hoping you can put me in touch with folks like that."

Father John sipped at his own coffee for a moment. His parishioners were still flowing around the table, leaving a space between the director and themselves. "Have you talked to Arapahos?"

"We got nowhere. Oh, they're very polite. Didn't tell us to back off or go away. Smiled, said they'd check with a few people who might know someone and get back to us. I know the old skiddoo when I see it. No sense in riling us up by saying you don't know anybody and if you did, you wouldn't be telling us. Just smile and smile. Works every time. Left us hoping every day that the next day we'd get an interview with somebody who had stories about Butch."

"I can make some inquiries."

"Ah!" Paxton threw up both hands. "I wish I had a dollar for all the times I've heard that."

"There's a white woman from an old family in the area. I can see if she'd be willing to talk to you. Do you have a card?"

"White?" Todd Paxton fumbled in his jeans' side pocket, withdrew a small metal envelope, and extracted a card that he pushed across the table. "I was hoping you'd suggest some Arapahos."

There were probably a lot of Arapahos with stories, Father John was thinking. Families that had straggled onto the rez with Chief Black Coal and Chief Sharpnose after the Arapahos had been hunted across the plains with nowhere to go, no more lands to call their own. The government had sent them to the Shoshones. They had asked Chief Washakie if they could come under his tent, and the Shoshone chief had taken pity. That was in 1878. Fifteen years later, Butch Cassidy had ridden into the area.

"I'll check around." He slipped Paxton's card into his shirt pocket and got to his feet.

The director had already stood up and was pushing the chair into the table. He glanced toward the door, as if he were plotting a path across the plains. "I'd appreciate it."

Father John watched the man weave through his parishioners and step outside, a dark figure against the sunlight. Then he started through the crowd, visiting, exchanging polite pleasantries. He stopped at the table where Elsa Lone Bear was sitting, pulled a vacant chair over with his boot, and sat down a little behind her left shoulder. She turned toward him. "That white man the film director?"

"His name is Todd Paxton."

"What's he doing here?" Elsa was in her twenties, part of the younger generation, teaching fifth grade and trying to find a way between the past and the present.

"At the mission?"

"No. What are they trying to prove? Butch Cassidy was a long time ago. Times have changed."

"The landscape doesn't change much." He was thinking that Butch Cassidy had seen the same mountains, the same rivers, the same prairie stretching into an almost always blue and cloudless sky.

"The people don't like a lot of attention, you know."

He nodded. He had come to realize that Arapahos liked to be the observers.

"Would it be all right to stop by later to see Eldon?"

"Oh, Grandfather would like that. Hasn't gotten out much lately. He's been having trouble with his ghost leg. The one that burns like fire even though he lost it in that automobile accident twenty years ago. The doctor says the nerves still think the leg is there, so they keep sending out pain signals."

"The past has a way of hanging around."

"Do we ever get free?"

"Is that what you would like?"

She turned her head and stared out over the hall. The crowd was smaller now. The plates of doughnuts gone. Coffee smells turning musky and stale.

"Sometimes I think . . ." She hesitated. "Not really."

A small crowd had bunched up at the door, straining forward, pushing past one another. From outside came a swipe of loud, angry voices. Father John stood up, crossed the hall, and shouldered his way outdoors. Warriors stood in a circle around the white man, advancing toward him, closing in. Todd Paxton looked calm, the effort stamped on his face. Shoulders back, eyes fixed on Lionel Red Bull, and the Arapaho shouting: "Get off the rez! Take your cameras and let us be!"

Father John lunged through the circle of warriors and stood next to Paxton. He could smell the fear rolling off the man. "What's going on?" He faced Red Bull, a troublemaker in the past, but lately he'd been coming to church with his wife, Lu, and the kids. Lu said he had stopped drinking. He was working again, a good job at the casino.

"This guy comes here." Red Bull hissed the words. "He's gonna make a film, show it all over TV. DVD forever. So folks out there"—he lifted both arms as if he could encircle the world beyond the rez—"they think Butch Cassidy's loot is buried on the rez. Gold and silver. Banknotes. Whatever he got from the railroads and banks. Could be a lot of money. We'll have a thousand treasure hunters, two thousand, roaming round, making nuisances of themselves, digging up the rez, crawling around the mountains, all thinking they're gonna get rich. Any loot Butch left here, he left for us. You get it, Paxton? It belongs to us. Maybe nobody has found it yet, but someday. Someday! We don't need outsiders roaming around."

"Look, what's your name?" A note of logic sounded in Paxton's voice. Searching for neutral ground. *Come, let us reason together.* He lifted his hands palms up, and Father John wondered if Paxton knew this was the Plains Indian sign of peace. There was the slightest trembling in his hands.

"I'm Red Bull." The man pulled himself to his full height and looked down on the director.

"Look, Red Bull. If some outsider, as you call the rest of us, got lucky enough to find Cassidy's loot, it would still belong to the tribes here. Nobody could take it away."

"Yeah." The Arapaho turned and spit onto the ground next to his boot. "What world do you live in?"

"Okay, enough." Father John took a step forward and the circle fell back. Red Bull shrugged and looked as if he were about to walk away. "Paxton and his crew are making a film about Butch Cassidy. Who he was. How he lived." He glanced back at the white man, clasping his hands now, rubbing his palms together.

"Right." Paxton nodded. "If nobody's found any loot in a hundred and thirty years, why would they find it now?"

"They'll come looking," Red Bull said. "Fools, all of them. Think they'll win the Butch Cassidy lottery. Take your cameras somewhere else."

The circle had broken. The warriors wandering off, Red Bull himself stepping backward, swinging around and hurtling back inside Eagle Hall. Little groups of people were making their way down the alley to the pickups and cars parked in Circle Drive. Engines coughed and sputtered. After a moment, Red Bull ushered his wife and two kids outside and into the silver pickup parked in the alley.

Father John turned to Paxton. "I'm sorry about this."

"It's what we've been running into. Most folks we've met are polite, but I guess they feel the same as Red Bull. Funny." He was smiling now, relaxed, hands hooked into the pockets of his blue jeans. "I never took that buried treasure yarn seriously. I'm starting to think I was wrong."

8

THE FRAME HOUSE sheltered under a lone cottonwood, branches swaying against the sky. White cottonwood fluff blew through the air. There was no other traffic on the narrow strip of asphalt that cut across the prairie. *Pagliacci* filled the cab. Father John pressed on the brake, turned right, and bounced across the borrow ditch into the bare-dirt yard. A blue sedan stood in the shade between the house and the cottonwood. Parked close to the sedan was a black truck.

He pulled up near the front stoop and turned off the engine. It wasn't polite to stomp up to the house and bang on the front door. If Ruth was up to having a visitor, she would open the door and wave. She would have heard the Toyota pickup coming down the road, rattling across the yard. The engine cutting off. He tapped his fingers against the steering wheel in rhythm to "Un tal gioco," giving her time to decide. The CD player on the seat beside him had a tinny sound, and for a moment he let himself imagine attending an opera again, the orchestra and the voices swelling around him, the sweep of the costumes and settings, the drama and heartbreak, the elegant opera house in Central City, a survivor of the past. The tickets were on his desk. He had looked at them this morning, then laid them back down.

The front door remained closed, the window shades pulled down halfway. A sense of abandonment lay about the place. And yet, Ruth's car was here. A truck was here. He wondered if the sheriff had released Robert's truck. A sense of alarm surged through him. You never knew what someone might do in the midst of grief. He got out and slammed the door hard so that, if by chance Ruth hadn't heard him drive up, she would know a visitor had arrived. He was on the stoop, rapping at the door, when a man emerged around the corner of the house. Slightly stooped into medium height, slim, a warrior look about him in cowboy hat, yellow Western shirt, blue jeans, and the kind of boots with toes turned up that had been worn a long time.

"Is Ruth here?" Father John stepped off the stoop. Arapaho, high cheekbones and hooked nose, dark eyes that took him in. A pockmarked face. He had been here the day Robert's body had been found. One of the relatives bringing casseroles, cakes and lemonade, and hope. The man had led them to the backyard and set up the lawn chairs.

"Dallas Spotted Deer." The man lunged forward and extended his hand. A single shake, that was the Arapaho Way. "*Hou!*" he said.

Father John had seen the man at get-togethers and powwows. Never at the mission, but some of the Walking Bears were traditionals, he knew. They worshipped at the Native American church. A few of his parishioners also worshipped there, he knew. Prayer was good, wherever you prayed.

"I been waiting for Ruth out back," Dallas said. "Figured she and Vicky . . ."

"Vicky?" Of course Vicky would be here to make sure Ruth was okay.

"Saw them out on the road in Vicky's car. Figured they were going to stop at the convenience store in Ethete. I been here most of an hour, and no sign of them."

Father John knew instantly where they had gone, as if Vicky and Ruth had left a note tacked on the door. Gone to the lake. Gone to see the place where Robert died.

"I guess she's all right, if she's with Vicky."

"She's all right."

"All the same, I worry. Robert was one of the relatives, you know, so I got an obligation to see that his wife is okay."

"It's good of you."

Dallas said something about Robert being the son of his step-father's cousin, and Father John realized he was explaining the relationship. "Not what you'd call close in the white world, but in the Arapaho . . ." He paused and looked away a moment. "Relatives matter." He looked back. "I hope they didn't go to the lake. She wanted to go, and I said, no way would that be good for her. She'd have the place burned into her mind the rest of her life. You think Vicky . . . ?" He left the question hanging.

"It's possible."

"I'm hanging around, in case Ruth needs to talk. You know what the head doctors say, process what she seen." He took another moment, jaw muscles flinching, words working on his tongue. "I just wish I'd gone with Robert. He had a crazy idea he was going to find Butch Cassidy's loot. I went a couple times with him and Cutter, but it was too weird for me. Robert had a copy of this old map he said he got from our grandfather. Passed down by Butch himself. You ask me, he bought it in one of them tourist shops in Lander. Everybody's trying to make a few bucks off the past." He was shaking his head. "I got me a good job at the BIA and I can't take off for a whole day. So Robert went up there alone."

"How could you have prevented what happened?"

"Ruth says it was an accident. Couldn't've been anything else, despite the fed going around and asking questions." He shook his head as if the investigation were an annoying inconvenience. "I can't get it out of my mind . . ."

"You mustn't blame yourself." Dallas Spotted Deer, Father John was thinking, would wait here until Ruth returned. They both needed to process what had happened.

"If I can ever be of help . . ."

"Yeah. Yeah." The man waved away the offer.

"Tell Ruth I'll stop by later."

"You do that, Father. Do her good."

HE DROVE FROM Arapahoe to Ethete, a few other vehicles coming at him out of the dust. Past little houses with white propane tanks and two-seat pickups and a smattering of plastic toys in the yards, laundry flapping on the lines. He turned up the volume on the CD player, and the music rose over the sound of the wind that rushed past the open windows. He tried not to think of Vicky. Still she lingered at the edges of his mind. Months would pass when he didn't see her. No one who needed their help—the lawyer, the priest—and he could almost forget about her. And then Robert Walking Bear died, and there she was in Ruth's living room. Old friends of hers, Ruth and Robert, from their days at St. Francis Mission School, ties that bind, the past that never lets go.

The hood was up on a tan pickup as Father John pulled into the yard in front of Eldon Lone Bear's place. Lawrence, the old man's grandson, lifted himself out from under the hood and squinted into the sun a moment before he came around the pickup, rubbing a black-splashed rag between his hands. A smile as wide as the outdoors creased his face. "Grandfather's been hoping you'd drop by ever since Elsa said she talked to you this morning."

"How is he?" One of his grandkids was always with the old man, he knew. Arapahos never abandoned the elders. Carried them on their backs in the Old Time, running from the soldiers and the guns that shot fire.

"For eighty-five years old, I'd say Grandfather is doing good. Complains about that ghost leg, but other than that . . ." He was still smiling. "Come on in. You like coffee? Sandwich? I think Elsa made a cake."

"Coffee sounds good." Father John followed the man up the steps and into the small living room. They always wanted to feed you, the Arapahos. It had taken some getting used to. He sometimes thought he would drown in all the coffee they poured for him. No one left an Arapaho village hungry in the Old Time. Visitors were sent off onto the plains with full bellies, because no one knew when they might eat again.

Eldon Lone Bear sat in a wheelchair in front of a small TV that stood on a chest against the far wall. Father John recognized Bette Davis and Glenn Ford. He wondered if Eldon's grandkids had heard of either actor.

"Hey, Father." The old man wheeled himself around in a couple of smooth strokes and tossed a glance over his shoulder at the TV. "I like the oldies," he said. "This is called *A Stolen Life*. Sit down. Take a load off."

"How are you, Grandfather?" He grasped Eldon's hand. The palm was weathered and roughened, like the old man's face, the residue of years in the outdoors, working horses, herding cattle, fixing fences. Then he pulled up a straight-backed chair and sat down. The sound of Bette Davis's voice purred between them.

Lawrence came back into the living room with two mugs of coffee, which he sat on a side table close to Eldon. He picked up a remote and turned off the TV. The sound of Bette Davis's voice faded like a wind blowing through. "Poured in a little milk like you like," he said. More than ten years on the rez now, Father John was thinking. People knew his habits. Peculiarities. Like family.

Then came five, ten minutes of pleasantries. The weather. Pow-wow season. Rodeos. Tourists on the rez, taking pictures, as if they had found themselves in a foreign country. Finally, a gradual move into more serious matters: The ghost leg giving him fits. Hurting all the time, and not even there anymore. From the past. He'd like to shoot it. Then he said, "Elsa tells me there was trouble at the mission over that Butch Cassidy film. Red Bull!" He made a hrrumph sound. "Hot head. From a long line of hot heads. I heard stories all my life of how the chiefs had to keep an eye on the Red Bulls or they would ride off, kill a rancher, steal the cattle, fire on troops, and lead them to the village. Get everybody killed."

"He believes the film will bring people here looking for Butch Cassidy's buried loot."

"Nobody's gonna find it." Eldon smiled and shook his head. "Folks have been digging holes in the mountains for a hundred years, and nobody's found it yet. My own relatives take it into their heads to go on treasure hunts every once in a while. We got a whole slew of maps. Maybe one of 'em came from my grandfather, Lone Bear, but Grandfather never said anything to me about a map." He gave a slow, thoughtful shrug. "Lone Bear and George was good friends. Went by the name of George Cassidy then, so he wouldn't bring shame to his family in Utah. Good Mormon people, last name Parker. His real name was Robert LeRoy Parker. I heard stories of how his mother grieved herself to death over her son taking to the outlaw trail. Always talked about going straight, my grandfather said. George took a stab at ranching for a couple of years, got to know everybody in these parts. Folks needed help building a barn, rounding up cattle, George would show up. Real neighborly like. White ranchers and Arapahos, didn't matter none to George. All people, trying to get on, he told Lone Bear. Later, after his partner framed him for stealing a horse and he served time down in Laramie, George hit the outlaw trail again. Robbed banks. Took to robbing trains. Now that took a lot of guts."

Eldon was nodding, an expectant look on his face. Father John agreed. A lot of guts.

"Always got away. They never caught Cassidy. You know why? Story I heard, he was a planner. The gang would switch to the fresh horses, grab fresh supplies, and keep riding, and the posses had to give up. Cassidy had friends on the rez, so he'd ride here. Nobody called the sheriff or the tribal cops. The people protected him, because he was a local. Gave folks money to keep the banks off their land. I think he had a fine old time giving folks bank money to pay off the banks. He showed up at Lone Bear's camp on the Wind River after a couple jobs. Spent a week or so helping with the horses and cattle. Made himself useful, like he was ranching again, going straight. Sometimes brought along one or two gang members. Suspicious characters, always watching the prairie. Never far from their guns. George told them to relax. Nobody was coming to an Indian camp on the rez looking for white men. Pretty soon the day came when they packed their saddlebags and rode off."

"What about leaving behind buried treasure?"

Eldon leaned forward, rubbing at the air above his missing leg, as if he could rub away the pain. "Robbing trains is where they made the big hauls. If he left behind any treasure, it was after robbing a train."

Father John took a moment before he said, "Robert Walking Bear was hunting for treasure when he died. Ruth says he had a map he'd gotten from his grandfather."

"Luther Walking Bear."

"Is it possible Cassidy hid out with one of his ancestors and left behind a map?"

Eldon gave a shout of laughter. "Walking Bears never owned any land, never wanted a place of their own. Liked roaming around, working on different ranches. Always wanted to be free to come and go, like in the Old Time." He paused, his gaze on some faraway point. "I heard George hid out one time at Jesse Lyons's place after robbing a train. I figure he was checking on Mary Boyd, Jesse's wife. Half-breed from the rez, a real beauty and lots of gumption, and George was sweet on her. Courted her when he was ranching up around Dubois. After he went to prison, she married Jesse. Settled down on a piece of land south of Lander."

"Did they have children?"

The old man shook his head. "Before she married Jesse, Mary had a daughter. Gave the girl to Gray Hair to bring up on the rez like an Arapaho. I hear descendants live around here somewhere." He went quiet for a moment. One hand moved over the empty space below his right knee. "There's stories about how the baby was George's, but Mary kept it secret. Didn't even tell him when he came back thirty years later."

"I've heard that he came back, but it's possible that he and the Sundance Kid were killed in Bolivia by the militia."

Eldon laughed. "Can't believe everything you read in history books. He came back, all right. Several times in the '20s and '30s. About 1934, he was here visiting old friends. Went on a camping trip looking for the loot he'd buried in the mountains. Looked up Mary and she went along. Oh, he never forgot her." He took a long moment, staring into the center of the living room, rearranging memories, Father John thought. "You know," he said finally, "there's a hundred maps on the rez. Everybody says his ancestor got a map from Butch Cassidy himself, when what they do is go buy a map in town. You ask me, if Butch gave a map to anybody, it would've been Mary. So she'd have something if she needed it."

The old man looked tired, his eyelids at half-mast. Father John got to his feet, thanked him, and said he'd be back soon. He started for the door, aware of footsteps behind him. On the stoop, he turned to Lawrence. "I forgot to ask if he'd be willing to talk to the film director about Cassidy visiting Lone Bear's camp."

"I'll ask him after his nap," Lawrence said. "I'll get back to you."

9

THE WARRIOR ON the other side of the desk was thirty years old, home from Afghanistan three weeks, divorced six months ago from his high school girlfriend, custody of child awarded to mother with weekend visitation rights to father. Anxious hands thumped the armrests, dark eyes skittered around the office. "Dorie told social services lies about me. Said I neglected Sam, didn't take care of him, wasn't vigilant enough when he was with me. Yeah, that's what she called it, vigilant."

Vicky jotted down notes below notes she had already made. At the top of the page she had written *Interview with Luke Wolf. Member of the Wolf family.* In the Old Time, the name was Soldier Wolf.

"Why would she allege neglect? Is there any history of your neglecting your son?" Vicky could hear the tenseness in her voice. So much neglect and abuse on the rez. Women beaten half to death, children beaten. Drugs, alcohol, always some excuse. Other clients had sat across from her, claiming innocence. Never would hurt the wife or kids. No reason for a judge to issue a restraining order, keep him away from his own home, his own family. She had checked out the stories and found the judge had made the right call. She had advised her clients to go into rehab, get a job, turn their lives around. Then they could go back to court. She knew when the client walked out of her office, shoulders slumped, head thrust forward, that he was walking back to the drugs and the alcohol.

"What did your ex-wife claim?"

"I'm telling you, I took good care of Sam when he was at my place." Vicky nodded. She wanted to believe him. She always wanted to believe. "Dorie's girlfriend called her and said Sam was running the streets. So Dorie calls social services and says, 'You got to get Sam away from that no-good dad of his.' She's got herself a boyfriend and she wants him to be Sam's dad now. She told me they're gonna be a family and she doesn't need me screwing things up. My boy's everything to me. All I thought about in Afghanistan was going home and watching him grow up."

Vicky scribbled more notes. *Denies social services allegation. Never neglected child. Wife has ulterior motive.* "You better start at the beginning," she said. "What made Dorie's friend call her?"

"The woman's a busybody. Lives next door to the place I'm renting in Riverton. Sam was outside playing in the backyard. No way was he running in the street. He's four years old. I was keeping an eye on him."

"You were sober?" The question hovered over the desk.

"I might've had a few beers. Don't mean I wasn't paying attention. Some lady from social services knocks on the door. She's got a cop with her and next thing I know, I'm getting a Breathalyzer test and the lady's driving off with Sam."

And that was critical, Vicky thought. The Breathalyzer test. She could guess the rest of it. Social services had entered the life of Luke Wolf and taken it over. "Did you admit to neglect?"

He was nodding slowly. "Through no fault of my own. I made it clear, no fault of my own. Now I have to go to rehab, therapy, counseling. I got to take off work, and if I take off any more, I'm gonna lose my job."

"Let me get this straight." Vicky set the pen down and looked at the man until he locked eyes with her. "The woman who made the allegation is a friend of your ex-wife's."

"She and Dorie was in cahoots. I'm pretty sure Dorie had her watching my place every minute Sam was there, waiting for something to go wrong. Now all I got is supervised visitation rights. Can't even see my boy without some old bag sitting there watching everything, listening to everything we say. And Dorie is claiming Sam has nightmares after he sees me, so she wants my visitation rights taken away."

She had seen it before, Vicky was thinking. A disgruntled spouse with future plans that didn't include the father of her child. Usually, the mother trying to push the father out of the picture. "Has Sam seen a therapist?"

"Oh yeah. Dorie takes him to some quack play therapist who says Sam acts scared and worried when he plays, 'cause he's been neglected. It's nuts. Sam's scared he's never going to see his dad again. You have to help me. I love that kid. I'd never neglect him."

"But you were drinking."

He nodded. "I had the TV on, but I was keeping an eye on the backyard. Sam was fine."

Drinking. It wasn't going to be easy to convince the court to dismiss a dependency and neglect petition. "I'll have to get records from social services and talk to the therapists," she said. "Any witnesses who would testify to your good character?"

"There's my sister. My mother. Sam misses his grandma. They need to reconnect. I need to reconnect with my little boy."

"Anyone else?" What else would family members say? *Luke's a good guy. Never neglected his son.*

"You can ask the neighbors in the village where Dorie and me lived." Vicky knew the housing area, Easter-Egg Village, with government houses painted pink, yellow, blue. "They'll tell you they never heard any disturbances. No domestic abuse calls from our house. I took good care of her and Sam."

"Okay." This was something to go on. She could confirm he had never been accused of neglect—or abuse—in the past. "I'll need the names and telephone numbers of your family members and neighbors. I can request a court hearing to review social services' finding." She waited a moment before she plunged on. "There are no guarantees, Luke."

Luke Wolf got to his feet, hope flooding his expression. He was moving backward toward the beveled-glass doors, thanking her, thanking her, as if she had already gotten the petition dismissed. She could hear the phone in the outer office start to ring. He gave her a little salute as he yanked open the doors, then swung around and walked into the ringing noise that abruptly cut off. She heard Annie's voice speaking to the caller, and the outside door slamming shut.

Then Annie appeared in the doorway. "Call for you. He won't give his name. Says it's about Robert Walking Bear."

"Where is he calling from?"

"The readout is Unknown. He sounds like he spoke Arapaho before he spoke English."

You could hear the familiar inflections on the rez, Vicky was thinking. She lifted the phone. "Vicky Holden."

"Robert sends you a message."

Vicky was conscious of her own breathing. In and out. In and out. She realized she was listening for what might come next, something that made sense, but the voice was silent.

Finally she said, "If you mean Robert Walking Bear, he's dead."

"His spirit's not at rest."

"Who are you?"

"The messenger."

"What's your message?"

"Be at the coffee shop at eleven forty-five."

Before Vicky could say anything else the line went dead. She got to her feet, went into the outer office, and told Annie to try to get the caller back. Annie jabbed at a couple of keys, then pressed another key for the speakerphone. First came the speeded-up sound of electronic blips, then the buzz of a ringing phone before the noise stopped, as if it had reached a natural end.

"My guess, it's a pay phone," Annie said.

"He wants to meet me at the coffee shop in thirty minutes." It didn't give her much time to get there. Her next appointment wasn't until two o'clock.

Roger had walked out of the back office and placed himself at Annie's shoulder, a sheaf of papers in his hand. "Who wants to meet you?"

"He wouldn't give his name," Annie said. "Most likely from the rez."

Vicky gave a nod of agreement "He says he has a message from Robert Walking Bear."

"You're not going, I hope." Roger leaned past Annie and set the papers on her desk. There was a self-assuredness about the man, the set of his broad jaw, the steadiness in his hands. "When you get a moment, I need these copied." He looked up sharply. "You shouldn't go."

"Ruth doesn't know what happened to her husband. She has the right to know. Maybe this caller . . ."

"Anonymous caller," Annie said.

"He may have information. The coffee shop will be crowded. I'll be fine."

"I'll go with you," Roger said.

Vicky smiled. "If he sees my bodyguard, he won't make contact."

It was close to noon and people were filing into the coffee shop. Vicky bought a cup of black coffee and carried it out to a small table on the sidewalk that two high school girls had vacated, leaving behind latte-smudged plastic glasses and crumpled napkins. She pushed them aside and sat down. A good place in full view of the door. People coming and going, white people mostly, a couple of businessmen in white shirts and blue jeans, a woman who looked Shoshone, swinging a briefcase. Chairs scraped the pavement as people sat down. A low tingling noise of conversation circled the tables. Vicky scooted her own chair out of the sun that beat down on the back of her neck and watched the traffic pass, half expecting a pickup or SUV to pull into the vacant space across the street and an Arapaho man to get out and hurry toward her. He had the advantage. She was the only Arapaho woman here.

Roger strolled across the street as if there were nothing on his mind but a leisurely cup of coffee and a sandwich. Straight into the coffee shop, without a glance her way. She could see him through the plate glass window, queuing up at the end of the line, checking on her from the sides of his eyes. She sipped at her coffee and tried not to smile. She had felt alone lately, disconnected from her own people, from the best part of herself. But here were Roger and Annie making sure she wasn't alone.

Roger came out with a coffee mug in one hand, a wrapped sandwich in the other, and took the last vacant table over in the corner. She looked away, not wanting to catch his eye. The girl who had waited on her inside came walking over. "You Vicky Holden?"

"Yes."

"You have a phone call." She rolled her eyes toward the inside of the shop. "Manager says to tell you we don't accept personal calls at the shop. He's willing to make a one-time exception."

Vicky pushed back from the table and followed the girl inside. The air was heavy with the sweet odors of baked pastries and fresh coffee. The phone dangled on a curly cord from the white box on the wall at the end of the counter. "Manager says to make it short," the girl said as Vicky walked over and picked up the phone.

"Vicky Holden. Who is this?"

"Robert sends you a message."

"Robert . . ." Vicky let the word hang on the line. Dishes clattered, a door slammed shut. "What is this all about. You know he's dead."

"Murder."

"What?"

"Robert can't rest until he gets justice."

"You're saying he was murdered? Who are you and how do you know this?"

"I seen it happen."

"You should go to Ted Gianelli, the FBI agent. He's handling the investigation."

"So he can investigate me? I don't think that's a good idea. I seen it, I know what happened, so I must've done it, right? He'll listen to you."

"I don't know anything about what happened." A man in a white apron standing behind the counter turned and glared at her.

"You're a lawyer. You know the fed and the coroner; they know you. You can tell them the truth."

"The truth? Who are you? This is crazy . . ." Vicky realized the line was dead, as inert as the countertop she leaned against. The man in the white apron was shaking his head at her. She replaced the phone and went back outside. An elderly couple had taken her table and stashed her coffee mug against the empty plastic glasses and wadded napkins. She kept going without looking at Roger. Down the sidewalk, around the corner to where she had left the Ford. A white truck gunned past. She wondered if the anonymous caller were behind the wheel, if he had been watching her go into the shop to take the call. Ruth was sure that her husband's death was an accident, and it looked like an accident. My God! Murder!

She slid onto the hot leather seat, started the engine, and rolled down the windows. The wind stirring around her was hot and dry. She couldn't shake the image of the lake where Robert had died. Water lapping the rocks, darkening the dirt and sand. Brush sagging into a swamp at the edge of the lake. And farther along the road, the ash-strewn circle of a campfire. Someone could have been watching the lake, watching the truck barreling toward the road and stopping. The driver's door opening, Robert getting out. A passenger getting out the other side. What if Robert hadn't fallen into the lake and drowned? What if someone else had been involved and whoever was at the campsite had seen the whole thing? *I seen it happen.*

She tried to shrug off the idea. An alternate story, that was all.

The oldest trick in the defense lawyer's handbook: feed the jury an alternate story of what could have happened, even if there was no evidence that it *had* happened, and the jury will find it difficult to convict beyond a reasonable doubt. Always the possibility something else *could have* happened. There was no evidence anyone had been present at the campsite when Robert died. But there were tire tracks to the campsite. Tire tracks that could have been a week old. Left over from last summer.

But if what the caller said was true, he had witnessed a murder, and if he had seen the murderer, chances were good the murderer had seen him. Which meant he was in danger. A man frightened of coming forward, frightened that Gianelli would scrutinize him instead of following up on what he had to say. Frightened the killer would learn his identity and come after him. Surely he would have identified the killer if he had recognized him. He would have given her something concrete to take to the fed. What he had given her was useless, a tiny spark catching in her mind. She knew she would not be able to ignore it.

She dug her cell out of her bag and tapped in the first numbers of Gianelli's office, then ended the call. She wanted to go back to the lake and have another look around, but first she wanted to talk to the white man who had found Robert's body.

The small, white shop with Fergus Auto Body painted in black letters across the front window stood on the south side of Main Street. A bell over the door jangled when Vicky entered. The place was all brown—vinyl floor, paneled walls, and counter. Voices came from behind the rear wall. Vicky stepped to the counter and pressed a metal bell. It was a couple of minutes before a large man with dark, curly hair and big arms came through the back door. "Help you?"

Vicky said she would like to speak to Alan Fergus, and the man nodded, as if to say, *You found him*. Then she told him she was a friend of Ruth Walking Bear's.

"Real sorry about her husband," Fergus said. "Sure a shock for my boy, seeing the body. I've told the FBI agent all I know."

"I went to the lake after Robert died," Vicky said. "There were a lot of tire tracks, but the coroner, the FBI agent, and other law enforcement had been there. I was hoping you might remember if there were tracks other than those from Robert's pickup."

The man tapped thick fingers on the countertop and squinted toward the window behind her. "Maybe," he said. "I wasn't paying real close attention. Might have been tracks around a campsite where I turned around."

"The campsite farther along the road?"

"Yeah. Hard to tell for sure."

10

THE ROAD SEEMED steeper, the curves tighter. Occasionally columns of deep, black shade blocked the sun. Vicky gripped the wheel, keeping an eye out for rocks that might have hurtled downslope since yesterday. She had called Annie before she started into the mountains and asked her to reschedule her afternoon appointments. "Where are you?" Annie had wailed. "Roger saw you leave the coffee shop. By the time he got to his car, you had driven off." She had told her secretary she talked to the man who had found Robert's body and was now on her way to Bull Lake. That had brought on another wail. "You're going alone?" She told Annie all of it then, what the caller had said, the fear that had come down the line like an invisible current.

Now it was the conversation with the anonymous caller that ran through her mind. Robert, murdered. It didn't make sense. Surely if he had been murdered, there would have been a sign of struggle. Something indicating his death had been violent. But the coroner had even suspected Robert might have drowned himself. And something else that didn't make sense: why had the caller waited so long to come forward?

Come forward? She gave a scoff of laughter. He hadn't come forward at all. He was hiding in anonymity, expecting her to go to the fed with his crazy accusation. And not even an accusation. He hadn't accused anyone, which meant he might not know the so-called killer. Or if he did know the killer, he hadn't wanted to name him.

She came around another curve and plunged into a long, black shadow that felt like an eclipse of the sun. Then out again into the clear, bright light. In the rearview mirror, she saw a white truck dart into the shadow. A lot of white trucks in the area. She had no reason to believe it was the truck she had seen at the coffee shop. But the feeling of unease crept over her like invisible insects. There hadn't been any other traffic on the road; she had been completely alone, just her and the mountain. Now someone was behind her. She pressed down on the accelerator and took the next curve so fast that the Ford rocked on the axles. She kept going, wanting to put as much distance as she could between herself and the white truck, and all the time telling herself this was a public road, she didn't own it.

But Robert hadn't come here to die. He had never been depressed, Ruth said. He was exuberant about life, excited about what he was doing. On a treasure hunt! He hadn't come to be killed! Had he known a killer was waiting, he wouldn't have come.

The lake below came into view, smooth and placid, rolling shades of deep blue and purple edged with silver in the sunlight. A beautiful place, she was thinking, to die.

God! She was as crazy as the caller, buying into his story. Most likely the cause of death was accidental drowning. Why couldn't she leave it at that? Refuse to take any more calls from Anonymous and let the fed handle whatever might come next.

But that was the problem. Something terrible might come next. The caller could be in danger. She had heard the terror running below the confidence in his voice. The same masked terror she had heard in the voices of witnesses testifying against their will, scared almost into incomprehension, eyes bobbing around the courtroom—the floor, the ceiling—everywhere except on the defendant they were condemning.

The road had turned downward, and the lake was coming closer. The white truck shimmied in the rearview mirror, and she forced herself to look away. She tried to remember what Ruth had said about Robert's treasure map. Ruth said Robert had gotten his map from his grandfather, but people who had purchased maps claimed they'd gotten them from some ancestor who had known Butch Cassidy. And what had become of Robert's map? Ruth hadn't said, as if the map didn't matter. An excuse to go treasure hunting. The map was probably in Robert's truck, and the fed hadn't yet released it.

Vicky tapped on the brake and turned into the two-track that ran parallel to the lake. Had she kept going, she realized, she could have driven straight into the lake. She had to concentrate. The Ford skittered over the troughs dug by other vehicles. The white truck had stopped at the turnoff and was making a U-turn. She felt the muscles in her stomach begin to relax. The truck had bothered her more than she realized. *Listen to your instincts,* Grandmother always said. *Your instincts know the truth.* She watched the truck complete the turn and start back. Why had the driver come all this way, if he didn't intend to go to the lake?

She drove toward the strip of land that jutted out into the lake, where Robert had parked his truck. Water lapped at the rocks on the thin strip of swampy, wind-stroked beach. She stopped about thirty feet from the strip and got out. The yellow tape that had been here yesterday was gone. Case closed, she thought. Accidental drowning.

She passed the strip and kept walking toward the campsite she had discovered. She wondered if she could find it again with the wind bending the grass and clumps of sagebrush. Easy for things to disappear in this landscape. So many stories of the Old Time that Grandfather had told about the people scattering across land-scape like this, hiding in the dirt and brush, scarcely breathing, not letting out a sound. The soldiers had ridden past, their white eyes unaccustomed to the play of sunshine and shadow, the wind mov-ing everything about.

She stopped to get her bearings. How far from the strip had she walked? Half a mile? She saw the slight depression then. She pulled over and started walking across the grass. Footprints were still visible, hers and Ruth's. She wondered if there had been footprints here when Gianelli and a forensics team were crawling over the area, and if they had made casts. In the Old Time, no footprints would have been left behind. Those who went last would sweep and brush the trail behind them. The people could cross the plains without leaving a sign.

The campsite looked the same as yesterday, and she wondered what she had hoped to discover. Something she and Ruth, as well as the investigators, might have missed? Something that might identify an anonymous caller? But there was no proof he had been here. He could have been farther along the lake, up above, looking down. Hiding in the grass where no one could see him. Except that someone had been at this campsite recently, and whoever it was had a full view of the strip of land.

She found a stick and started prodding the ashes. The forensics team would have done the same, scattering them about as they prodded. If anything had been left behind, they would have found it. A few feet from the fire pit was a flat-topped boulder. She sat down, thinking that the caller could have sat here and looked out at the lake. And did nothing! If Robert was murdered, the caller had done nothing to help him. Now she had a better sense of the man: scared to death for his own life; unable or unwilling to help someone else.

Out of the corner of her eye, she saw the white truck coming around a curve above. She could feel the knot tightening in her stomach as she watched the truck pull to the side and stop. The driver wore a cowboy hat, wide brimmed and tan-colored, that shaded his face. It was a man, she was sure. Powerful shoulders, a red plaid shirt.

She was certain it was the caller, as certain as if he had walked down the slope and announced himself. He must have been waiting near the coffee shop and had followed her, expecting her to go to the fed. Wasn't that his instruction? But she had come here hoping to find something—she had no idea what it might be—to take to Gianelli, other than the claim of an anonymous caller.

She fought back the impulse to jump up and start running. Take the diagonal route through the grass, run all out for the Ford. She glanced over her shoulder. The Ford was a long ways away. It would take a few minutes to get there. And then what? Drive back along the road, around the curve where the white truck would be waiting? She got to her feet, feeling slightly shaky and disoriented. She was alone here. Annie and Roger were the only ones who knew where she was, and they were in Lander.

Now she was pushing the stick through the ashes, as if this were the most ordinary thing to do, the white truck a blur in her peripheral vision. She would not let the man in the cowboy hat see her fear. She dug past the ashes and into the burned ground, forking up chunks of dirt. An exercise in futility that proved nothing. Forensics would have swept the campsite clean, taken anything they found.

She tossed the stick aside and started for the Ford. It struck her that the white truck could turn downhill, barrel through the brush and grass and spindly stalks of trees, and cut her off. She willed her legs to stretch out, go faster, as if the Ford were an oasis where she could hide, a dirt cave from the Old Time where she could make herself small and invisible.

She saw the small, white flash under a sagebrush, scooped up the torn, half-burned piece of paper, and kept going. Not until she had gotten into the Ford, locked the doors, and maneuvered through a U-turn back to the junction of the two-track and the dirt road, did she open her palm and examine the piece of paper. A faint scribbling of boxes and X's and lines with arrow signs. It looked like part of a tourist map, but different. The paper dingy with age; the scribbling almost formal, deliberate. The piece had been torn off from what looked like the right corner of a larger piece. The torn edge charred and burned.

She drove up the incline to where the road started bending around the mountain, the white truck out of sight, but still there, she was certain. Except that when she came around the curve that overlooked the strip of land and the campsite, the truck was gone. She could make out the tire tracks at the edge of the road where it had parked. The in and out of her breathing sounded loud and shallow around her. He could still be ahead, waiting. She slowed down, peering around each curve as she drove, half expecting to see the white truck stopped in the middle of the road, where she would have to brake hard. Every possibility of flying off the road.

She kept going until she emerged onto the flat road that sloped gently down into Lander. Still no sign of the white truck. She tried to shake away the unpleasant sense of having been shadowed by a cowboy she didn't know, a cowboy who knew her. A few cars and pickups on the road now, the usual traffic between the houses in the foothills and town. Even if the white truck were nowhere in sight, she had the feeling she was still being watched.

TED GIANELLI WAS a big man with a thick neck inside the open collar of a denim shirt. He had black hair streaked with gray and gray eyes that gazed at her with curiosity. He had kept her waiting a few minutes in the entrance to the FBI office building, staring at wanted posters on concrete walls. Finally the metal door had swung open and the fed had beckoned her inside. Down the wide corridor past a warren of offices, the sound of his boots bouncing off the walls, and into a roomy office with paper and file folders stashed around the open laptop computer on his desk. Opera music played in the background; she recognized "Caro nome" from *Rigoletto*. John O'Malley had been playing the aria once when she had visited his office, and for a long time afterward the melody had stayed in her mind. She smiled. Two opera lovers, John and the fed, in the middle of Wyoming.

"What brings you here, counselor?" Gianelli motioned her to a side chair and sat down behind the computer. "Which one of your clients did I arrest in the last day or so? What kind of deal are you hoping to make?"

Vicky stopped herself from laughing out loud. Gianelli had never been willing to make a deal. He was as hard-nosed as they came. He tapped a ballpoint against a folder in rhythm to the aria while she told him she had come about Robert Walking Bear's death.

"It might not have been an accident." That caught his attention, and he stopped tapping, his gaze locked on her. She told him about the anonymous caller and the message he had delivered. Then she told him that she had driven up to Bull Lake and that she was sure the caller had followed her in a white truck. "I found this near the site where Robert died," she said, reaching into her bag and pulling out the piece of paper. Tiny flakes of blackened ash rose in the air. She slid the paper across the desk. "It's part of a map. Ruth said Robert had a map with him when he died."

Vicky waited while Gianelli placed the piece of paper inside a clear plastic bag and sealed the top. Then she went on, explaining before he could ask why she had removed evidence from a possible crime scene. "It was under sagebrush close to a campsite," she said. "It would have blown away."

"We combed the area. Nothing to suggest the fire pit had been used at the time of Robert's death."

"The ashes looked recent."

"You know that how?"

She wanted to say: from years of sitting around campfires when she was a kid, listening to old stories. "Ashes remain in place for days," she said. "They could have been warm when Robert's body was found."

A fixed, concentrated look came over the man's face. "Even if the campsite was used recently, there is no way to know exactly when. Campers could have been there days before Robert Walking Bear's death." He drew in a big breath and tapped the ballpoint several times, staring across the room. Finally he looked at her. "This investigation is ongoing. If someone claims he witnessed a murder, I'm going to take that seriously."

"If I hear from the caller again"—and she would, she was

thinking; the scared, desperate cowboy would call again—"I can try to convince him to come forward."

"Good luck with that," he said.

THE HEAT OF the day settled over the parking lot and sucked at the asphalt. Vicky could feel it grabbing the soles of her shoes as she raised the tailgate on the Ford and lifted out the sack of groceries she had bought on the way home. Salad for dinner, bread, a carton of milk that squished against the bread. She closed the tailgate and headed down the sidewalk toward the glass entryway to her apartment building. From the distance came the faint hum of going-home traffic, hardly rush hour traffic yet, but heavier than during the day. A faint, intermittent breeze carried odors of exhaust and hot asphalt.

"Hello!"

She flinched, almost dropping the sack of groceries. Where had he come from? She hadn't seen anyone in the parking lot, no one near the building. She could hear her heart thumping against her ribs. She looked around, wondering how she could not have seen a white truck. But there was no white truck among the parked vehicles. It was a moment before she recognized the man coming toward her.

"Cutter," he said. He was smiling, a big, lazy grin. "Didn't mean to startle you." He leaned toward her, reaching for the bag. "Let me help you."

"I'm fine." She swung the bag out of his grasp.

"Tried to call you this afternoon. Annie said you were out of the office. Anything I can help you with? You're not sick, are you?"

"No. No. Nothing like that."

"It's just that, well, you look a little tired, and I was wondering . . ."

"It's been a long day." She started to step past him. "So if you'll excuse me . . ."

"Hold on." She could feel the strength in his fingers as he gripped her arm. "I've been waiting for you. I was hoping we could have dinner."

"I don't think so." She felt herself beginning to relax. The white truck had put her on edge, that was all. Here was someone from the past, returning to his own people. "Not this evening. As I said, it has been a long day."

"All the more reason to have a nice, relaxing dinner. It's been years since I've had a steak in Hudson. How about it? What's in that bag? A container of salad? You can do better in Hudson."

It was foolish, she knew, even as she started nodding, smiling at this man who was smiling at her. She had no memory of Jimmy Walking Bear, called Cutter now. And yet he had been in her past, a fellow student at the mission school. And here he was, handsome and thoughtful, wanting to take her to dinner.

"I'll meet you at the restaurant," she told him.

"I can wait for you upstairs." He threw a glance at the top floor of her building, and she wondered for a moment if he knew her apartment number. "I'll drive."

"I'll meet you at the restaurant in thirty minutes." She shouldered her way past him.

11

THE RESTAURANT WAS crowded. An undercurrent of voices mixed with the clank of dishes and the noise of the kitchen door swishing on its hinges. A hostess with blond hair and freckled face led Vicky through the dining room past the tables with families and couples bent over baked potatoes, salads, and steaks that overlapped the edges of the plates. Cutter shifted out of a booth along the wall, his face set in a wide smile. "Thank you," Vicky said to the hostess, but the woman was nodding at Cutter, as if she expected a pat on the back for having delivered the right woman.

"You look good," he said, his eyes on Vicky. He gave an absent-minded wave to the hostess, who turned and started back. "I'm glad you changed your mind."

"I should be home catching up on work." She was thinking of the reports on Luke Wolf that social services had sent over this afternoon. A lot of reading to get through.

"Work will always be there." Cutter took a long look around the restaurant. "This place brings back memories. Whenever Dad sold a beef, he'd bring us here for dinner. Only happened once a year. Times were tough on the rez. How about you?"

"We hardly ever ate out." Grandmother's house, the closest they came to going "out." Buffalo stew and hot fry bread, a campfire, stories around the campfire. It was better than any restaurant. Memories kept rearing up in front of her, those old days, and she realized how much she missed them. The man across from her had been on the rez at the same time, a brown-faced boy, probably experiencing the same things.

A waitress who looked like a younger version of the hostess— blond hair and freckles, a slash of red lipstick— took their order. Vicky waited until the woman had walked away before she asked Cutter what it was like to leave the rez as a kid.

He was quiet a moment, staring off into the restaurant as if he were trying to pull memories out of the tables and booths, the red wallpaper. "I never liked Oklahoma," he said. "We had family there, but it wasn't the same. I had cousins here, and grandparents. I always felt the relatives in Oklahoma wished we would go home. I left soon as I was old enough. Went to Texas and got jobs in the oil fields. Finally wised up and enrolled at Texas Tech. Took six years, but I came out a petroleum engineer. Went right back to a job in the oil fields in management for a lot more money."

He smiled at her, expecting her to pick up her own story, she guessed. She looked away. Cutter Walking Bear was a handsome man, long black hair flecked with gray, and black deep-set eyes that she could feel boring into her. She would have to keep her balance. It was too soon after Adam to become involved in a relationship. She caught sight of the red-haired man at the table across the dining room and, for a disconcerting instant, thought he was John O'Malley. With a wife and two little kids. She shook away the notion. It was absurd the way she thought she saw him—on Seventeen-Mile Road, at a powwow—when he was nowhere in her life.

She realized Cutter was reciting her own life to her: divorced from Ben Holden, seven years in Denver earning a law degree, another couple of years at a big law firm there, and finally—home. He left out the rest of it: Susan and Lucas growing up on the rez with her parents, the snatched weekends with her children getting so tall, growing away from her, the sadness inside her that she had missed the best part of her life.

"What is it?" Cutter said. "Did I get it wrong?"

"You got it right." She forced a smile and waited while the waitress delivered the steak dinners.

"I regret I didn't come back sooner." Cutter sliced off a piece of steak and began to eat. He studied the table, examining something she couldn't see. "Robert was sure he was going to find a lot of money. I went along a few times. Chance to get to know my cousin, and now he's dead. I had a job interview that day with Fowler Oil in Casper. I keep thinking if I had been with him, I could have helped him . . ."

"How could you have helped him?"

"Talked him out of going up there by himself."

"Ruth said he's been going treasure hunting by himself for years." Vicky took a bite of steak. Tender and delicious. There was no mistaking fresh meat, Grandfather always said.

"Ruth didn't know he brought me along."

"I'm surprised he wanted someone else around when he found Butch Cassidy's treasure."

"Butch Cassidy's treasure! Who really believes that? Robert just liked getting away."

"From Ruth?" Vicky waited before she took another bite. Ruth had never given any hint that she and Robert were having trouble.

"From everything. Haven't you ever wanted to get away? It's peaceful in the mountains." Cutter dipped his fork into the baked potato and the rivulets of butter and sour cream. After a moment, he said, "Ruth told me you took her up there yesterday. I refused to take her when she asked me. 'What's the point?' I told her. What good would it do? I had no intention of going back there. It's a sad place, a place of death."

"She wanted to see where Robert died."

"So what did she see? Nothing. The investigators have already checked the place. They should let Robert's spirit rest in peace."

Vicky continued eating, half-aware of the sound of Cutter's voice going on about Ruth and Robert. It was the second time today someone had mentioned Robert's spirit being unable to rest. She thought about telling Cutter she had gone back to the lake this afternoon, then pushed away the impulse. This afternoon, there had been something—a torn, charred piece of map. There had been the white truck and the anonymous caller who said he had a message from Robert. She felt a chill run through her. Spirits sending messages made no sense in the world where she lived now, the white world, a law office, the courts. And yet the old ways were still part of her. Robert's spirit would not rest until his body had been properly buried and sent to the ancestors. She wondered if the Arapaho across from her would understand; he had been away so long.

"Are you okay?"

Vicky tried for a reassuring smile. Yes, of course, why wouldn't she be okay? Straddling two worlds, not at home in either. "What were you saying?"

"It's best if Ruth can put this behind her, instead of dwelling on it."

"Put behind her husband's death?"

"Sooner or later, she has to. I think we can help her start now."

Vicky ate a little more, then set her fork down. "How do you propose we do that?"

"By not encouraging her to ask so many questions. I understand she wants to know how the accident happened . . ."

"How do you think it happened? How could Robert have accidentally drowned?"

"See? That's what I mean. Those are the questions Ruth keeps asking. No one else was there, so no one knows."

"What if someone else was there?"

"What? Are you saying someone else was there?"

Vicky could hear the low, tense voice of the caller. *My name don't matter. He was murdered.* "I have no idea," she said. "Any time someone dies alone in what appears to be an accident, there are always questions."

Cutter pushed his own half-eaten dinner aside and leaned toward her. "Look, Ruth needs to start healing. The longer this investigation goes on, the harder it will be for her to move forward. We're her friends, and we have to help her."

Vicky didn't say anything. She wondered if Ruth was the reason he had wanted to have dinner with her. She could see Ruth on the day Robert had died, pivoting toward the front door every time someone new arrived, tense with expectation. Who else had she been expecting except Cutter, the cousin who had come back to them, made himself welcome in their home?

"How well do you know Ruth?"

"Like I said, we were just getting reacquainted when Robert died. All I remember about Ruth from when we were in school is that she was annoying. Robert was my cousin. I want to help his widow in any way I can."

"Walking Bear? That you?" A large man in a tan cowboy hat and a blue-striped shirt stopped at the booth. In his hand were a dinner check and a credit card that he waved at the table. "I heard you were back. Good to see you."

"Help me out." Cutter smiled up at the man. "You look familiar, but I've been away so long I've forgotten more names than I ever knew."

"Wayne. Wayne Shadow. Hell, we used to shoot hoops over at the mission school."

"Wayne! Sure I remember." Cutter stuck out a hand and gripped the other man's hand. "You know Vicky Holden?"

The man gave her a dismissive sidewise glance. "Ben Holden was a good friend of mine," he said.

Vicky remained quiet. People on the rez still remembered Ben Holden—handsome, friendly. He could do anything, tame a wild horse, ride a bronco, round up a herd of cattle. Bring the world crashing down around her. They didn't know him.

"You back to stay?" The man gave his full attention to Cutter, as if she weren't there, and she realized that, in some way, when she had divorced Ben Holden, she had ceased to exist on the rez.

"That's my plan. I have a line on a job with Fowler Oil in Casper, but I'm hoping to work in the oil fields on the rez. I'm here to make up for lost time. What have you been up to?"

"Hired on with the school district as a bus driver couple years ago. Still live in the family place. You remember how we used to race the ponies out in the pasture?"

"Yeah, but I'm drawing a blank. Where was the place?"

"White Horse's place west of Ethete. Been in the family since

Arapahos came to the rez. Butch Cassidy himself used to hide out there after a job. You see that movie bunch on the rez? Making a film about old Butch? Hell, we got stories in the family that film crew would like to get ahold of. They offer enough money, I'd be glad to talk to them." He turned to Vicky, a slow, reluctant motion. "You know how I could get in touch with them?"

Vicky shook her head. "Sorry."

The man rolled his shoulders in a shrug. "Lot of stories on the rez about Butch and his gang. Trouble is, people are going to give them away. I'm thinking about getting up a union of all the old families with stories. We agree on a price, and everybody's paid the same or nobody talks. What do you think?" He gave Vicky a half glance. She remained quiet.

"Makes sense to me," Cutter said.

"Sorry to hear about your cousin. Is it true he was looking for old Butch's buried treasure?"

"So I've heard."

"Claimed he had the original map that Butch himself drew up. What a crock of you-know-what. Walking Bears was poor as prairie mice. Never had a place where Butch could've hid out. My bet is, no Walking Bear ever laid eyes on Butch except if he happened to ride by. Hey!" He stuck out his hand again. "Don't be a stranger. Stop by the place for dinner next Sunday."

"Thanks." Cutter looked at Vicky. "I may have other plans."

Wayne Shadow gave a two-finger salute and started for the front of the restaurant. A black-haired woman with a baby on her back and a toddler in hand hurried after him.

The waitress cleared the plates and brought cups of coffee. Vicky sipped at the hot liquid a moment before she said, "Ruth said Robert got his map from his grandfather."

"I hear you can buy maps lots of places."

"You think that is what he had? A map for tourists?"

"Listen, Vicky, I tried to talk him out of looking for treasure. It's a fool's game. But the man was obsessed. Let's forget Robert for a while, okay? I want to talk about you."

Vicky finished her coffee and set the mug down. "I'm a lawyer with a pile of work to review, and I'm afraid it's time for me to say good night." She slid to the end of the booth and got to her feet.

Cutter stood up beside her. He picked up the check the waitress had laid at the end of the table. "Let me take care of this first and I will follow you home."

"That's not necessary." She thanked him for dinner and headed for the front door.

SHE WAS COMING around the curve into Lander when she realized the dark truck had been behind her for the last couple of miles. Cutter behind the wheel, she knew, by the tilt of his cowboy hat, the straightened set of his shoulders. He was taking the long way to the rez. He was following her.

She eased up on the accelerator and turned into the residential area. Past brick bungalows with lights flickering in the windows, in and out of circles of light from the streetlamps. She pulled into the parking lot, hurried to the glass-enclosed entryway, and jabbed a finger at the elevator button. There was the truck again, parked at the curb, Cutter waving as she stepped into the elevator and pressed the floor button. Then she hit the close button and braced herself against the metal railing as the elevator clanked upward.

Cutter Walking Bear, she was thinking. Making sure she reached home safely. A warrior looking out for women and children, the helpless. God, she wasn't helpless. When she saw him again, she would thank him and make it clear she wasn't helpless. When she saw him again, she thought. He would be back.

She hurried down the corridor, let herself into the apartment, and flipped on the light switch. She walked over and looked out the side of the window. The truck was still at the curb.

12

1899

MARY SPRINKLED A handful of flour on the dough and thumped it onto the table. She leaned into it, rolling, pushing, and kneading until the dough became soft and pliable, then added more flour and repeated the process. Finally she plunked the dough into a metal pan and spread a cloth over the top. The kitchen was warm and muggy, filled with the smells of simmering meat, potatoes, and onions. She put another chunk of wood into the stove and stepped out onto the back porch. The hot breeze washed across the floor planks and rattled the thin metal chairs where she sat sometimes in the afternoons, getting her breath before Jesse and the hired hand came in from the pasture. This last week, there had been four men to feed, but she hadn't minded. It had been nice to settle in with George at mealtimes. The evenings, sitting out here, George and his friend Sundance on the steps, she and Jesse in the chairs. George as sunny and friendly as she remembered. He had lit up her life once, before she met Jesse.

She stretched her legs and massaged the cramps in her fingers. This was a hard place, but it was all they had. They had started from nothing, a patch of dry dirt scrambled with sagebrush and buffalo grass. They had built the house and barn and the outbuildings themselves. At times she had feared the place would kill them, with the hot winds that blew all summer and the blinding winter blizzards that piled snow against the doors and locked them inside for days. Jesse had gone to the bank a few years ago, desperate to keep what they had built. Borrowed enough money to buy hay to keep the cattle alive over the winter when the snows raged and the temperatures stayed below zero. Paying the interest had eaten up every extra nickel. And now the principal was about to come due.

She swatted at a mosquito. Banks were getting rich all over the county by foreclosing on ranchers who couldn't pay off their loans. If that happened, Jesse would have to hire out on other ranches. She would have to try to get work somewhere. They could lose the place, lose everything.

"Mary! What is it?"

Mary shifted around. George stood at the end of the porch, holding his hat in one hand, patting the top of his head with the other, as if to brush off a nest of mosquitoes. His hair looked thinner, lighter than she remembered. It was ridiculous, the way old times kept jumping in front of her.

"Just taking a little rest before dinner."

George walked around and sat down on the step. He looked up at her. "Are you happy?"

"What a silly question."

He turned toward the pasture. "I like to think of you as happy. Jesse's a good man."

Mary was quiet. She stared at the back of his head, the round, sunburned bald spot getting started. Finally she said, "I waited for you to come back like you promised."

He was staring out at some point far away. "Didn't have anything to offer you, Mary. No kind of life to give you. Around these parts, I was a horse thief, and that's all I was."

"You were a rancher."

"Didn't work out, so I went back to stealing horses. On the run from the law all the time. You were a lady. Deserved better."

"I guess that was my decision." She started to say that he never said good-bye, then stopped herself. George Cassidy hated good-byes.

"I had to decide for both of us. Soon as they let me out of prison, I took off. Been running ever since." He leaned back on the palms of his hands and turned his head toward her. The familiar smile creased his face. "Leastways I got a plan now. Get myself a big-enough stake and take off for parts unknown where nobody ever heard of the Hole in the Wall gang. Get me a nice spread and settle down. Nice place like this. No more running."

"This will be the bank's soon."

"What are you talking about?"

"Principal due on a loan Jesse had to take out to keep body and soul together a couple winters back."

George sprang to his feet and slapped his cowboy hat against his thigh. "I'll speak to Jesse."

"Not your business, George. You got your own worries. The law could come riding out here anytime." She thought she had heard the hooves pounding the ground last night. Lying there, next to Jesse, staring into the darkness, and wondering if that was the posse coming and if they'd shoot first and ask questions later. She stood up, smoothed her apron, and made an excuse about having to check on dinner. Jesse would not have wanted her spilling their business to strangers.

GEORGE SEEMED THE same at dinner, as if he didn't know the place was collapsing around them. The wide grin, the big laugh that rang around the walls, the way he thumped his fist against his thigh as he told about the bank teller who had turned to stone, eyes bugged out, mouth stuck in a circle, when bank robbers told him to hand over the cash. How one robber had held a gun on the customers while another had jumped over the counter and scooped the cash into a canvas bag. How the bank teller had stood there like a statue, except for the big puddle at his feet that the robber tried to avoid when he jumped back over the counter.

"What bank was this?" Anthony, the hired hand, was the only one not laughing.

"Just a story I heard around," George said.

Anthony mopped up the last of his stew with a piece of bread, then sat back and folded his arms across his chest. "Seems to me you and Sundance here live a right dangerous life."

George let out a shout of laughter. "Nah. Pretty tame life, isn't that right, Sundance?"

Sundance hadn't said anything during supper, but he had been a man of few words since he and George had arrived. Sitting back, watching. It was George who made the party.

"You say so," Sundance said after some consideration.

Anthony scraped his chair back and got to his feet. "I thank you, Mary, for a fine meal. If you don't mind, I'm gonna retire now. We're branding calves tomorrow."

It was like a cloud drifting out of the house, Mary thought, as the hired hand's boots clicked across the kitchen floor. The screened door opened and snapped shut.

"What do you know about him?" Sundance set his elbows on the table and leaned toward Jesse.

"Never asked questions," Jesse said. "Law of the West. Man does his job, that's all that matters."

"I was thinking the Union Pacific has probably put up a nice bounty on us by now."

"Any man works for me and blabs our business to the outside is a dead man."

Now it was Sundance's turn to get up and thank Mary for the supper. He was going to take a walk, he said, and have a smoke. When the door slammed after him, George turned to Jesse, and Mary felt her neck muscles tighten into the familiar knot that usually brought on a headache. She rubbed at her neck.

"How can I help you, my friend?"

"You're helping me plenty. Got the fences fixed, cattle rounded up. Finish the branding tomorrow."

"I mean help you keep this place."

Jesse shot a glance down the table at Mary. "We got our problems, but I intend to work things out with the bank." The words sounded empty and hopeless. "Anyhow, it's our business."

"Well, I don't mean to interfere. But this is a real nice spread that you and Mary have put your sweat into for how long now?"

"Four years."

"You have Mary here to think about, and I don't want to see you lose what you've worked for like a lot of other ranchers in these parts. Banks are a bunch of vultures. They always know when to swoop down." George took his time getting to his feet. Without saying anything else, he went outside.

"You shouldn't have told him," Jesse said.

"It's been on my mind, Jesse. Nothing else I been able to think about, so I blurted it out."

She could hear George's footsteps receding across the porch. The tension in her neck was shooting into her head. Then the footsteps came back, the screened door opened and closed, and the footsteps reverberated across the kitchen and into the dining room.

George walked over to his place at the table and set down a metal box. The lid squealed as he lifted it, as if the hinges needed oiling. Stacks of bills sprang free around columns of gold coins. "How much you need to get free of those vultures?" He had fixed Jesse with that determined stare he had used when he meant business.

"I can't take your money," Jesse said.

"Well now, it's not exactly my money, is it?"

"If the railroad catches up to you, they'll want their money back."

"Let them get it out of the bank. Here's an idea. Let them rob the bank." George threw his head back and laughed. Then he started counting out bills. "What's it gonna take? Thousand? Two thousand?"

Mary put her hand to her mouth. "You said that was your stake," she said, the words muffled and queer against her fingers.

"There's lots more where this came from." George leaned across the table and set the bills in front of Jesse.

Jesse stared at the bills for a long moment. Then he peeled off the top two and pushed the rest back toward George. "This is all I need, and I thank you. Soon as I'm able, I'll pay you back."

"You'll have to find me," George said. "I'll be off on my own place somewhere." He set the bills back in the box, closed the lid, and held the box against his chest. "All the same to you, I'm going to ride into the mountains first thing in the morning and find a safe place for this loot. I'll be back in time to help finish up the branding."

"Safe place?" Jesse's head jumped back in surprise. "What are you fixing to do? Hide it under a tree? Bury it?"

"Only other safe place I can think of is the bank. And we all know, banks aren't that safe these days." He was still laughing as he retraced his steps across the kitchen and outside.

Jesse didn't say anything for so long that Mary wondered if he would ever speak to her again. Sitting there, staring at the table, ruffling the bills. "I did this for you," he said after a moment, his voice low and sad. "I made you a promise I'd take care of you, and if this is what I have to do to keep that promise, I'm gonna do it."

"You can't take that money to the bank." The truth of it made her heart skip about. She narrowed her eyes with the pain that spread through her forehead. "The bank knows we don't have the money. The whole county knows George and Sundance are hiding out around here. You show up with that kind of money, the bank will put two and two together. Somebody will figure out that we've got visitors. They'll send the posse out here."

Jesse seemed to mull this over. "I'll come up with a story," he said. "Tell 'em my rich brother came to visit and gave me the money. That ought to be good enough. For a while," he added. "George never stays anyplace very long."

13

A HAZY SUN shone through the white clouds that drifted across the sky when Father John left the church and headed toward the residence. He and Bishop Harry took turns saying morning Mass, and today had been his turn. The sound of sputtering engines floated from the cottonwood tunnel as cars and pickups drove toward Seventeen-Mile Road. His parishioners, the same wrinkled brown faces that looked up at him every time he said Mass, fingers turning the pages of missals, working the rosary beads.

When the bishop had first arrived, Father John had suggested the old man sleep in the mornings. After all, the bishop had come to St. Francis to recuperate. Father John had assured him that he could handle the Masses. The bishop had reared back as if he'd taken a punch in the stomach, and in a way, Father John guessed that maybe he had, that his suggestion was a polite way of saying the old man was no longer up to the job. "Far as I know, I'm not dead yet," the bishop had said. "When I'm dead, you can say Mass every morning, nobody to stop you."

Walks-On had been asleep on the front stoop. Now he came bounding down the path, the red Frisbee clamped in his jaws. It was the golden retriever's morning routine. Either Father John or the bishop had to throw the Frisbee a few times before he could go inside for breakfast. But the dog never wanted to let loose of his prize, and it took Father John a little while to snatch away the Frisbee and toss it beyond the grass. The dog followed the red blur that sailed through the air, hip hopping on three legs, head and neck stretched forward.

Father John threw the Frisbee a few more times, then ran up the concrete steps of the stoop and let himself into the entry, Walks-On trotting behind him. The bishop was in the kitchen, bent over the *Gazette*. "Investigation into Robert Walking Bear's death still going on. Up at the lake all by himself. What else could it be except an accident. Might've had a heart attack before falling into the lake."

"Heart attack! Accident!" Elena let out a loud snort. She stood at the stove, ladling oatmeal into a bowl. The same breakfast every morning, but this was a routine Father John had settled into. Not long ago, the housekeeper had decided to make pancakes, and he remembered exchanging glances with the bishop. The pancakes were delicious, but a change in the routine didn't seem right.

"What do you mean?" Father John took his place at an angle to the bishop, who had set the paper down and was staring at the housekeeper's back.

Elena took her time. Filling the bowl to the brim, carrying it over to the table, moving the small pitcher of milk closer to the bowl. "Don't like to say anything about the dead with Robert's spirit still roaming until he gets buried and sent off to the ancestors."

"But you don't think his death was an accident."

"When people get sad, they do unexpected things."

Father John didn't say anything. He could hear the quiet, raspy breath of the bishop. Elena turned back to the stove, lifted the pan over to the sink, and turned on the faucet. Eventually she looked around. "Like I say . . ."

"You don't want to speak of the dead, but you believe Robert was sad."

"He had a dream that would never come true. He was going to find buried treasure, and that was going to change his life, make him happy. Now if that isn't sad, you tell me what is."

"Maybe the fun was in the hunting, even if he never found anything."

"Nobody's going to find that treasure. Butch Cassidy himself couldn't find it."

Father John thought about what Eldon Lone Bear had said. That Butch had returned to the reservation some thirty years after he supposedly buried some money. That folks in the area had seen him, met with him, gone camping with him in the mountains. "You don't believe Butch Cassidy and the Sundance Kid were killed in Bolivia?"

Elena blew out a puff of air, then poured a cup of coffee and set it in front of Father John. She went back to washing the pan in the sink, scrubbing hard, elbows flying with determination. "I guess we know what happened on our own rez," she said, almost under her breath.

"A familiar quandary." The bishop sounded as if he had been mulling things over and had reached a conclusion. "The past has many truths, depending upon how it lives on in the minds of the living."

Father John sipped at the coffee and watched the old man over the brim of the cup. He had enormous respect for Bishop Harry Coughlin, philosopher, theologian, pastor with a deep understanding of the human heart. But he had been taught to find the evidence, and you will have the truth. One truth, not many. He said, "Either Butch Cassidy and the Sundance Kid died in a shoot-out in Bolivia, or they didn't. If they died, Butch Cassidy was not on the rez in the 1930s." He could hear Lone Bear's voice playing in his mind: *He came back, all right.*

The bishop held out his hand and wriggled his fingers. "Evidence is elusive, is it not? Like sand running through your fingers. A new piece of evidence surfaces, and old beliefs are wiped away, proved wrong."

It was true, Father John was thinking. The truth could be found in stories passed down through the years. He had heard so many stories on the rez that differed from the history books, until the history books were proven wrong. A battle on the plains where the official records claimed belligerent Indians had killed dozens of soldiers, but descendants of Arapaho warriors had said, no—only Arapahos had died. Warriors, women, and children. One day letters turn up in an old trunk in an attic, written by troopers who had witnessed the events, disclaiming the official reports. Only then did historians change their minds about what had actually happened. They had a way of believing what had been written down.

"Butch himself was here." Elena pivoted about and faced him, drying her hands on her apron. This was how she stood when he had pushed too far, doubted too much: straight, shoulders back, head high, daring him to contradict her again, like one of the women warriors in the Old Time, as brave and determined as the men. "Go talk to Mary Boyd's granddaughter over at White Pines. Might give you a gift."

*   *   *

HE HAD STARTED the pickup and was about to back into Circle Drive when Walks-On came running over. Lately the dog had insisted upon going along whenever he headed out to visit parishioners in the hospital or have coffee with the elders. Sometimes he wondered if the dog understood the conversations around him. Before he had excused himself from the table, the bishop had nodded in his direction and told him he would hold down the fort. Which made Father John smile at the idea of Bishop Harry, rifle in hand, on the battlements of an old log fort on the plains, fending off any attackers, holding it down. Walks-On had sprung off his blanket and started for the front door.

And now here was Walks-On, such a mixture of disappointment and hope flashing in his black eyes that Father John put the car in neutral, pushed open the passenger door, and waited for the dog to jump inside, which he did with alacrity, pushing off his single hind leg.

By the time he headed into the tunnel of cottonwoods, Walks-On was licking his ear. He turned up the volume on "E fra quest'ansie" and made a right onto Seventeen-Mile Road. The voices of Nedda and Silvio soared over the wind blasting across the open windows. "Good boy," he said, hoping the dog would get the message and stop licking.

FATHER JOHN FOUND a parking place in the shade in front of the low-slung, tan brick building with the sign next to the door that said, White Pines. The nursing home had a familiar feeling about it. Any number of parishioners had spent the last years of their lives there since he'd been at St. Francis. Morning was usually the best time to visit.

He left the windows down and told Walks-On he'd be back in a few minutes. Inside was the stilled hush of important things happening in a routine manner. Several elderly patients sat in the upholstered chairs arranged around the vinyl floor. Odors of antiseptic mixed with the faint odors of coffee and fried eggs. He stopped at the counter on the left and waited until the receptionist swung her chair around. She gave him a wide grin. "Father John! Good to see you. Who is the lucky resident you've come to visit?"

"Julia Marks. Is she available?"

"Oh, I believe so. Julia spends most of the day watching old movies on TV. You'll find her in the recreation room." She gestured with her head toward the sunny space that opened off the far end of the reception area.

He knew the way. Most of the time it was in the recreation room where he found his parishioners who had moved into White Pines. The wall of windows that ran along the west side looked out across Riverton to the rolling brown foothills of the Wind River range. He often found the elderly Arapahos staring out the windows at the trees and roofs of Riverton, as if they were seeing the wide spaces of the reservation nestled beneath the foothills.

Julia Marks sat slumped in a padded recliner, clicker in her lap, eyes glued to the TV a few feet away. A black-and-white movie was playing, the volume so low that the buzz of conversations drowned out the staccato movie voices. Julia stared at the screen with an entranced, faraway look. A howl of triumph went up from a nearby table where three gray-haired women and a bald-headed man were playing cards. Father John found a vacant chair and pushed it close to Julia. "How are you, Grandmother?" he said.

She lifted her gaze from the world unfolding on the screen and turned toward him. Her eyes were wide spaced and dark, with pinpricks of light. She had tightly curled white hair, the whitest hair he had ever seen, untouched by any other color, as if the curls had been painted onto her head, and the clear, unwrinkled skin she must have had forty years ago. "Buster?" she said. The light in her eyes flickered on and off.

"Father John. It's good to see you again."

She waited a few seconds, her jaw moving around inaudible words. "My friend from the mission."

"Yes, that's right." It had been about two months since he was last here. Two of his parishioners had died six months earlier, leaving only Julia and Will Morningstar, and Will had been in a coma for weeks. He had meant to visit Julia; it had been on his list of things to do. He told her how glad he was to see her.

"Is Charlotte here?"

Charlotte? Oh yes. Charlotte, her daughter, who lived somewhere in the area. "I haven't seen her," he said.

The old woman was looking around now, craning her neck and twisting her head sideways, eyes scanning the room. Another shout of triumph rose from the card table. A man moved past on a walker, nodding at Julia as he went. "You have a good morning, you hear?" he said.

Father John decided to take a chance. Sometimes the present faded away, but the past . . . the past had a way of remaining. "Do you remember your grandmother Mary Boyd?"

"Mary." The old woman settled back into her chair and stared at the TV, as if she were trying to reconcile this new thought with the story she had been lost in. It was a long moment before she looked back. "Grandmother taught me my ABCs, taught me to read. I used to slip off her lap, it was so big and round."

"Did she talk about Butch Cassidy?"

Julia went quiet. "Who?" she said eventually.

"The outlaw, Butch Cassidy. I've heard he and your grandmother were friends."

"Oh?" she said. "Is that a fact?" Nodding, staring at him, the light gone from her eyes. "What would she be doing with an outlaw? Charlotte!" She stretched herself in the chair and tossed her head again. "Where's Charlotte? She'll tell you Grandmother never knew any outlaws. Where is she? Charlotte!" She was shouting, and the buzz of conversation died around them.

Father John took the old woman's hand. It was as light and smooth as a moist leaf. "It's all right," he said. "I'm sure Charlotte will be coming soon."

A nurse in green scrubs with a stethoscope around her neck materialized beside them. "Are you all right, Julia?"

The old woman gave a series of quick nods, like a child eager to please. Then a dark shadow passed across her eyes. "You're not Charlotte," she said.

"Your daughter called. She will be here later. Would you like to go back to your room and take a rest?"

"Oh no. I must watch my movie. I don't know what might happen. Anything might happen in the movies, you know."

The nurse patted the old woman's shoulder. "You call if you need anything." She bestowed a complicit smile on Father John, as though they shared something that had eluded Julia. "I'm sorry, Father, but . . ."

"I'll come by another time." He laid Julia's hand on the armrest and got to his feet. "I'll see you soon," he said, but the old woman had entered into the movie story, the muted voice of a politician at a podium, waving his arms.

The nurse walked him to the reception area. "Sometimes she remembers the past as if it were yesterday," she told him. "The next time you come, she may remember everything."

14

FROM BLUE SKY Highway, Father John could see the trucks and vehicles, the crowd gathering along the riverbank like a cloud of mosquitoes, the white tipis and the crossed poles framed against the sky. He made a right onto a dirt road and parked behind the food van. One side had been pulled up and braced on metal rods. Inside a man in a white jacket was turning hamburgers on a grill while a plume of gray smoke sputtered out of a vent on the roof. Smells of charred meat and coffee hung in the air. Walks-On jumped down from the pickup and lifted his head toward the aromas.

Before he and the dog had walked very far down the road, a man in a pink shirt and blue jeans, clipboard in one hand, stepped in front of him. "You got a pass?"

Father John put up both hands, palms out. *I come in peace.* "Father O'Malley from the mission," he said. "Todd Paxton asked me to stop by."

"Todd looking for a three-legged dog?"

"The dog's with me."

The man in the pink shirt slipped a phone out of a case on his belt. He pushed a button, stared at the phone, then said: "Todd? Got a priest here with a dog, says you told him to stop by."

"Send him over." The director's voice echoed around itself, as if he were speaking inside a barrel.

"We're pretty busy today. Got a lot of shooting ahead. Keep that dog under control and make it short." The man in the pink shirt said all this while motioning Father John forward with the phone. A small plane passed overhead, leaving a rumbling noise in its wake.

He found the director in the center of a crowd, heads bent in his direction. After a minute or two, the people around him backed away and hurried off in different directions. All around were the clanking and scuffing noises of busyness. Todd dropped into a canvas chair, an air of exhaustion about him. Father John could feel the man's eyes on him as he walked over.

"Get a chair." The director waved to a man standing nearby, then turned back to Father John. "Glad you could stop by," he said as Father John perched on the canvas chair that had appeared behind him. Walks-On settled on the bare dirt, turning his head side to side at the kaleidoscope of sights and motion. "We're shooting Lone Bear's camp today," Todd said. "The old maps say this is the exact place on the Wind River where it was located."

Father John took a minute. After ten years with the Arapahos, the white ways of putting business first jolted him a little. Finally he said, "Eldon Lone Bear's grandfather was a friend of Butch Cassidy. Eldon's grandson told me the old man would be glad to talk to you."

The director slapped a hand against his thigh. "Great news! Let's hope his grandfather passed along stories about his buddy Butch." He leaned over and held his hand above Walks-On's head. "This guy friendly?"

"Pretty much likes everybody."

He patted the dog's head. "More than I can say for the Indians around here."

"I've also spoken with Maris Reynolds," Father John said. He had called the woman yesterday and asked if she might be willing to talk to the film crew about Butch's ranch near Dubois, next to her grandfather's place. She had sounded excited that somebody cared about her stories. She told him she had gone to the shooting site, but some guy with a clipboard had blocked her way, which she found insulting. Nobody in these parts blocked the way of a Reynolds, she announced. Her family had been here before . . .

He had interrupted. "Would it be okay to give the director your number?"

"Yes, of course," she had told him. He could feel the subject of the opera tickets clinging to the line like a live creature, and just as he expected, Maris asked if he had made plans to use the tickets. When he said he was still thinking about it, she told him to stop lollygagging. "A very good word," she said. "No reason for it to go out of use. I expect you to do your part to bring it back."

He had promised to try, then hung up and looked at the opera tickets held down by a paperweight. A tempting thought, the opera, but it would mean leaving the bishop alone for three days. He had pushed the thought away.

Now he told Todd Paxton that Maris Reynolds's grandfather and Butch Cassidy had been good friends. "They ran adjoining spreads," he said, tearing off the top page from the tablet he carried in his shirt pocket. He had written down Eldon's telephone number as well as Maris's. He handed over the paper.

Todd stared at him with surprise-widened eyes. "This is good stuff," he said. "I regret not coming to the mission sooner."

"When people hear that Eldon and the descendant of one of the old families are talking to you, others might step up." It was possible, Father John was thinking. Arapahos had always been friendly with outsiders. In the Old Time: the friendliest tribe on the plains, the tribe that collected the stragglers lost from the wagon trains, took them to their village, fed them, and led them back to the trains. It wasn't like Arapahos to turn away from strangers.

Todd Paxton slipped the paper into his shirt pocket, patted Walks-On's head again, then leapt out of the chair so fast the dog gave a little twitch. "Come on. I'll show you around the camp while they're rearranging props."

Father John followed the man past an array of cameras on tripods, people hustling about, arms loaded with eagle-feathered headdresses, painted shields, quivers of arrows and armfuls of bows, tanned, fringed shirts, a black metal pot banging on a tripod.

And then they were in the village. A collection of white tipis that from a distance resembled tanned skins, but close-up he could see were canvas. Painted on the walls were red, white, yellow, and black figures of horses, buffalo, and warriors charging an unseen enemy, headdresses flying behind. All meant to depict the events in Lone Bear's life. Somebody in the crew had done the research. The tipis encircled a campfire, logs latticed on one another, as if the fire might alight at any moment. Except, on closer inspection, he saw the logs were made of Styrofoam.

Between the campfire and the Wind River stood a brush shade that looked genuine, with stripped lodgepole pines and young cottonwood trees forming the walls and the roof. There was a wide opening in the wall facing east. Sunlight shone through the branches and cast leaf shadows over the dirt floor inside, a sight that Walks-On seemed to find fascinating, since he kept nosing at the shadows.

Inside the brush shade the temperature was twenty degrees cooler, an engineering marvel that had made it possible for Arapahos and other tribes to survive the burning summers on the plains. The cottonwoods muffled the shouts and the pounding footsteps outside, as if the activity were far away, leaving the clear sounds of the river brushing the rocks and lapping at the shores.

Father John felt as if he had stepped into the past, as if Lone Bear himself might appear, invite him to a feast, and Butch Cassidy might stroll in. Grinning, slapping everyone on the back.

"What do you think?" Todd Paxton stood in the opening, a blurred shadow backlit by the light outside.

"I'm looking around for Lone Bear himself."

The director laughed. "It's going to be even better when we add the old stories. Everything will come to life. That's what I love about documentaries, the you-are-there feeling." He stepped backward, and Father John joined him outside. The director threw out his arms and framed an imaginary scene with his hands. "I can see Eldon in the brush shade, reminiscing about his grandfather. Or maybe seated around the campfire out here." He pivoted toward the fire pit. "Yes, that might work best. Telling stories around the fire that plays across his face. We'll have to adjust the lights."

Father John had to move sideways past two men hauling a narrow cot into the tipi, covered with a buffalo robe that dragged on the ground. Other crew members jostled past, carrying more buffalo robes. "Almost ready, Todd," one called.

A dozen women were milling about, dressed in skin dresses, with black hair that hung in braids beneath the beaded bands around their foreheads. Other actors started walking over: warriors, naked to the waist, blue and red slashes painted on their brown chests and faces. They gathered near the tipis, around the campfire, inside the brush shade. Everyone moving into a pre-assigned place. Warriors sat down cross-legged on the ground and began carving arrow points. Women bent over the pots and pushed large bone spoons around whatever was inside.

A sharp clack sounded, then quiet fell over the camp. Todd had moved behind the cameras, and he and the crew members stood very still. The only people in motion, the actors and the cameramen who turned the big lenses toward a clump of trees farther down the river. Out of the trees rode a big man in a cowboy hat and what looked like tan corduroy pants and jacket. A rifle lay in a scabbard next to his right leg. He rode close to the camp and dismounted with the ease of a man who had spent years on a horse. The cameras locked on him as he looped the reins around a willow branch. A small boy ran out from a tipi, shouting, "*Hou! Hou!*" The cameras turned on him now. The boy shouted something else in Arapaho and the camp sprang into life. Everyone hurried over to the white man, warriors with arms outstretched, women bowing, tapping the ground, making the ululating sounds of joy.

An elderly man stepped out of a tipi. Dressed in a white shirt decorated with beads, quills, and fringe, leather trousers with fringe down the sides, white moccasins. He waited, arms at his sides, until the crowd of Indians parted and the white man came toward him. Then he went to meet him and gripped the white man's hand. "Good to see you, my friend."

They turned back and dropped cross-legged at the campfire,

bending heads together, conversing in low voices, and Father John understood this would be where a voice-over explained how the man who called himself George Cassidy used to visit the camp of his Arapaho friend, Lone Bear.

"Cut!" Todd yelled. He went over to a man with a clipboard and conferred for a moment, then stopped at the campfire and spoke to the actor playing Cassidy. Then he was back beside Father John. "We're going to do another take. Cassidy's too stiff. Butch was at home with Lone Bear; he liked the Arapahos, got along fine with them. I want to see more warmth and excitement, old friends getting together after some time."

"I'm looking forward to the film," Father John said. "Thanks for the preview." He checked around for Walks-On, but the dog was already bounding toward the pickup, as if he had figured out it was time to go.

"One more thing." The director's fingers dug into his arm, and he turned back. "We did a shoot in the mountains on the possibility that Butch buried his loot hereabouts. I picked up a treasure map at the bookstore in Lander. Figure the maps must mean locals believe the loot is still there."

"It's a good story." One of those Western yarns, Father John was thinking, that grew in the telling and retelling. "I don't know whether there's any truth in it."

The director gave a quick look around and, still gripping Father John's arm, led him farther from the camp. "One of the warriors"—he nodded back at the actors—"overheard some gossip at a bar in town last night. Is it true an Arapaho was drowned in the mountains last week looking for the loot?"

"The man liked getting away," Father John said. "The idea of buried treasure was a good excuse."

"Something else." The director stayed with him along the dirt path. "The actor heard that the man—what was his name? Robert . . ."

"Walking Bear."

"Yeah, Walking Bear. Rumor is he might've been murdered. Found the loot and somebody took it from him."

Father John was quiet a moment. This was news he hadn't anticipated. "The rez is full of rumors," he said. "Most likely, Robert's death was an accident."

Todd stopped walking and turned toward him. Excited, the color flaring in his cheeks, light bristling in his eyes. "We could have a mystery here. Nothing better to promote the documentary than a modern-day murder linked to Butch Cassidy. See what I mean? Not just a tour through the past with a fascinating character, but repercussions today. Look"—he tightened his hand on Father John's arm—"anybody around here with family stories about Butch Cassidy burying his loot? Now that would be a find. That would make the film. I hear Robert was married. Do you think his wife might . . ."

"The woman is grieving, Todd."

"Sure, sure. Naturally." He shook his head and looked off into space. "Still, if her husband was murdered, she'd want to know who did it."

Father John freed himself from the director's grasp and left him standing in the middle of the road, thumbs hooked in his jeans pockets. He walked past the man in the pink shirt with the clipboard to the pickup where Walks-On waited at the passenger door, wagging his tail.

Murder! Over stolen treasure that may or may not have been buried in the mountains. Treasure that no one had found in more than a hundred years. It seemed preposterous that Robert Walking Bear had actually stumbled on Butch Cassidy's treasure. Shrugging off the idea, Father John let Walks-On into the pickup, then slid in behind the steering wheel. Anything to promote the film. He regretted giving Todd Paxton the telephone numbers.

15

STILLNESS GRIPPED THE white frame house and the dirt yard with the gray sedan angled close to the front stoop. Vicky parked behind the sedan, rolled down the windows, and turned off the engine. Ruth would have heard the Ford, the tires skidding to a stop. The door remained closed. Tight red buds on the geraniums next to the stoop looked withered in the dry heat.

Several minutes passed before Vicky got out and slammed the door hard, in case Ruth hadn't heard the Ford after all. She walked up to the front door and knocked, aware of her muscles crimped with tension. Something wasn't right. The sedan was here, which meant Ruth was probably home. A woman in shock, grieving, alone. Maybe she didn't want company, but that didn't make sense. Vicky had called before she left the office and Ruth had wanted to know when she could come over. "I'll get away this afternoon," Vicky had told her.

She knocked again.

"Cutter?" The voice came from the side of the house. Then Ruth appeared around the corner, dark red hair piled on top of her head, a yellow blouse with long, wide sleeves flowing in the breeze. "Oh, Vicky! I thought you were Cutter." She stopped next to the geraniums and tried to smile past the look of confusion on her face. "Sorry, I didn't hear you drive up. It's cooler out back."

Vicky followed the woman around the corner, along the side of the house, Ruth racing ahead as if she were trying to outrun the disappointment. A tarpaulin had been set up over two lawn chairs, creating a block of shade. On the small metal table between the chairs stood a pitcher of iced tea and two glasses. "Cutter promised to stop by this afternoon. You know how it is—always something to fix around the house. Now the kitchen sink is leaking. He's been such a good friend. Can I pour you some tea?"

Vicky nodded and took one of the chairs while Ruth filled the glasses. She handed one to Vicky. "He was just getting to know Robert," she said, and Vicky realized Ruth was still talking about Cutter. "Family was important to both of them. Robert wanted to make sure the relatives all accepted Cutter."

"And did they?"

"Oh yes. I mean they're surprised Cutter came back. But most of the cousins welcomed him back." Ruth dropped into the other chair, took a sip of iced tea, then patted at her hair and pulled her lips into a tight red line, as if she were testing the words erupting in her throat. Her face looked puffy, at the edge of pale. Her eyes shifted from side to side, as if she weren't sure what they should focus on. Eventually she looked at Vicky. "You've heard the news, I guess."

Vicky didn't reply. News traveled on the moccasin telegraph at lightning speed, but it didn't always reach her. "I came to see how you're doing," she said finally. "If there is anything I can do . . ."

"All over the telegraph." Ruth held up her glass and rolled it back and forth, staring at the tea that sparkled and changed from brown to golden in the bright light. "Everybody sticking their noses in my business, making up gossip, spreading it all over the rez."

Vicky took another drink of her tea. Sweeter than she would have liked, but cold and refreshing. The wind had picked up, and the tarpaulin made a loud thwack as it billowed upward. The metal poles at the corners skidded a little in the dirt, like debris caught in a lake.

"Don't worry," Ruth said. "It won't fall down. Cutter put it up for me, said I needed a cool place in the yard."

"You'd better tell me what's going on."

Ruth drank most of her own tea. She had gone back to looking around, hunting for a place upon which her gaze could land. Then she shifted toward Vicky again. "The fed showed up yesterday with a lot of questions. Did Robert have any enemies? Had he been in any altercations? Anyone threaten him? How do I know he was alone in the mountains? Who might have gone with him? Could I be sure he told me everything?" She took another drink of tea, then reached over, lifted the pitcher, and refilled her glass. She held out the pitcher, but Vicky shook her head. "He'd pretty much stopped asking questions, and now he's started up again. I've been holding on the best I can." She blinked back the tears forming in her eyes. "Now, a bunch of new questions. Well, not exactly new. The same questions but with more . . . I don't know. Meanness. And the fed has been bothering Robert's relatives and friends again, wanting to know what they might've forgotten to tell him. Went to Dallas's house. Asked so many questions Dallas was late for work this morning. Talked to Robert's cousin Bernie and her husband, talked to Cutter and I don't know who else."

She leaned closer. "That's not the worst. The coroner won't release Robert's body. Robert should have been buried by now; instead his spirit is wandering the rez. Oh, folks have seen him! Talked to him! Last night I heard a loud pounding noise in the yard. I got up and looked out the window. The pounding got louder. I couldn't see anything, but I knew it was Robert. He's confused and upset, doesn't know what to do, where to go. Vicky, help us. Get the coroner to release his body."

Vicky looked away. She had caused this pain and stress. An anonymous caller, a self-proclaimed witness to murder. Of course Gianelli would double down on the investigation. And yet, part of her felt relieved. If Robert Walking Bear had been murdered, then a killer was walking around free. The truth should be known; justice done.

She pressed her lips together to keep from laughing at the thought. Justice, so seldom done. Truth, rarely known. She made herself look at Ruth: "I'm afraid I may be responsible."

"You? Responsible? Why, Vicky? What did you do?"

Vicky told her about the anonymous caller and what he had claimed. She told her about going to the lake again and finding a piece of a torn, burned map. And she told her about giving the information to Gianelli.

"Anonymous caller? He must hate me."

"Hate you?"

"To keep me on edge like this. Nothing settled, Robert's ghost wandering around, and I can't get on with my life. I have plans, you know, things I always wanted to do that Robert didn't give this much about." She snapped her fingers. "He did what he wanted, chased after his dream, and I sat here, waiting. Well, now it's my time." She settled her back against the webbing. "Anonymous caller," she said again, almost to herself. "Some crank. It will blow over. Will you talk to the fed, explain how Robert needs to be buried?"

Vicky finished her tea and set the glass on the table. "Gianelli is in charge of the investigation. I'm sorry, Ruth, but it will have to run its course."

"You don't believe an anonymous caller, do you?" Ruth gave a little laugh out of the side of her mouth, as if she were spitting out gum. "Please! I can't handle this nonsense."

"Why would he have called me?"

"I just told you. He has it in for me. Maybe Robert told him something . . ."

"Like what? What could Robert have said about you?"

Ruth pinched her lips together a moment before she said, "Nothing. There was nothing to tell. So I nagged him to do things around the house, stop spending so much time in the mountains, take me to Denver, take me dancing. What difference does it make? What couple doesn't have their differences? We hung together for twenty-one years, Robert and me. Now he's gone. He's gone, and some hateful man wants to make my life miserable."

Vicky didn't say anything. She wasn't sure how to bring up the subject, the uneasiness she hadn't been able to ignore. Cutter, sitting across from her at the restaurant last night. *Robert was sure he was going to find a lot of money. I went along a few times. Chance to get to know my cousin . . .*

"I thought you told me Robert went treasure hunting alone. But Cutter told me he went with Robert several times. Is there anybody else who might have gone with him? What about Dallas?"

Ruth was shaking her head. "I don't care what anybody says. Robert always went alone. He didn't want anyone around when he found the treasure. Like he was ever going to find treasure!" She gave a sharp laugh.

"Why would Cutter say he had gone if he hadn't?"

Ruth sprang out of the chair. She stepped to the edge of the shade, the wind whipping her skirt around her legs, then turned back. "I thought you were my friend. You were on my side. You're working for the fed."

"You know better than that, Ruth. I got to thinking that if Robert took Cutter, he might have taken someone else."

"He never took Cutter! Why do you doubt me? When did you talk to Cutter?"

"We had dinner last night."

"Really!" Ruth pushed back a clump of reddish hair that had blown over her forehead, then mopped at her forehead with the back of her hand. She was breathing heavily, chest rising and falling beneath the yellow blouse. After a long moment, she seemed to will herself to calm down. "I get it now," she said. "Cutter has been trying to reconnect with people. He's trying to find his roots here. But you have to understand your anonymous caller is a liar. Robert was alone when he died. Nobody else was there. I challenge the caller to come here and lie to my face."

Vicky took a moment before she said, "He sounded like he knew what he was talking about, Ruth. I believe he was telling the truth, and I think he's scared."

"That's crazy." Ruth started pacing, from one metal pole to the next, eight steps forward, eight steps back. "I'm starting to think you're crazy, too."

"If there is any truth to what he said, you would want to know, wouldn't you?"

Ruth stopped and glared at her. "There is no truth to it."

"You said Robert had a map handed down in the family. What about the other cousins? Did they know about the map?"

"My God. The map! You can buy a map in any town in Fremont County. Yeah, the map was in the family, all right, and Robert got it from his grandfather, who"—she laughed—"bought it in a store somewhere. They've been selling Butch Cassidy maps for a hundred years. All phonies. There's no buried treasure, except in the dreams of people like Robert."

"But Robert's map predated the maps available today, and the piece of map I found was on rough, yellow paper. It looked old."

"Yes. It came from a store that predated the tourist shops today. Please, Vicky." Ruth held out both hands, palms up. "No more of this nonsense. If you want to help me, talk to Gianelli. Talk to the coroner. Tell him to release Robert's body. I have to get through this. I have to get him properly buried."

HIGHWAY 287 SHIMMERED beneath the little clouds of dust and tumbleweeds blowing off the prairie. Except for the sound of the wind and the occasional scratching noise of a tumbleweed against the Ford, it was quiet. Traffic was light; a few cars passing, a truck ahead. Vicky had rolled the windows partway down, and now she drove with one hand on the wheel, the other holding her hair out of her eyes. She thought about talking to Gianelli again, but what did she have? Nothing. Except a small disagreement. Ruth insisting her husband always went treasure hunting alone, and Cutter saying he had gone with him. A problem between Robert and Ruth, probably. Let Gianelli figure out the reason behind the discrepancy.

She squinted in the bright glare coming toward her, the sun

glinting off the bumper of a truck. A loud roar as the truck passed, and then, the quiet of the plains again. It filled her with memories, as if the past were here, all around. A little girl in the back of Grandfather's pickup, driving down this very road, narrower then, the paving rough and broken. Riding her pony across the fields, the wind in her face, cousins racing alongside. Always cousins, always family. She understood why Cutter had come back. Yes, it made sense. She had come back herself.

She spotted the dark truck halfway down the block to her office. Parked at the curb, as if a client had dropped by, but it wasn't a client. Cutter was here.

16

HERE, IN THE middle of the day? He hadn't made an appointment, hadn't said anything last night about stopping by. Vicky left the Ford in the driveway next to the brick bungalow she had turned into an office. She let herself through the front door and stopped.

A ladder open in the middle of the reception area, and Cutter on the top step, setting a fluorescent lightbulb into the sockets. Balanced on the ladder top was the long, plastic light covering. "Hey, Vicky," he said, without looking down.

"What's going on?" Stupid question, she thought. She could see what was going on. Annie jumped up and inched herself between the desk and the ladder. All black hair, shiny under the new light; dark, smiling eyes.

"We're finally getting that bulb replaced. Isn't it great?" She pushed her hair back behind her ears and grinned. "Cutter offered to help, and I said, 'Sure, why not.'"

"You called the landlord? It's his responsibility."

"Called and called and called." Annie lifted both arms, as if she were beseeching heaven.

"I'm glad to be of help." Cutter fit the plastic covering into place and started down the ladder, a sureness about him. He snapped the ladder together and said, "I'll just return this to the garage."

Vicky moved away from the open door as he hauled the ladder past her, out across the small porch. She could see the ladder bobbing outside the front windows. "When did he show up?"

"He has been here an hour waiting for you. As long as he was hanging around, he wanted to know what he could do. I immediately thought of the bulb." Annie glanced up at the white light streaming out of the fixture. "I really needed the light."

"Did he say why he came by?" Vicky threw the question over one shoulder as she walked past the beveled-glass doors into her private office. She could hear Annie's footsteps behind her, and something hesitant in them now, second-guessing.

"It's okay, isn't it?" Annie had rearranged her face, erased the grin as Vicky dropped into her swivel chair.

"That he came by?"

"I mean replacing the lightbulb. He's so friendly and helpful."

"What did he want?"

Annie stepped forward, set her hands on the edge of the desk, and leaned forward, as if whatever shadow had fallen between them had now vanished. "To see you. He waited and waited. The man is nothing if not patient." She paused and leaned closer. "He's interested in you, Vicky. He's such a nice guy, and he's a warrior."

"Got a minute?" Cutter poked his head past the beveled-glass doors.

"Hold on," Vicky said, and Annie stepped back and shut the

doors, smiling at the man on the other side as she did so. "Anything else this afternoon?"

Annie walked back to the desk. "Anonymous called again," she said, her voice low. Sound traveled through the beveled glass. "He said you should be at Miner's Café at five o'clock. He will call."

Vicky spun a ballpoint pen over the top of a legal pad. This was crazy. And yet, and yet . . . he could be telling the truth. "What else did he say?"

"Nothing. I just took the message. Oh, I almost forgot." Annie drew in a long breath. "I filed the motion with the district court to review the social services finding on Luke Wolf's custody case. And Bernie White Horse made an appointment for four o'clock. She didn't say what it was about."

Bernie White Horse, one of Robert's cousins. It was almost four now. "Okay. Tell Cutter to come in."

Annie walked back and flung open the doors. "Vicky only has a few minutes."

The man hurried past her: the trademark grin, the longish black hair that he pushed back with one hand. "A few minutes is all I need to convince you to let me take you out tonight."

Vicky shook her head. "I'm sorry. I have other plans."

"Break them. There's a fair down by the river. Food, art, music. We'll have a great time."

Vicky got to her feet. Just wanting to reconnect, she told herself, and yet something about his insistence, the way he had inserted himself into her life made her feel off-balance, a little dizzy. "I appreciate the invitation . . ."

"Say yes."

Vicky hesitated. She was being foolish. Annie was right. A good man, a warrior. There was no reason not to say yes; no other pressing plans, no plans at all. It would be the chance to ask Cutter if Robert had ever mentioned taking anyone else along on his treasure hunts. There was the sound of the outside door opening and closing, the hush of voices in the outer office.

Cutter must have seen her hesitation, sensed it in the half minute of silence, because he said, "Pick you up at seven?"

"I'll meet you on the corner at Third Street."

He bowed, as if in acknowledgment of a great performance, smiled, waved, and backed out of the office. She sat down again and waited for Annie to announce Bernie White Horse.

THERE WAS A family resemblance. Bernie might have been Robert Walking Bear's sister; the same stout frame, thick arms and neck, narrow eyes sunk above rounded cheeks. A serious look in her eyes. Grayish hair pulled back into a bun, pink beaded earrings that matched the pink dress she wore. "You've met my husband." She indicated the heavyset man a few steps behind her. "Big Man White Horse."

Vicky nodded and gestured them to the chairs in front of the desk. She had probably met Big Man at a powwow or fair; most likely he was at Ruth's the day of Robert's death. She had no memory of him. "I'm sorry about your cousin," she said, trying for the polite pleasantries. Expected, even in a law office. "How are you doing?"

"That's why we're here." The woman scooted back in the chair and clasped her hands in her lap. The pink fabric folded over her fingers. "Robert stole from me. I want what belongs to me." The man beside her nodded his massive head and clapped his cowboy hat over one knee.

"Wait a minute . . ."

"Let me take it from here." The man interrupted. "This is hard for Bernie, accusing her own relative, but Robert was a sonofabitch. Ask anyone, they'll tell you. Bernie's grandfather wanted her to have the treasure map."

"That's a fact." Bernie jumped in, leaning forward now. "I remember when he brought me out to the barn and took a brown box off the shelf. He opened the box and . . . I can see it today. There was a real old map, the only thing in the box, and Grandfather said, 'This is yours. It belongs to you, and don't you forget it, and don't you let any of them thieving relatives take it from you.'"

"Talking about Robert, you ask me," Big Man said. "Soon as her grandfather died, Robert hightailed it out to the ranch and cleared out everything. Took the map. Been looking for the treasure ever since."

"Listen, Bernie." Vicky held up her hand. "I can't help you. I'm a friend of Ruth's, and it would be a conflict of interest."

"I don't get it." Bernie shifted toward her husband, who snorted but didn't say anything. Then she turned back to Vicky. "You know a lot of people on the rez. You grew up there. Probably related to half the population. You help people all the time. You telling me when you help other clients, you don't have a conflict of interest? I can prove the map is mine, you know. I can prove it."

"I'm not sure anyone knows where the map is."

"Robert kept it on him."

"Robert's death is still under investigation." Vicky shifted forward and forced herself to meet the burning looks of the couple across from her, as if she were looking into a campfire. "I doubt you need a lawyer. If you have proof that the map belonged to you, you should take the proof to the tribal police. They can help you recover stolen property."

Bernie pushed herself to her feet. "I thought you were one of us." She was sputtering. Little flecks of spit littered the top of the desk. Big Man stood beside her and patted her back, murmuring something like, "We don't need her. We'll take care of this matter ourselves, like I told you. We got our own ways."

Vicky stood up. "I strongly advise you not to do anything illegal."

"Don't look like you're our lawyer, so we don't need your advice," Big Man said, guiding his wife toward the beveled-glass doors. Vicky could see the woman's thick shoulders trembling under his hand, then Bernie burst into sobs that trailed behind them until they had crossed the reception area and the front door had slammed shut.

Annie took a step into the office. "Everything okay?"

Vicky sat back down. She closed her eyes against the image of Bernie's husband, the mask of hatred on his face. The words reverberating silently around her: *We got our own ways.* What had he done? Killed a man for an old map that had already been destroyed? She forced the thought to the outer reaches of her mind. The anonymous caller had given an alternative story, and now that story, against all reason, had taken hold of her. She was like a juror: well, something else *might* have happened.

She realized Annie was waiting, and she opened her eyes and tried to concentrate. "Everything's fine," she said.

"Well, Roger and I will be at the café at five. If you're going."

"It's not necessary. The caller will have to come out of the shadows if he wants to talk to me."

Annie didn't say anything for a moment. "We'll hang around here past five o'clock."

"Thank you." It was kind, Vicky knew. Kind and thoughtful, and God knew, she had been longing for kindness and thoughtfulness. "But no sense in your leaving late. I'll finish up some work before I meet Cutter." The court might set the hearing at any time, and she had to be ready to argue that Luke Wolf's reports were positive. The man hadn't had a drink since he had lost the right to see his son unsupervised. The neighbor who had called social services happened to be a friend of Luke's ex-wife's. And the ex-wife, planning to marry her boyfriend, had every motivation to remove Luke from their child's life.

"You're meeting Cutter?" Annie said, a smile of approval now, all worry wiped from her face. "I like him, Vicky. To tell you the truth"—she lowered her voice and gave a backward glance toward the reception area—"if it weren't for Roger, I'd be tempted to give you some competition."

AT FIVE FIFTEEN, Annie stuck her head into the office and said she and Roger were off, but her cell was on in case Vicky needed anything. Vicky heard the front door close, the lock snap, and went back to working on the arguments she intended to make on Luke's behalf. He had told the truth. No police calls to the house he and his wife had occupied, no record of any domestic abuse. She thumbed through a second report from the investigator she had hired. All the neighbors, except for the ex-wife's friend, said he wasn't a troublemaker. Stuck to his own business. They had seen him outside playing with his son, giving the kid horseback rides on his back.

She realized some part of her was waiting for the phone to ring, muscles clenched, hand ready to grab the receiver. Once she thought she felt the tiny surge of energy before it was about to ring, but it hadn't rung. She imagined the phone ringing at the Miner's Café, a waitress picking up. *Vicky Holden? No one here by that name. Wrong number.*

At twenty to seven, she shut down the computer, cleared her desk, and locked the papers in the filing cabinet. The wind was blowing, knocking at the eaves. A cottonwood branch scratched the window, an eerie sound, like that of a small animal trying to get inside. She turned off the lights and looked out the window. Clouds moving across the mountains were outlined in shades of purple and orange. A white carpet of cottonwood pollen lay over the backyard. She could probably ask Cutter to rake it up, she thought. He would do anything she needed. He wanted to help, just as he was helping Ruth. He wanted to be useful.

She lifted her bag out of the desk drawer and walked through the office, turning off the lights in the reception area as she went. It was silly, this uneasy feeling about Cutter Walking Bear.

17

CUTTER STOOD ON the corner like a statue with people flowing around him toward the fair at City Park. Families with strollers and toddlers, couples holding hands, teenage girls in cutoffs and tee shirts, boys in blue jeans and cowboy hats—Cutter stood his ground. Cowboy hat tilted back, hands on his waist, a friendly, fixed smile on his face. Vicky had parked in a residential neighborhood several blocks away. Now she hurried around the groups of people and waved. Cutter waved back and started toward her.

"Glad you could make it." He took her arm. "For a couple minutes there, I thought maybe you'd . . ." He took a moment, then hurried on: "Maybe something had come up."

"It's been a long time since I've gone to a summer fair." Why had she told him that? It made her sound pathetic, chained to her desk, tied to legal briefs.

She was aware of the warm pressure of Cutter's hand on her

arm, guiding her across the sidewalk and onto the lawn that ran along the Popo Agie River. Crowds milled about the food and craft booths under white tents that swayed in the evening breeze. Still more crowds poured off the sidewalk and filled up the benches that flanked the wooden tables. Music was playing over by the riverbank, drums pounding, flutes singing. Through the crowd, Vicky could see the Arapaho dancers, blue, red, and silver regalia flashing in the sunlight.

"I've checked out the place," Cutter said, his grip tightening on her arm. "What's your pleasure? Meatball or pork sandwiches, fried chicken, stew, Indian tacos."

"Definitely Indian tacos," she told him.

"I knew you'd say that." Out of the corner of her eye, she saw him grin.

They joined the line in front of the booth, a cacophony of sounds around them, the drums, the singers, the people chatting and calling to one another. Vicky recognized the two grandmothers behind the counter, Irene Hunting and Mo Fallsdown, punching small circles of dough until they were the size of a dinner plate, then dropping them into a pot of boiling oil for a moment or two, then flopping the tacos onto two paper plates. Spreading cooked, seasoned ground beef followed by chopped onions and tomatoes and sauces. Cutter ordered two iced teas. Together, the two of them, each balancing a taco plate and plastic glass of cold tea, made their way to a table that four teenage boys had vacated. They sat across from each other at one end, while a family filled in the rest of the benches—a white family with plates of chicken nuggets and glasses of Coke.

"Your law practice must keep you busy." Cutter worked at his taco with a white plastic knife and fork he'd taken from a glass on the table. "All work and no play . . ." He shrugged. "You know how it goes. When do you have time to spend all your money?"

"All my money?"

"Come on, don't be coy. You're an attorney. The attorneys I know live pretty high. Big houses, fancy cars. Why not? You work hard for it."

"Attorneys in the oil regions of Oklahoma and Texas? Maybe so." This was a small, rural community, she wanted to say. Instead she took a bite of the taco and wondered what difference it would make to Cutter Walking Bear that few people lived high here, that most of her clients came from the rez, that a lot of them couldn't pay.

She sliced off another bite of taco. Hot and spicy, the way she remembered her grandmother's Indian tacos, the way she used to make them for her own kids, a lifetime ago. After a moment, she said, "How about you? Any luck with the job hunting?"

"Still waiting to hear from Fowler Oil in Casper. Job's perfect for me. Managing the drilling on the rez." He looked out across the fair grounds, as if his thoughts had wandered somewhere else. The drums had gone quiet, and the dancers were strolling about, crowding in front of the booths, digging bills out of small, beaded bags. A small plane buzzed overhead and cut through the hum of conversations, the swish of people passing by.

"Anyway . . ." Cutter looked back at her. "The interview went pretty well. God knows I have the right résumé. Engineering degree, years of experience. It helps that I started out working the rigs. I know the oil business from the ground up." He smiled. "No pun intended."

Vicky took a drink of the icy tea and let a moment pass before she said, "I spoke with Ruth this morning."

"I know. She told me. I went over to help her out with a few things."

"It's good of you, Cutter."

He shrugged and bent over the last of his taco. Vicky went on: "She claims Robert always went alone to the mountains."

Cutter kept chewing. He took his time before he said, "Has it occurred to you that Robert didn't tell his wife everything?" He leaned over the table, so close that she could smell the spicy odor of his breath. "Maybe Ruth didn't tell him everything, either. Couples keep secrets from each other. This isn't a perfect world."

Vicky drew back, surprised at his sharp tone, and he went on: "Don't tell me you and Ben Holden never kept any secrets. I suspect you kept quite a few, and I'll bet he had his."

"What does that have to do with anything?" Now the sharpness was in her voice, which surprised her. But wasn't that how it went? The anger in Ben's voice, the shouting and yelling, and she had given it back, everything she received. Not the blows. She hadn't been able to give those back.

"I apologize." Cutter moved his glass around, making small wet circles on the table. "It's just that I don't lie, and I don't like being accused of lying."

"I haven't accused . . ."

"Ruth did, if she said I never went with Robert. I can give you dates and times. I can tell you exactly where we went. The parking lots where we left his truck, the trails we hiked, the time we went to the lake. Evidence, isn't that what you call it? He was always so sure that this was the day he was going to dig up the treasure. He kept saying he was getting so close he could smell those old bills. Thousands and thousands of dollars. Enough to set him up for the rest of his life. Said he'd give me a share. I told him I didn't want any of it. I was along for the ride, you might say. Making up lost time with my cousin." He watched her for a moment, as if to make sure she understood. "Tell you the truth, I started to think the phantom treasure had driven my cousin round the bend."

Vicky laughed. She could feel the tension dissipate into the atmosphere of the fair, the booths and people, the music starting up again. "Did Robert carry a map?"

"You ask me, he never went anywhere without his precious map." Cutter shook his head and allowed a half smile to play around his mouth. "An old map, practically falling to pieces. I don't know how he could make sense out of it. Ruth probably has it. She could show it to you."

"Robert's truck and his things are still impounded." She had found a piece of the map, she was thinking. Burned and torn, and for a moment, she considered telling him, then decided not to say anything. The old piece of paper she found might not have anything to do with Robert's map. It was Gianelli's business now. She changed the subject. "I worry about Ruth. She's eager to have Robert buried in the traditional way, but with the investigation still going on, the coroner won't release the body. I assume you've heard the rumors."

"Robert was murdered." He shrugged. "The fed's been talking to the family and everyone else that knew Robert. Showed up at the house I'm renting first thing this morning. Asked crazy questions. Anybody have a problem with Robert? Want revenge? Want him dead?" Cutter was leaning forward again, elbows planted on the table, the empty taco plate and glass pushed aside. "Ticks me off the way he's trying to work the cousins, pit us against one another, trying to turn us on our own relatives. You ask me, who hasn't gotten mad at a relative over some stupid thing? Anybody could say anything. Accuse anybody."

"What if there was a witness?" Vicky drank the rest of her tea, watching over the rim of her glass at the way his face changed, as if another storm were brewing inside him.

"A witness? What are you talking about?"

"Someone who claims he saw the murder."

Cutter threw his head back and laughed. "What's he smoking?"

"Maybe Robert took someone else with him the day he died. A couple of other people. How do you know he didn't?"

Cutter kept his head back, looking up at a sky that had turned steel gray, the laugh silent in his throat. "Okay, I give you that, counselor." He looked back at her. "We don't know for sure, except Robert didn't trust a lot of people. He said the cousins were always trying to get their hands on his map. You understand why I'm ticked off at the fed? He talks to the cousins that wanted the map, no telling what they're going to tell him."

"You mean, about you?"

"Sure, about me, since Robert took me up there a few times. About any of the relatives. Pitting one against the other—it's a dirty trick. Doesn't mean people are going to tell the truth." He drummed his fingers on the table. "What witness?"

Vicky hesitated. The anonymous caller was hardly a secret. Gianelli knew, Annie and Roger knew. Almost nothing could be kept secret on the rez; if one person knew, sooner or later, everyone knew. She drew in a long breath, then told him she had heard from someone who claimed he witnessed Robert's murder.

Cutter clenched and unclenched his fists a moment, then clasped his hands together, as if he wanted to contain the force. "Does this so-called witness have a name?"

"He didn't give one. If he had, I would have told Gianelli. It's his investigation."

"So you know nothing about a man who called you out of the blue. You believe him?"

"It's not up to me."

"So that's why the investigation never quits. Jesus, Vicky. I'm surprised you took a nameless caller seriously. You tell Ruth about this?"

Vicky nodded. "I'm sure she would have heard anyway."

Cutter stood up and surveyed the crowds circling about. "Let's take a look around," he said, as if the possibility of murder had been set aside, forgotten.

A PALE DARKNESS had descended when Vicky drove home through the quiet residential neighborhood that lay between City Park and her apartment building. The sky was clear and gray, the stars beginning to come to life. Streetlights cast wavering circles of white light onto the asphalt. John Fullbright singing "When You're Here" on the CD mixed with the shush of the wind blowing across the half-open windows.

She held on to the steering wheel with one hand and thought about the times she had spent with Cutter. Yesterday evening in Hudson, this evening at the fair, strolling along the booths, looking at the jewelry, the paintings, stained glass, carved wooden figures. Cutter beside her, strong and dependable. An Arapaho like herself, struggling to find his place among his own people. And yet, there was something odd about him, off-putting, as if he moved in his own impenetrable space. He had walked her to her car and offered to follow her home. *No thanks*, she had said. This was good, this was enough, slowly getting to know each other.

Vicky slowed for the turn into her parking lot and drove to her space past the shadowy rows of cars. Light glowed from the glass-enclosed entry to her building and trailed out onto the sidewalk. She let herself out, locked the car, and glanced about. A habit she had cultivated, all those dark nights working late at the office and coming home alone. She had started up the sidewalk into the edge of the light.

"Vicky Holden."

The man's voice came from nowhere, from the air, the lawn, the bushes. She swung about, scanning the area. There was no one.

"You disappointed me. I waited an hour at the café."

"Who are you?" She hurried up the sidewalk; she was almost to the entry door when she spotted the white truck parked across the street. The man was in the shadows somewhere, crouched down among the bushes, where she couldn't see him.

"The fed is making a fool of himself, playing for time so it looks like he's done his job. Don't step inside!" Vicky had pulled open the front door. She stopped, aware of the tension in her shoulders. Her eyes fixed on the elevator button. It would take a couple of minutes to get the elevator, minutes in which whoever was out there could rush inside. A hundred scenarios ran through her head: push her into the elevator, drag her down the corridor, force her to open the apartment door. She dug into her bag for her keys and fitted them between her fingers like brass knuckles.

"Listen to me. The killer is getting desperate. He's getting ready to kill again. If you don't convince the fed that time is running out, you'll have to pay."

Vicky let the glass door slam behind her, lunged for the elevator, and jammed her palm against the button. Somewhere inside the building, wheels and pulleys emitted small screeching sounds. Inside the elevator, she found her cell and called the FBI office. "This is Vicky Holden. Put me through to Agent Gianelli," she said, half running down the corridor, the cell in one hand, her apartment key isolated in her other hand.

A minute passed before the voice said, "He's not picking up. I'll keep trying."

"It's an emergency!" Vicky heard her own voice shouting. "I have to talk to him immediately." She jammed the key into the lock, pushed through the door, then slammed it shut, turned the lock, and leaned against the hard surface, finding her breath now, the quick intakes of air burning her chest. The apartment was dark except for the seams of light from the streetlamps that lay across the floor, the desk, the chairs and sofa. The cell was cool and inert in her hand.

It was five minutes before it rang. Call from Unknown flashed on the screen. Her legs had turned to liquid, scarcely holding her up. Anonymous calling from outside somewhere, watching the building, watching for her lights to come on. She realized she was still leaning against the door; the door holding her up.

She slid her finger over the screen. "Yes?"

"Vicky?" The fed's voice. "What's going on?"

"The anonymous caller was just at my apartment building." The words tumbled out, bunching against one another. She could feel her heart racing, and she made herself draw in a deep breath. "He said that the killer is getting desperate. He'll kill again. The caller could be heading back to the rez now. He drives a white truck. You can have the tribal cops pick him up. He's your witness, Gianelli. He saw the murder!"

18

A CIRCLE OF light fell over the stacks of papers, notebooks, and laptop that littered the surface of the desk. At the edge of light stood the chair Father John kept for parishioners who tracked him to the residence. The notes of "Vesti la giubba" rose and fell against the nighttime creaks and groans of the old house. The bishop had gone upstairs to bed an hour ago. Walks-On snoring at his feet, twitching in a dream. A good time, the last, quiet minutes of the day.

Father John tried to ignore the tiredness running through him. It had been a busy day, driving to the nursing home and the film set, having lunch at the senior center with some of the elders, visiting the sick, the dying, at the hospital in Riverton, driving, driving. Walks-On had either trailed along on the visits or slept in the pickup under a shady tree.

Following him through the day were thoughts of the man who

had once lived in the same area—ridden a horse along the trails that were now asphalt roads, and who might have returned, when everyone thought he was dead. Risen from the dead. He smiled. It had happened only once.

Father John turned the desk lamp toward the bookcases and ran his finger over the spines of Western history books until he found what he was looking for. *Outlaws and Other Legends.* A clear imprint outlined by dust clung to the shelf when he removed the book. It must have weighed two pounds; the cover, a tooled, navy blue leather, the title printed in gold. He ran his fingers over the cover a moment, then opened the book carefully. A delicate thing, like film that might disintegrate in his hands. The end sheets were cream-colored, stamped with tiny light blue half circles. He thumbed through the heavy, ragged-edged pages: desperate, narrow-eyed men looked out from sepia-toned photographs. Then he turned to the table of contents. Butch Cassidy and the Sundance Kid appeared halfway down the list. He turned to page 70.

The photograph of Butch Cassidy smiling out at the world took up the top half of the page, light-colored hair slicked back from an open, friendly face, eyes deep set, amused yet watchful, full cheeks and square jaw. In his thirties, hard-driven, experienced. The caption read: *Robert LeRoy Parker, known as Butch Cassidy, about 1899.*

On the lower half of the page was the photo of another man, smaller and slimmer, also in his thirties, but with black hair and dark complexion and the wary eyes of a man who had seen and absorbed too much. *Harry Alonzo Longabaugh,* the caption read, *known as the Sundance Kid, about 1904.*

He turned the page and found a photo of five men in suits and ties, black fedoras, and polished shoes, a successful bunch of merchants or bankers, perhaps, photographed at a wedding. Except the caption identified the men as members of the Wild Bunch. Butch Cassidy and Sundance were seated in front, on either side of Ben Kilpatrick. Behind them stood Will Carver and Harvey Logan. A tiny smile played around Butch's mouth, as if he were the only one in on a highly amusing joke.

On the opposite page were crowded lines of black type that ran into narrow margins. Father John skimmed through the text, then turned to the next page and the next. Looking for the dates, the details that grounded a life. Butch Cassidy, born Robert LeRoy Parker in Utah in 1866. Large Mormon family, honest and hardworking, so Butch changed his name to spare them the embarrassment and heartbreak at the turn his life had taken. Rustled cattle and horses at first, and Butch was good at it. Bank robberies came next, more dangerous and more lucrative. The San Miguel Valley Bank in Telluride, the Denver National Bank, and more robberies whenever a bank looked promising. Then the train robberies, the big payoffs, $50,000 or more at a crack, more than a man could make in a lifetime of ranching. Often he hid out with friends in Wyoming. He was generous with the money he had stolen, helping friends pay taxes and mortgages to save their ranches.

And Butch Cassidy was a man of meticulous planning. He planned the bank robberies and the train robberies by working out every detail. He left nothing to chance.

Still, at times, Butch had tried to leave the outlaw life behind. Homesteaded a ranch north of Dubois, Wyoming, about 1890. Became part of the community, another rancher at the carry-in dinners, a dancing partner for the single girls. Handsome and fun-loving, popular with everybody. Always willing to lend a hand on the neighboring ranches. It lasted almost two years, those normal days, until the lure of horses waiting to be rustled became too strong to resist. Arrested for rustling a horse in the Bighorn Basin, which he claimed he had purchased legitimately, and sentenced in 1894 to two years in the Wyoming penitentiary in Laramie. Released in January 1896.

Father John skimmed the next page: How Butch went back to robbing banks. Idaho, Utah, South Dakota. How Harry Alonzo Longabaugh joined the Wild Bunch sometime in the 1890s. How the gang was hardly a gang, forming and reforming, taking in new outlaws as others rode off. Then, halfway down the page, Father John stopped skimming and read the text:

On June 2, 1899, the gang turned to robbing trains. As the Union Pacific Overland Limited Number 1 thundered down track near Wilcox, Wyoming, an emergency lantern swung ahead. The engineer stopped the train and the gang rode out of the shadows. They ordered the train crew to cut off the baggage and express cars and move them across a bridge ahead. Using the new explosive, dynamite, they blew up the bridge first, then proceeded to blow up the express mail car and the safe. No one was killed. They rode north with $50,000 in gold, silver, and banknotes.

Butch Cassidy himself did not take part in the actual robbery, but he had planned the event and the getaway route. He rendezvoused with the gang nearby, and they divided the loot and went their separate ways. It is believed that Cassidy and Sundance hid out for a time on a nearby ranch with friends Butch had made in his ranching days.

The Wilcox robbery led to the largest manhunt in Wyoming history. One hundred men—posses, state militia, private

*citizens, and Pinkerton detectives hired by the Union Pacific—
rode across the state, but the gang had disappeared into the
wide, empty spaces of the West. Posse leaders believed the gang
had gone to Brown's Park, a narrow, remote valley on the
Utah-Colorado border controlled by outlaws. The posses gave
up. No one wanted to venture into Brown's Park.*

Father John skimmed the following page on how Butch had
tried to leave the outlaw life behind. Petitioned the Wyoming governor for a pardon on the condition that he would join the Rough
Riders and go to Cuba to fight in the Spanish-American War. The
governor refused. Still other attempts to clear his record and live a
lawful life. A possible deal with the Union Pacific. In exchange for
a pardon, he would work for the railroad and provide security
against outlaws like himself. But negotiations went no further, and
in 1900, Cassidy and the gang robbed another Union Pacific train
west of Rawlins.

Cassidy's friends in the Lander area claimed that Butch and
Sundance were tired of being hunted and eager to start a different
life. In 1901, they went to South America, where they reside today.
However, they remain outlaws in the United States and should
they return, they will still face justice.

Father John went back to the front of the book and read:
Printed 1907. New York City.

He closed the book, set it back on the shelf, and went into the
kitchen. The old wooden floors sighed under his boots. He made a
pot of fresh coffee, measuring out the grounds, pouring in the
water, his thoughts with the man looking out of the sepia photo.
Smiling and friendly, well liked in these parts, generous with whatever money he had. The book confirmed—at least it didn't deny—

everything he'd heard so far. Butch had helped local ranchers, and they helped him. Provided safe places for him to hide after the robberies.

He filled the dog's water bowl—the tap of paws coming down the hall breaking into his thoughts. Walks-On looked sleepy, a little disoriented as he lapped up the water. Father John poured himself some coffee, stirred in a little milk, and went back to the study.

It took a moment for the laptop to find its bearings and click into life. Eventually Web sites on Butch Cassidy and the Sundance Kid materialized. He glanced down the first couple of screens and clicked on the headline: *Did Butch and Sundance Die in Bolivia?*

Generally historians accept that Butch Cassidy and the Sundance Kid had robbed the Aramayo mine payroll in Bolivia on November 4, 1908, and fled to the small town of San Vicente. A small military detachment surrounded the house where they were hiding. The shoot-out lasted for hours, and when it ended, two bodies were found inside the house, mortally wounded. The bodies were buried in unmarked graves.

The end of Butch Cassidy and the Sundance Kid? Wyoming friends of Butch Cassidy who had known him well do not believe that he died in Bolivia. In the 1920s and 1930s, these friends maintain that Butch visited the area several times. He went by the name William T. Phillips, but the people around Lander and the Wind River Reservation recognized their old friend, whom they had known as George Cassidy, and who had, at long last, made a life on the right side of the law in Spokane, Washington. On one visit, Butch and a group of friends took a camping trip into the mountains, where Butch

spent several days looking for treasure he had buried after the
Wilcox train robbery.

Historians argue about the accuracy of such stories. Many
believe that Butch and Sundance could not have escaped the
hail of bullets they encountered in Bolivia and that the Wyo-
ming visitor was an impostor. But Butch's friends in Wyoming
never faltered in their belief that their old friend had re-
turned. Indeed, their stories raise the question: could an impos-
tor convince a dozen or more people he was someone they had
known well?

Reports of the Sundance Kid in Mexico after 1908 suggest
that he also survived. But there are no reports of him in Wyo-
ming.

So what is the truth? Did Butch Cassidy return to Wyo-
ming, as his friends said, or did he and Sundance die in Bolivia?
Perhaps the point is that the past yields only some of its secrets,
never all.

Father John closed the site, then opened several others. On two
sites, Butch Cassidy smiled out at him again from the same sepia
photograph, but now something new in the deep-set eyes that
Father John hadn't detected before, a mocking look. *Find me, if*
you dare.

The other sites reiterated the information: the shoot-out in Bolivia, the emergence of a man who visited Butch's old friends in
Wyoming. And in the third site, a mention of Mary Boyd:

Butch Cassidy courted any number of women in Wyoming, but
he seemed most attached to Mary Boyd, who was half Indian.
In 1892 she gave birth to a daughter. Unmarried and unable to

care for the infant, Mary placed her with an Arapaho family on the Wind River Reservation. Some historians believe the child was Butch Cassidy's and that Mary hoped he would marry her and take care of her and the child. Instead Butch was arrested for horse stealing and sentenced to prison. After his release, he left the area. Mary married a rancher named Jesse Lyons. They did not have children. Mary never publicly named the father of her daughter.

Father John shut down the computer and watched the screen go dark. Walks-On was dreaming, making little mewling noises. The internet sites confirmed the stories, the pieces of the past he had heard. Eldon Lone Bear had said that if Butch Cassidy left behind a map, there was only one person he would have left it with: Mary Boyd. One of her descendants was still on the rez. Living at the White Pines Nursing Home. And her name was Julia Marks. The generations of stories she must have heard about Butch and Mary and a map, all of it locked in her mind.

19

THE NOISE CAME from a far distance. Clanging and incessant. Vicky fought her way upward to the surface of wakefulness. It took a moment before she realized the phone was ringing. She reached toward the bedside table, pawed past the clock radio, the lamp, and gripped the receiver. The ringing stopped. She pushed herself upright on the pillows and tried to concentrate. The yellow numbers on the clock read 2:18.

"Vicky Holden," she said. Her voice sounded scratchy and sleep-logged. She squinted at the ID: R. Walking Bear.

A long sob came over the line, followed by gasps of breath, followed by coughing. Finally, Ruth's voice, the words jumbled. "I can't believe what they did to me. It's terrible." She started gasping again, coughing.

"Ruth, are you hurt?"

"Robert's dead, and I don't have anyone. They're all against me." She was crying hard, sputtering and sobbing. "They want me dead."

"Are you hurt? Do you need help?"

"Nobody can help me now."

"Are you at home?" She could be anywhere, Vicky was thinking, calling on a cell.

"What's left of it," Ruth said.

"I'm on my way."

VICKY DROVE OUT from the streetlights of Lander and plunged into the darkness of the reservation. The sky was overcast, a dark veil drawn over the stars that usually shimmered like a field of diamonds. Lights twinkled in a few of the small houses set back from the highway. A pickup came toward her, headlights bucking, then passed. She was alone, following the beams of her own headlights through the darkness. She kept going until the houses began to fall away, and she was plunging through wide, dark spaces of pastures and barns and ranch houses. She turned into Arapahoe. The Walking Bear place was ahead, lit up like a carnival.

They want me dead! The words kept looping through her mind, and with them, the sense that something terrible had happened.

Vicky parked near the front stoop, slammed her door, and ran up the steps. She knocked on the door, then tried the knob. The door sprang open into the living room: chairs upended, chest overturned, and drawers thrown on the floor, papers and broken pottery and glass everywhere, sofa cushions ripped open with the foam shooting out.

"Ruth! Where are you?" She stepped through the debris to the kitchen, looking around, half expecting someone to jump out. Her heart pounded in her ears. "Ruth!" she called again. The kitchen looked like the living room; cabinet doors flung open, and dishes, pans, cans of food, and boxes of cereal scattered over the floor.

She heard the whimpering then, like an animal in pain, and she picked up a knife and started down the hall to the bedrooms. A pair of bedrooms across from each other, doors open, and everything inside tossed about: clothes, bedding, chairs. Mattresses pulled off the beds. The whimpering noise came again, and Vicky followed it to the bedroom at the end of the hall.

Ruth sat cross-legged on the floor, leaning into a pillow stuffed in her lap, surrounded by piles of clothes and towels and broken bottles. The air reeked of perfumes and lotions. Vicky went down on her knees, set the knife on the floor, and grasped the woman by the shoulders. "Are you hurt?"

Ruth lifted her eyes and blinked, as if she couldn't bring anything into focus. Reddish hair loose, flying about in curly chunks, lipstick smeared, lines of black mascara running down her cheeks. "Vicky?" she managed.

"Look at me," Vicky said as the woman's eyes trailed off to some vacant space. "Tell me if they hurt you."

A series of thoughts seemed to flitter through the woman's expression before she finally fastened on to one. An odor of whiskey drifted about her. "This is how it was when I got home. Everything ripped apart and trashed, like they wanted to kill me. If I had been here, they would have killed me."

Vicky felt herself relax, the tension in her muscles letting go. "Okay," she said. "Let's go into the kitchen. I'll make coffee and you can start at the beginning." She got to her feet, took Ruth's arm, and tried to steer her upward, but the woman was like dead weight, her legs dragging over the clothes and blankets. She was in shock, sunk into the chaos that was her home, unable to lift herself out of it. It took all of her strength to guide Ruth down the hall and into the kitchen.

She had to clear a chair for Ruth to sit down, then she located a can of coffee and a metal coffeepot in opposite corners of the kitchen. She rooted through a pile of dishes before she found the black cord. After pushing several cans to one side on the counter, she filled the pot with water, measured out the coffee, and plugged in the cord. Eventually she found two serviceable mugs, one with a handle broken. She pushed the papers off the chair across from Ruth and sat down.

"Tell me what happened."

Ruth seemed to be waking up, struggling toward a semblance of calm. Tears bunched in the corners of her eyes. "It's all I have left, this house," she said. "Why'd they have to trash it?"

"Where were you?" The smell of fresh coffee blended with the odor of whiskey.

"Bernie, Robert's cousin, said we should go out. You know, have a girls night out, let down our hair. I never should've trusted her. All she wanted was for me to get out of the house so that no-good husband of hers could trash it. So we went to a couple of bars in Riverton. Danced a little with a cowboy. It was fun, getting away from everything, forgetting for a while. We went back to Bernie's place and had a nightcap. Pretty soon, Big Man came home, after he finished wrecking my house, and drove me home. Dropped me off and drove away. Just drove away and let me find what he'd done all by myself."

"What makes you think Big Man did this?" Of course it was Big Man, Vicky was thinking. Bernie and Big Man determined to get their hands on Robert's map. They must have concluded that

Gianelli had returned Robert's things, and the map was some-where in the house. A map that was in pieces, blown in the winds, burned. Which meant Big Man knew Robert had had the map the day he died. But, even if he had been at the lake, he didn't know that someone had destroyed the map. She felt a chill run through her, as if a blast of cold had burst into the house. How many people had watched Robert die?

"They hate me, that's the reason. Robert's cousins hate me." She waved a hand at the debris on the floor, the mess in the living room. "They didn't want me to marry Robert, thought I wasn't good enough. Only one that's been decent is Cutter." She stopped and looked around, as if Cutter might step out of the shadows. "Where is he? He said he'd be right over when I called."

"I'm sure he's on the way." Vicky sipped at the hot coffee. Al-ways on the way, Cutter. Always ready to help out. "Have you called the police?" She knew the answer. Ruth had called her and Cutter, and probably Cutter first. No one else. Ruth was an out-sider, in a way, with all of her own people gone. She didn't belong anymore. Funny, when she thought about it. Ruth, Cutter, and herself, all outsiders in different ways.

"What will the police do?"

"You can tell them your suspicions about Bernie and Big Man. They'll talk to them."

Ruth took a drink of coffee. "It'll just make people hate me more."

"I think you should talk to Gianelli."

"What?" Ruth stared at her over the rim of the mug.

"It's possible Bernie and her husband were looking for the map."

Ruth gave a shout of laughter. The mug shook in her hands and she set it down firmly, taking a moment to make sure it had connected with the table. "Always the map! The famous map! If Bernie wants a map she should go buy one."

"But it wouldn't be the map from Butch Cassidy himself."

"If you believe that, you're as big a fool as the rest of the people on the rez. Always looking to get rich quick. That was Robert. Traipsing all over the mountains with a piece of paper, thinking he was going to dig up a fortune." She took another sip of coffee, set the mug down, and pulled herself upright, as if she had entered a new space. "Oh my God. I get it now. You think Big Man killed Robert for the map, but he didn't find it. So he came here looking for it. They'll come after me next, make me tell them where it is." She started to tremble, her hands shaking against the table.

"Gianelli will want to know that someone ransacked your house. I'll go with you in the morning. Now you need to call the tribal police and get this on record."

Ruth had retreated into herself again, staring out into the distance, defeated. "What difference does it make?"

"What difference does what make?" A man's voice, behind them.

Vicky jumped up, adrenaline pumping through her. When had Cutter come in, walked through the living room, planted himself in the doorway? How long had he been there?

"Cutter!" Ruth was on her feet, flinging herself into the man's arms. "You see what they did? Big Man and Bernie? They're trying to destroy me. What took you so long?"

"Why would they do this?" Cutter said, ignoring the question, holding her close.

"Vicky says they're looking for Robert's map."

"It's possible the map no longer exists," Vicky said. "I found a torn piece of a map at the lake."

Cutter lifted an eyebrow. "You didn't tell me about that. Why would anyone tear up a treasure map?" He left the question un-answered and walked Ruth over to her chair. "Vicky's right. You should notify the police. Big Man and Bernie shouldn't get away with this. Go see Gianelli if you like, but you ask me, it won't change anything. The fed and the coroner refuse to believe that Robert's death was what it was—an accident. All of this"—he threw a glance around the kitchen—"is about greed and jealousy over the fact you and Robert lived better than the cousins. Wouldn't surprise me if Big Man thought he could scare you off the rez."

"What am I going to do?" Ruth ran her fingers through her hair, pushing back the curls, tidying up. She gave Cutter a weak smile mixed with hope and dread.

"I'm going to help you clean up this mess, and you're going to do whatever you like. Don't you worry. Bernie and Big Man aren't the only cousins. You got me and Spotted Deer."

Vicky stood up. Things seemed to be under control, with Cutter here. He would call the tribal police, help Ruth clean up the house. He was capable, decisive, comforting in the way he took charge. She could see Cutter's calmness taking root in Ruth, the regular rhythm of her breathing, the way she settled into her chair and took a sip of coffee. "Shall I meet you at Gianelli's office tomorrow at ten o'clock?"

Ruth nodded, as if everything were all right now, everything settled.

Vicky headed back through the debris-strewn living room and started to let herself out the front door. "Thanks for coming." Cut-ter's voice in her ear, startling her. "Ruth needs friends. I'm trying to be a friend to her."

"It's good of you." Vicky stepped out onto the stoop, conscious of the weight of Cutter's hand on her arm.

"That's all it is, you know," Cutter said. "She's my cousin's wife, and she needs friends. You . . ."

Vicky waved off the rest of it and hurried down the steps to the Ford. Back on the highway, the darkness dissipating, a few stars twinkling in a sky that had turned mossy gray. More pickups and cars coming and going, lights shining in the windows of more houses, the reservation starting to come to life. Something that Cutter said had stopped her, dug into her mind. *Why would anyone tear up a treasure map?*

Why indeed. Unless the map was no longer needed. Unless the treasure had been found.

20

THE WOMAN ON the other side of the desk was small, barely taking up half of the chair. Probably in her fifties, with thin blond hair and large eyes set in a narrow, reddened face that tapered to a pointed chin. She smiled often—smile lines appeared at the sides of her mouth—exposing a row of white teeth too large for her face. "I'm Charlotte Hanson," she had said when she walked into the office, hand outstretched. "Julia's daughter." The sounds of *Pagliacci* drifted through the air.

Father John had risen to his feet, walked around the desk, and taken her hand. The strong, forceful grip of a woman accustomed to hard work, mostly in the outdoors. He offered her a glass of iced tea, and when she said that sounded good, he went into the closet-kitchen off the back hall, poured two glasses of tea from the pitcher he kept in the under-the-counter refrigerator, and dropped in chunks of ice. He handed her a glass and sat down in the swivel chair behind the desk.

"I hear you stopped by to see my mother. Sorry she wasn't having a good day." Charlotte Hanson talked with her hands; the ice in her glass clinked over the notes of "O Colombina." "Sharp as a tack some days, remembers every detail. She can tell a thousand stories. Of course I never know which ones she's made up." She laughed. She was used to laughing, Father John thought.

"I was hoping she might remember family stories about Butch Cassidy."

The woman nodded. "I stopped by the site on the river where they're filming. The security guard wouldn't let me get very close, but I saw Butch himself riding into a camp. Takes you back in time. Made me feel like I was there, the way Butch lit up the scene and made everything seem exciting. I imagine that's the way my great-grandmother Mary must have felt when he came around."

"I've heard he hid out with Mary and her husband after a train robbery."

"The Wilcox robbery. Mom's told me about it a thousand times. Famous robbery in Western lore. Took place down on the Wyoming border. Stopped a Union Pacific train, blew up the mail car and the safe after the express agent refused to open the doors. The gang made off with sacks of money." She was shaking her head, smiling, as if she were recalling an event she had witnessed herself. "The way Mom figured it, if the agent had opened the doors, the railroad would have blamed him for not protecting his precious cargo and deducted the stolen amount from his paycheck, which would have put him in hock the rest of his life. Anyway, the railroad had the memory of an elephant. They never forgot Butch Cassidy or the Sundance Kid, either. From then on, they only wanted one thing: to see them dead."

She leaned forward. "Mom told me Butch didn't actually take part in the robbery. Had he been there, she said, the gang wouldn't have set explosives on a car with the agent inside. Butch didn't go for violence. Oh, he was the brains behind the robbery. And he met up with the gang to divide the loot before they got away. Oh yes." She stared off into space, as if the gang were riding away in front of her eyes. "I can imagine how excited Mary was when Butch and Sundance rode up after the robbery. She knew Butch quite well, you know. In the biblical sense, you could say. About 1890 Butch was running a ranch out by Dubois, and Mary Boyd caught his eye. She was real pretty. Petite with long black hair. She was a half-breed from the rez."

The woman sat back in the chair, considering. He could see the conflict moving like a storm over her face. Eventually she said, "I don't know if Mom would want this known. There's no evidence, no historical proof. Just a story handed down in our family."

"I won't say anything."

She shrugged. "What does it matter? It happened a hundred and twenty-five years ago, so who cares? Correct?"

Father John nodded. She was probably more correct than she imagined. So many things that had happened last year, last week, yesterday, were already forgotten. When he was a kid in Boston, adults were always talking about something important. All forgotten now, like dust blown in the wind.

"They planned to marry, Butch and Mary," Charlotte went on. "But he got arrested for stealing a horse and was sent to prison in Laramie." She was smiling again. "Seems he just couldn't go straight, hard as he tried. Well, Mary found out she was pregnant. Imagine a woman with no husband, pregnant, in the 1890s. Lucky she was from the rez, because an Arapaho family took her in and welcomed her baby girl, who was also named Mary. The child grew up with the Arapahos. Mary found work wherever she could on the ranches in the area. I mean, she had to support herself. That's how she met Jesse Lyons and married him."

"What became of her child?"

The woman was still smiling at the memories. "She married a man from Riverton named Edward Levelts. Mom was their only child. She was still a baby when her mother died, so we don't know my grandmother's story. But Mom always said we were descended from Butch Cassidy. There's no proof. Only an old family story." She paused before she said, "Mom grew up in Cheyenne with her father's family. Later she came back here—something about this place that draws people back—and married my father. I was born on their ranch across the border from the rez, same ranch Mary and Jesse had owned a long time ago. Of course it had gone through several owners after the bank repossessed it."

Father John sat back. What a tangled web, the past. Lives lived in the midst of heartache and loss. Somehow the hard times—leaving a child, losing a ranch—often turned into the stories that were passed down. But what about the joyous times, the moments of sunshine and lightness? Surely they also existed. Moments of hope and love that Mary must have felt for a man she knew as George Cassidy, and that he had felt for her.

"Have you ever heard . . ." he began, picking his way. "Whether Butch Cassidy gave your great-grandmother a map that showed where he had hidden money from the train robbery?"

"The old map story." Charlotte shook her head, looked away, and gave a different smile, quiet and inward, as if she were contemplating something impossible to understand. "Everybody around here believes Butch left behind a map. Folks have been hiking through the mountains the last hundred years with a version of the so-called original in their hands, sure they were about to strike it rich. It's like gold fever. Rumors of gold brought thousands of people out West. Some actually struck it rich, so their stories kept people coming."

Father John smiled. "Anybody strike it rich with Butch Cassidy's map?"

She let out a snort of laughter. "That never kept people from trying. In fact, it encouraged them. Nobody has found Butch Cassidy's treasure yet, so it must still be there, waiting for them. Greed," she said, allowing the word to hang in the air. "It never changes. I heard Robert Walking Bear was looking for the treasure when he died." She paused, forehead wrinkled in a new thought. "I've heard rumors he was murdered."

"As far as I know, the FBI hasn't concluded the investigation."

"I suppose he had one of those bogus maps."

Father John shrugged. "He believed it was the original, according to his wife."

"There was no such thing." Charlotte Hanson took a long drink of tea, then examined the glass a moment. "If Butch Cassidy did draw a map, would he have given it to anyone? I didn't think so. Why would he do that? Then I thought, if he got caught and the posse found the map on him, they would steal his treasure. So it makes sense that he might have given a map to someone he trusted."

"Such as your great-grandmother." Father John could hear Eldon Lone Bear's voice in his head: *If Butch gave a map to anybody, it would have been Mary.*

Charlotte shook her head and sipped more tea. "Logical, I suppose. The only problem is, logic can be wrong. Mom has never mentioned a map, not in all the stories she's told through the years. Oh, Butch and the Sundance Kid hid out for a while with Mary and Jesse after the train robbery and helped out on the ranch.

Butch may even have given Mary the money to keep the bank from foreclosing." She gave a quick shrug. "The hard times came soon enough. Jesse died, the bank eventually foreclosed, and Mary was left alone with no way to take care of herself or her little girl, even if she had wanted to take her child from the only family she had ever known."

"You're saying that if Butch had given her a map, she would have used it." The woman across from him was nodding, as if they had circled to the same place. "If she'd had the money, she could have saved the ranch and made a home for her little girl."

"Logical," Charlotte Hanson said again. "Butch would have wanted her to find the treasure if she needed it. But she had no idea where to find it." She set the glass on the floor and laced her fingers together in her lap. "Butch came back in 1934, you know. Despite what the history books say. A lot of people here knew George Cassidy, and they welcomed him back. They spent days with him, reliving old times, reconnecting."

"It was thirty-five years later. Some historians believe Butch's friends were mistaken."

"Folks around here? They never forget people. Butch and his friends went on a camping trip in the mountains. You ask me, Butch was hoping to find his treasure." She looked at a point across the office. "Mary went along. She was living in Riverton then. She'd married a rancher after Jesse died, but her second husband had also died, and she was alone again. She and Butch were reunited on that camping trip. If she had kept a map all those years, never using it to help herself, wouldn't she have given it to him? He was old then, probably could have used the money. After that trip, Butch sent Mary a beautiful ring. You must've seen it. Mom never takes it off. It is the only thing she has of her grandmother's."

Father John didn't say anything. He tried to picture Julia,

slumped in the chair, lost somewhere inside her own mind, gaze fixed on the flickering black-and-white images of an old movie, clasping her hands together and perhaps . . . Was he imagining it now? Had she been running a finger over the ring on her left hand?

Charlotte was saying something about the ring being a sign that Butch had always loved her. "He never forgot her," she said, "and she hadn't forgotten him. Don't you think she would have known if he weren't Butch Cassidy?" She lifted herself to her feet, the matter settled. "I'll be in touch if Mom has a good day. I'm sure she would like to relive the old times for you."

Father John stood up and walked the woman out into the corridor. She barely came to his shoulder; her boots made a soft clicking noise on the wood floor. "Do you think Julia might be willing to relive the old days for the film?" He pulled open the heavy door and waited as Charlotte brushed past and stepped out onto the stoop.

"Are you kidding?" she said, turning back. "My mother has always wanted to be in the movies."

21

THE PHONE WAS ringing. Before Father John could locate the receiver under the piles of papers on his desk, the bishop had picked up. "Yes, yes, hold on a moment." The old man's voice drifted down the corridor.

Father John got up from his desk and hurried toward the back office before the bishop could head his way to tell him he was wanted on the phone. He found the old man working his way upward out of his chair. Throwing Father John a grateful look, he sank back down. "The man on the phone sounded as if you were expecting his call. I'm afraid he has hung up."

I wasn't expecting any call, Father John thought as he retraced his steps down the corridor to his own desk. People called and dropped in unexpectedly. Every day a surprise. The phone had started ringing again, and this time he located it under the papers. "Father John," he said.

A clicking noise sounded on the other end, as if the caller were grinding his teeth. Father John could sense the concentration, the effort. "How can I help you?"

"I'm a dead man."

The statement demanded respect. Father John took a moment before he said, "What is your name?"

"It don't matter. I don't want to die." He sounded Arapaho, the cadence of his words.

"I understand. What can I do?"

"He'll listen to you, a priest. You tell the fed that Robert's death was no accident. I seen him murdered. I told the Rap lawyer . . ."

"Vicky Holden."

"I told her twice now. She's a lawyer; she knows Agent Gianelli. She's always talking to him. I figured he'd believe her. Oh yeah, he acted like he did, went around talking to the same folks he'd talked to before. Didn't learn anything new. He's overlooking the most obvious thing. The map. I told her, he finds out what happened to the map, he'll find the killer."

So this was where the rumor that Robert had been murdered started, Father John thought. Someone on the rez claiming he'd seen the murder. Someone seeking attention, like people who confess to murders they've read about in the newspapers. Imagining things, telling stories.

But he didn't believe the caller was making up a story. He'd heard confessions now for nearly twenty years; he could hear the truth beneath the camouflage of words, the sense of desperation, the shades of fear. "Why don't you start at the beginning. What did you see? Tell me what happened."

"You're like that lawyer. You want all I got, but you offer me nothing. I give you the . . ." He struggled with the rest of it. "I give you the details, I'm the one that goes to jail. The fed will say, 'How's he know that? He must be the murderer. Nobody else would know.'"

"And now you believe you're in danger."

"You bet I'm in danger. The killer's coming after me next."

"I can go to Agent Gianelli with you. I can tell him your fears about coming forward. He'll under . . ."

The laughter came like the blast of a horn. It was a moment before the caller said, "I'm begging you, Father. I went to school at the mission. I wish I could've played on your baseball team. What is it, the Eagles? There wasn't any team then. I've come to your games though. Yeah, saw the Eagles beat the Rangers. Not having the best season so far."

It was true, Father John was thinking, but there was every reason to believe the team would start winning. He'd had to miss the practices this week, and one of the team mothers, Marcy Hawk, had been coaching the team, and she was a better coach than he was.

Father John leaned into the receiver. "Let me help you. Tell me the name of the killer." He was speaking into a vacuum. Nothing on the line, no human presence; then, the electronic beep of the disconnect signal.

He pressed the numbers for Vicky's office, aware of his heart thudding in his ears. Annie answered—calm and controlled, businesslike: "Holden Law Offices."

"This is Father John. I have to speak to Vicky."

"Sorry, Father. She's on the rez, but I can try to reach her. I'll give her the message."

He thanked her and hung up, then he flipped through the Rolodex until he found the number for the local FBI office. In a moment, another cool, controlled voice came on. He told the voice who he was and said he had to speak to Ted Gianelli about Robert Walking Bear's death. Gianelli would return his call, the voice said, still unperturbed. Another death to investigate; there were so many.

He hung up and went over to the window. The wind had picked up; a cottonwood branch knocked against the side of the building. The other branches stayed in perpetual motion, white billowy clouds moved across the blue sky. The caller's words kept running in his head. *I'm a dead man. I'm a dead man.* If he had told the truth, if he *had* witnessed a murder, it was only a matter of time before the killer would come for him. Dear Lord, the caller could be a walking dead man. He stepped back to the desk and checked the caller ID; the last call had come from Unknown. A pay phone, most likely on the reservation. He had no way to trace the call, no way to help the man.

He sat back down and thumbed through the papers until he found the budget he'd been working on. He pushed it aside. *I'm a dead man* kept drumming in his brain.

Father John grabbed his cowboy hat, went down the corridor, and told the bishop he was going to take a walk. Send any calls to his cell.

A hot, dry wind pressed against his shirt and tugged at the brim of his hat as he started for the alley that separated the administration building from the church. At the far end of the alley, a path ran through a grove of cottonwoods to the Little Wind River where the Arapahos had camped when they first came to the reservation. It was cool and quiet there, a good place to walk and think. The spirits of the ancestors gathered there, the elders said, and the place had a holy, set-apart feel that was hard to fit into any logical syllogism.

He was about to turn into the alley when he noticed the pickup in front of the old school building that was now the Arapaho Museum. Visitors came throughout the day; more visitors in the summer, with the tourists. And this pickup belonged to a tourist, judging by the Texas license plate. A tall man in cowboy hat and blue jeans came through the front door and stepped onto the porch that stretched across the front of the museum. Probably in his forties and agile, the way he hooked an arm around the post and glided down the steps. "Hello!" he called. "Father John?"

Father John started over. The man was already coming along Circle Drive, gravel spitting under his boots, a wide smile on his face. An Indian, possibly an Arapaho, with the high cheekbones and hooked nose, dark complexion. A large turquoise-and-silver bracelet gleamed on his wrist. "I was hoping you'd be here." He stretched out the hand with the bracelet. "Cutter Walking Bear. I've heard a lot about you."

Father John shook the man's hand and tried to place the name. He had it: Ruth had mentioned Robert's cousin Cutter recently moved back to the rez. The man was saying something about having come home after a long time away.

"Ruth mentioned you had moved back."

"What a tragedy." Cutter shook his head and lifted his gaze toward the foothills, still hazy and indistinct. "I was just beginning to get to know my cousin again after thirty-five years when he had the accident. I blame myself."

Accident? The word reverberated through Father John's mind. An anonymous caller claimed he had seen Robert murdered. *I'm a dead man.*

"Can't help thinking," Cutter was saying, "if I'd been there, I could have prevented it somehow. Kept him from going near the lake. He could be unsteady on his feet sometimes." He nodded in emphasis. Ruth hadn't mentioned anything about that, Father John thought. He wondered if she had realized it. "Oh yes," Cutter went on. "Surprised me, Rap like Robert, ranching and breaking horses, outdoors every day, a little unsteady at times. Loved the Wind Rivers though. Nothing could keep him from searching for buried treasure." He tipped his head back and laughed at the sky. "I have some good memories of us hiking together."

"You went with him?" Robert always went alone, Ruth had said.

"Sure did. I was planning to go with him the day he died, but I had a job interview in Casper." He paused and glanced around the mission. "Robert was showing me around the rez, helping me get my bearings. We had plans to come to the mission, you know, relive old times. Well, I decided to come here on my own."

"Did you and Robert go to school here?"

"Sure did," Cutter said. "Got a whole bunch of great memories of this place."

Father John smiled. So many Arapahos had gone to school at the mission. Like a community center, the mission, a gathering place. Children, parents, volunteers, teachers, all coming together. Sometimes when he looked at the old stone building, especially on quiet days like this with no one about, he tried to imagine what it must have been like, people coming and going, school buses rounding Circle Drive, a half dozen or more Jesuit priests teaching classes, kids spilling over the grounds, shouting and laughing—the sounds of children everywhere. A hundred years the school had been here, then it was gone. Closed down for lack of money and replaced by the BIA school close by. The old stone building vacant and crumbling, a ghost from the past.

"Hard to leave home and board at school," Cutter said, "but once we got here with our friends, we had a great time. Although, if I remember right some of the proctors . . ."

"Proctors?"

"The older students in charge of the boys' dorm. Some of them could be tough. I guess they'd had tough proctors in their time, so they passed it on." He laughed and shook his head. "Didn't keep us from raising hell. I mean, Robert and I used to jump into that old fire escape tube on the back side of the building and slide down. More fun than an amusement park, but what did we know about amusement parks? No such thing in the entire state." He turned partway around and looked at the building. "If I remember, the boys' dorms were on the third floor. I got that right? Which floor were the girls' on? Second? Or were they at the other end of the third floor?"

"Before my time, I'm afraid." Something wrong here, Father John was thinking. Like a dissonant note in an aria.

Cutter was going on about how he used to climb the trees and swing from the branches. "I remember Vicky. She was as gutsy as any of us boys. Used to be up in the tree with us. Priests would come out and tell us to get down before we fell and broke our heads. I always had the feeling . . ." He stopped at that, then pushed on. "I felt like they would have liked to climb those trees themselves. Maybe they did after we went home at the end of the semester."

"What other memories do you have?" Father John said, still trying to grasp the off-key note.

The man drew in a long breath. He hooked his thumbs in his jeans pockets and looked down, as though he were reading a book. "That's what Robert and I planned to do, recall the old days, relive the good times. I hated it when my father took us to Oklahoma to be with Mom's family. The Walking Bears were here. I was about eleven. We moved in the summer when my cousins were getting ready to go back to school. But I remember—I remember." He looked up. "Wasn't there some kind of basketball hoop up around here? We used to scrimmage, and we were pretty good, too. Wasn't there a shop? Yeah, we made things out of wood and metal. Over there, wasn't it?" He nodded toward the white building next to the church, set back from Circle Drive. A storage shed now. "In the spring, there was baseball. I already walked around the diamond out back." A nod now in the direction of the redbrick residence. "Brought back a lot of memories. I'm glad to see it's still here."

Baseball? Father John saw it now, as if he had opened a photo album with pictures of a mission that hadn't existed, not when Cutter and Robert Walking Bear and Vicky Holden had been in school. There was no baseball diamond. Ten years ago, his first summer at St. Francis, he and the kids had cut down the wild grasses and stamped out the bases. The parents had helped him build the dugouts and the benches. It had taken all summer.

The sound of ringing cut into the quiet. Father John took the phone out of his pocket and glanced at the ID. Federal Gov. "Sorry, I have to take this." He stepped away a few feet and pressed the answer key. "Father John."

The voice on other end: "Ted Gianelli, returning your call."

Father John thanked him and started to tell him about the anonymous caller, aware of Cutter Walking Bear off his shoulder. He took another few steps. "The caller could be telling the truth."

"Anything else that would give me something to go on?" The fed sounded as if he believed in the possibility. "Any names? Anything at all?"

"He sounded frightened. I got the impression he wants you to locate the murderer without any specific help from him. He doesn't want to be involved."

"If he's a witness, he's involved." There was a long pause, the sound of rustling paper, a pen or pencil—something solid—tapping a hard surface. "I've talked to everybody around Robert Walking Bear, all the relatives. They all have alibis. This investigation is over, unless I find something new. It makes me sick to think"—there were several rapid intakes of breath at the other end—"there's a killer walking around in my jurisdiction. If he calls again, see if you can get him to come in."

Father John said he would do his best. He might not hear from the caller again. In fact, he thought, ending the call, it was highly unlikely that he would. It would make more sense for a frightened witness to walk away, go where the murderer couldn't find him.

"Trouble?" Cutter said.

"Could be." Father John slipped the phone back into his pocket and turned around. He had the sense the man hadn't taken his eyes from him throughout the call. He told him to feel free to continue looking around, then he headed back to the office. A dozen thoughts clanged in his mind. An investigation into a possible murder, with no evidence. Nothing except an anonymous, scared voice on the phone. A detective eager to wind things up, stamp *closed* on the file. And a stranger back on the rez, trying to find his roots, looking around the mission, remembering things that hadn't been here. How fragile memories were, like air or music, hard to grasp. It was easy to misremember, to be jolted into an imaginary past by the things around you. The baseball diamond behind the residence—maybe it had made Cutter think there had been a baseball diamond in the past because there should have been a baseball diamond. The boys' dormitory. There had been a dormitory when the mission was founded, but not in the last fifty years. And maybe there should have been, instead of the creaking, chilly buses Cutter and Robert and Vicky had ridden across the rez. Maybe memories were just that, the longing for a better past.

22

1899

MARY HEARD THE horses' hooves out on the dirt road. She swished the last shirt in the washtub and ran it through the wringer that Jesse had set up on the back porch. Then she stepped outside, pinned the shirt to the line with the other shirts and jeans and unmentionables flapping behind the house, and went to see who was passing by. Not many people on the road, especially in the middle of the day. Folks in these parts didn't go visiting at high noon, not with fences to fix, cattle to round up and brand, chickens to look after. An endless stream of chores, just to stay alive, and you never knew, oh, you never knew, when the bank or the tax man would slap a piece of paper on the front door and tell you to move on. That was one worry she and Jesse no longer had, now that Butch was here.

She spotted the billowing dust as she started around the house. Coming down the ranch road were two men in floppy black hats, rifles in scabbards next to their right legs. The horses looked winded and hard used. She had never seen either man before, and she could feel her mouth go dry. Jesse and the others were in the high pasture. Even if she rang the cowbell hanging on the front porch, it would take Jesse fifteen minutes to reach the house. And that was if he heard the bell. "Don't take chances," he had told her. "Use the rifle if you have to."

She ran up onto the front porch, went inside, and grabbed the Springfield off the rack by the door. She went back outside and walked to the top of the step, where the riders would be sure to see her.

"Halt," she shouted. "Halt, I say." The riders pulled up on the reins and the horses danced about, front hooves pawing at the dirt. "Identify yourselves."

"Name is Siringo. Charles Siringo," the man on the left shouted, sitting taller in the saddle. "This here's my partner. Don't mean you any harm. We come on official business."

Mary walked down the steps, keeping the rifle trained on the man named Siringo. The faces of both men were in shadow, but everything about them looked seasoned and experienced. There was an unhurried steadiness in the way they sat the horses. They wore leather vests that hung open and exposed the sidearms on their belts.

"State your business."

"Now, ma'am." Siringo made as if to dismount.

"Stay where you are." Mary moved in closer. Not too close, just enough that they could see she was serious. "Don't let anyone underestimate you," Jesse always said. "You're the best shot in the county." Now she could make out the faces in the shadows of the hat brims: Siringo had a long, narrow face, sunken cheeks, with a big nose; the other man, a smoother face, round with slits of dark eyes.

The men exchanged quick sideways glances, then settled back into their saddles. Siringo said something, but his voice was low, the words lost in the breeze.

"Speak up!" This was a trick, she could feel it in her bones. He would lower his voice until she came closer, and somehow they would overpower her before she could fire.

"We're lawmen," he shouted. "With the Pinkerton Detective Agency, here on business for the Union Pacific Railroad. You can put the rifle down. You have nothing to fear."

"I guess I'll be making that determination."

"You got menfolk around here?" This from the other man.

"What business would that be of yours?"

"Just thinking. Looks like a big spread for a little lady like you to run all by yourself. Might be you had some strangers stop by and offer to help out for a spell?"

Mary moved the rifle a little until it was pointed at the other man's belly. "If I had to fire this gun," she said, keeping her voice steady, "the menfolk would be here before you knew you got hit."

"Listen here, ma'am." Siringo leaned forward and crossed his arms over the saddle horn. "We're here to help you. You and your menfolk could be in a lot of danger with outlaws on the loose hereabouts. You hear about the train robbery down in Wilcox?"

"What's a train robbery got to do with me?"

"I'm asking if you heard of it."

"I heard about it in town. It still doesn't have anything to do with me or my menfolk. We got our own business to tend to."

"Butch Cassidy, you heard of him?"

"I heard he ran a ranch around here some time ago."

"Well, he's still got friends in these parts, and we believe Butch and his partner, the Sundance Kid, stopped off with some of those friends. Could be they're here on this spread, helping out."

"If they were here, I'd know it, wouldn't I?" Mary could feel her heart jumping about. She struggled to keep her words steady. Her tongue felt like a piece of wood. "I'm the one that does the cooking. I guess I know how many mouths I feed, and I'm not feeding any extra mouths."

"You mind we have a look around?"

"You heard what I said, so ride on out of here. There aren't any outlaws on this ranch." God! Jesse, the hired hand, Anthony, Butch, and Sundance, all of them rounding up cattle in the upper pasture. If the Pinkerton men were to ride up there, Butch and Sundance would be arrested.

Arrested! For a moment, she couldn't catch her breath. They would be killed.

Siringo was still leaning over the horn. "Maybe you didn't hear all the news in town. The Union Pacific wants these outlaws bad. They caused a lot of damage to railroad property. Blew up cars, cleaned out the safe, blew up a bridge. Cost the railroad a lot of money in repairs and canceled trains. This whole country depends on railroads. Can't have outlaws stealing and interfering with the service. So the Union Pacific is making folks a helluva offer. Reward of eight thousand dollars per head for Butch Cassidy and his gang."

Mary realized she must have flinched, because the man went on: "You heard that right. Enough money for you and your menfolk to live happily ever after. Hell, you could buy your own island out in the ocean somewhere. No more worries."

"I told you, there's no outlaws on this ranch. No strangers." My

God, the reward was a fortune. Enough to tempt a lot of people to turn in Butch and Sundance. "Ride on out of here," she said, "before I have to use this gun."

"I don't believe you're going to shoot us." Siringo smiled and shook his head.

Mary shifted the rifle on him and looked into the sights. He didn't move. She sighted the rifle on the high branch of the cottonwood next to the road and pulled the trigger. A gray squirrel exploded into pieces and landed in front of the horses. They reared back, ears flattened against their heads. It took a moment for the riders to steady them.

"You got two seconds to turn around and ride out of here."

Mary kept the rifle on the two men as they turned the horses and galloped to the main road. Still she waited until they had taken the diagonal cut and headed south, past the sage-marked hillocks and the clump of willows. She stared out across the plains, hazy in the hot sun. There wouldn't be enough left of the squirrel for dinner. In the distance she could hear the muffled thuds of the horses' hooves. She kept the rifle pointed at the road. If the Pinkerton men decided to return, they would not take her by surprise.

Eventually the sounds of the hooves disappeared into the low shushing roar of the wind, and she walked back along the house to the washing tub and wringer. Ducking past the clothes that flapped on the line, she made her way to the porch and set the rifle on the table, not more than an arm's stretch away. She put another shirt into the water, still warm from perching in a stream of sunshine. In case the Pinkerton men were watching from a high bluff, she would go about her business as usual. If she saddled a horse and rode into the pasture, they would come back. Besides, Jesse would be here in another five or ten minutes, if he heard the rifle shot.

She had hung up the wet shirt when she spotted two riders coming across the north pasture, dark, blurred figures that gradually began to take shape and color. She knew Butch by the way he sat the saddle, straight-backed and shoulders squared, his body moving in rhythm with the galloping horse. Anthony rode close behind. Mary hurried over to the fence, let herself through the gate, and ran toward them.

"You okay?" Butch shouted when she was still a barn's length away. "We heard the shot."

They pulled up beside her, and she told them about the two detectives. She was breathing hard, partly from running, partly from fright, she realized. "Pinkertons," she said. "Man named Charles Siringo and his partner. The Union Pacific hired them to find you and Sundance. They're killers, Butch, I could smell it on them."

Butch turned in his saddle toward the hired hand. "You take Mary back to the house. Don't leave her, in case they come back. I'm going after Sundance."

Mary handed the rifle to Anthony and swung up behind him. "I'll take my gun back, if you please," she said. She laid it crosswise between her and the saddle. Then she clasped her arms around his waist and held on tight as he spurred the horse into a fast gallop. Over her shoulder she could see Butch riding back across the pasture.

IN THE KITCHEN she made sandwiches from the beef she had roasted yesterday and the week's supply of bread she had baked this morning. She wrapped the sandwiches in packing paper and put them in two canvas saddlebags. Then she added hardtack, oranges, a loaf of bread, two jars of beans, and peaches she had put up last fall. She filled tin bottles with fresh spring water and laid them on top. Enough food, she hoped, to get Butch and Sundance to the Wyoming border and all the way into Brown's Park. Not even Pinkerton detectives would lay siege to Brown's Park. Or maybe Butch and Sundance would head to the Hole in the Wall in the Bighorn Mountains. Another place where they would be safe.

She saw the three riders out in the pasture: Butch in the lead, Jesse close behind, and Sundance in the rear. Anthony opened the gate for the riders, who slowed the horses into the yard and dismounted. They stood there talking, making plans. Butch would have already formed one in his mind, she was sure. He would know which direction they had to go in order to avoid the Pinkertons, who had ridden south. While she had prepared the saddlebags, Anthony had saddled fresh horses. Now he led them out of the barn. Butch and Sundance would ride their own horses, with two fresh horses roped behind.

She knew all this, standing by the half-dry laundry on the line, watching with one hand shading her face, because it had happened before. She had never been sure when Butch would leave. Looping through her mind was what she did know, had always known: Butch didn't like good-byes, so he just left. She picked up the saddlebags, carried them out into the yard, and set them on the ground by the horses.

"You have to go," she said to Butch.

He nodded. "Pinkertons never give up. We have to stay ahead of them."

"It's because of the money, just like I said. The minute Jesse took that money to the bank, somebody figured out where he must've gotten it. The railroad put a big price on your heads."

When she told him the amount, Butch whistled. "Makes me think about turning myself in," he said. "Now don't you blame Jesse for saving the ranch. He did it for you." He held her eyes a long moment until she thought she could read the real meaning in what he had said: *I did it for you.*

"We wish you luck," Jesse was saying. "You've been a big help to us. Which way you think you'll go?"

Butch looked around, as if spies might be hiding in the grass. There were only the five of them, Butch and Sundance, she and Jesse, and Anthony. "I reckon we'll go where the wind blows," he said.

Jesse took her arm and walked her across the yard to the house. It was as it should be, she thought, she and Jesse alone in the house, Anthony helping on the ranch. She had never thought she'd see Butch Cassidy again. After he had gotten out of prison, he rode off. Didn't even come by to say his good-byes. It was his way.

She sank down at the kitchen table as Jesse poured two big mugs of coffee. "Those boys'll be fine," he said when he set the mug in front of her, but the way he said it, she knew he was trying to cheer her up. And maybe cheer up himself. "Looks like they're about ready to take off." Jesse was at the window, looking out. Then he set his mug down and went back outside.

Mary stayed at the table and sipped at the coffee. She had said her good-byes years ago. Let him go with the Great Spirit.

She got to her feet at the sound of boots on the back step. The screened door flew open and Butch hurled himself inside. "I want to leave you something." He took a folded piece of paper out of his shirt pocket and spread it flat on the table. She knew in an instant what it was: the pencil marks, pressed down hard, that resembled four trees set in the four corners. On the south tree was what looked like a horseshoe. Beyond the north tree was a clump of boulders that lifted off the top of the page. Over to the right, the banks of a lake and an odd, squiggly line, like a strip of land jutting into the lake. Yesterday morning, he was gone when she had served breakfast. She thought he had left forever, but by midafternoon, he was back, and she had understood.

"You want me to keep this safe for you?" If the Pinkertons found him, they would find the map, and they would take the treasure.

"If you and Jesse need the money, you know where it is."

"I would never take it," Mary said. "It's yours, and I hope someday you will come back to claim it."

"Maybe so. But you promise me, Mary, you'll use it if you need it. You'll keep your ranch and take good care of yourself and Jesse. You promise?" He was smiling at her, and she had never been able to resist that smile. She promised.

23

"HEARD ANYTHING MORE from the anonymous caller?"

Ted Gianelli nodded Vicky into a hard-backed chair, inched past the desk in the closet-sized office, and dropped into his chair. He clasped his hands over his stomach, a calm, unhurried look about the man, the inexhaustible patience of an experienced investigator. The music of an opera drifted across the office. *Rigoletto*, Vicky guessed, although she didn't recognize the aria.

"I'm here about Ruth Walking Bear," Vicky said. She perched on the chair and allowed the music to wash over her. Feeling calmer, more settled. She had waited in the parking lot a good fifteen minutes, watching the vehicles streaming down the street, unsure of what Ruth might be driving. The sun beating down, white clouds skimming through the blue sky. There was no sign of Ruth. Finally she had gone into the small entry, pushed the button on the metal communicator in the wall, and said she was here to see

Agent Gianelli. A few moments later, she was following the agent down the long corridor to his office in the back.

Now she told the agent that someone had broken into Ruth's house and ransacked it. Ruth should be here, she was thinking, telling her own story.

Gianelli's eyebrows lifted a quarter inch. "She report it to the tribal cops?"

Vicky said she wasn't sure.

The fed leaned into the laptop, tapped a few keys, and stared at the screen. "Reported at two forty-five this morning. Officers responded at three fifteen. No sign of burglar. Homeowner said nothing had been stolen. She believes dead husband's cousins, Bernie and Big Man White Horse, are responsible."

He looked up, and Vicky said: "I think Bernie's husband was looking for the map." She could still see the couple seated across from her, the greed flashing in their eyes. The hard look of disgust when she told them she couldn't help them. And Big Man saying there were other ways to get the map. "Bernie took Ruth out last night and kept her out late. Ruth thinks she was giving Big Man time to ransack the house. Any results from forensics?"

Gianelli drew in his cheeks as if he were sucking on a cigar. "Paper dates from the last part of the nineteenth century. Not enough pencil traces to provide a conclusive date. So the scrap of paper doesn't prove anything definite. Pencil marks could be from last week."

"Or from the 1890s. If the pencil marks can't be dated, then we don't know when they were made."

The fed beat a rhythm with his pen on the desk, and Vicky went on: "It's possible Robert had the original map drawn by Butch Cassidy, and Big Man was desperate to find it. Which means . . ."

She had his full attention; she could feel the intensity in his gaze. "Whoever ransacked the house didn't know the map could have been destroyed."

Gianelli was nodding, his gaze still fastened on her. Finally he said, "The anonymous caller called Father John this morning. If a lawyer can't spur us in the right direction, he thinks a priest might be able to."

Vicky looked away. It made sense the caller would get in touch with John O'Malley. The caller was desperate and frightened. He needed help, and that's what her people did when they were butting their heads against the wall of white officialdom, the impersonal, automatic machinery of the law—they called the white man they could trust.

"Even if the burglar didn't know the map had been destroyed," Gianelli was saying, "it doesn't mean he wasn't at the lake. He could be the anonymous witness if"—he lifted his hands—"Robert was murdered. The coroner says there is little evidence of trauma, but Robert was wearing a bulky vest that could have prevented any bruising. There was muddy debris under his fingernails, but that could have resulted from his trying to lift himself out of the lake. We haven't found any real evidence he was murdered."

He waved a hand now and started to his feet. Vicky remained seated. "There's only one reason anyone would destroy the map."

Gianelli dropped back down, curiosity working through his expression. "Are you going to tell me that Robert found the treasure and somebody killed him for it? What's the killer going to do with gold coins and bills from the 1890s? The minute he walks into a bank or visits a coin dealer, questions will be raised. Word will get out, people will know an old treasure had been found. Quite a risk to take, when the guy might be involved in murder."

Vicky took a moment before she said, "He won't do anything. Not until the investigation is closed and Robert's death is declared an accident. Then he'll go to another state and cash in a treasure where no one is likely to connect it to Butch Cassidy or Robert's death."

The fed lifted his eyes to the ceiling. "For how long? A hundred years? Folks have trekked through the Wind Rivers looking for buried treasure based on a rumor that an outlaw had hidden his loot hereabouts." He leaned forward and clasped his hands over the desk. The edge formed a crease across the front of his shirt. "Everybody loves the old outlaws of the West like Butch Cassidy and the Sundance Kid. Why? Because they outwitted the law? That's part of it. But the most important thing is, they robbed the banks and railroads that ordinary folks considered bloodsuckers. So folks cheered them on. They were heroes. And they live on because no one wanted them to die in a shoot-out in Bolivia. I'm sure you've heard stories about Butch visiting friends in Fremont County in the 1930s. That is all they are, Vicky. Stories of treasure buried by an outlaw who never died."

He stood up this time and made a point of checking his watch. "Sorry, Vicky. I've got an appointment, so unless there is something else . . ."

Vicky got to her feet. "You'll be the first one I call."

SHE HAD TO shield the phone from the sun in order to read the text message from Annie. "Father John called." Still gripping the phone in one hand, Vicky crossed the parking lot to the Ford, started the engine, and rolled down the windows. Heat emanated off the leather seats and accumulated in the air like a compressed fireball.

She tapped on John O'Malley's name and waited a half minute until the buzzing noise sounded. Then the familiar voice was on the other end: "Vicky. Thanks for getting back to me." She asked if he had time for lunch. He was about to head to Ethete to visit elders at the senior center, he said, but he could meet her first. She suggested the restaurant at the casino.

VICKY FOLLOWED BLUE Sky Highway north, then zigzagged east toward Ethete when she spotted the crowds ahead, the traffic stalled. She slowed behind a pickup and looked out the open window. The documentary film crew, filming horseback riders trotting over the prairie, crossing the road, and trotting on toward the mountains.

The line of traffic began inching forward along the road the riders had crossed. She started to follow the pickup truck when a man stepped out and held up a red stop sign. She slammed on the brake and rapped her fingers on the steering wheel. No telling how long the delay would be.

The riders were coming back. No special order now, no cameras trained on them, and she understood the director must have decided to reshoot the scene. One of the riders looked like Butch Cassidy, broad shouldered, muscular, and confident in the saddle, blond hair escaping from the rim of his cowboy hat. She must have seen a photo of the man, she was thinking, or maybe the actor crossing the road just happened to look the way she imagined Butch Cassidy. Riding close behind was a thin, smaller man, darker complexioned, impatience stamped on his features. Sundance Kid, most likely. She wondered if the real Sundance had looked as surly and restless. Other men followed, and on their faces, the haunted, desperate looks of men on the run.

A short gap, then another group galloped past: Arapahos, riding tall and easy in the saddle, the horses at their command. They were good with horses, her people. Experts. She recognized several of the men from the powwows, and a few had been at Ruth's the day Robert died. Dallas Spotted Deer rode past. Then he spurred the horse and galloped around the other Arapahos. In the last bunch of riders was Eldon Lone Bear, staring straight ahead, as if the road that interrupted the endless prairies had never existed.

Behind them rode a bunch of cowboys, silver badges on their shirts glinting in the sun, holsters moving up and down on their hips. Still more cowboys followed, horses snorting and prancing. And in the rear, two official-looking men with broad cowboy hats, holstered guns, rifles in scabbards.

She put the scene together now: they were filming a getaway following a robbery, Butch and the gang on the run, and behind them a posse of deputies and civilians and finally, Pinkerton agents. She tried to remember what she had read about Butch Cassidy, how Pinkerton agents had tracked him and Sundance to Bolivia. But Butch had once been part of this place, a friend to her people. Riding behind the outlaws came Arapaho warriors. Shielding Butch from the posses and Pinkertons. Throwing them off the trail.

Finally, all the riders crossed to the other side, and the man stepped back and turned his sign around: Slow. Vicky inched forward, then pressed down on the accelerator and drove toward Ethete.

24

IT WASN'T THE Wind River Casino on Highway 789 that drew tourists from across the West, but a smaller casino in Ethete, with flashing neon lights, clanging slot machines, and the quiet concentration of people pulling levers and pushing buttons in front of dancing colored lights. Most of the players were Arapahos, but some white faces bobbed about, tourists in shorts and tee shirts, who had ventured off the highways and into the center of the reservation. The restaurant was in a back room, booths and tables with a few people working on hamburgers and toasted ham-and-cheese sandwiches. John O'Malley sat at a table for two against the left wall. He stood up as Vicky walked in.

"How are you?" He took her hand, his palm warm against her own, and guided her onto the chair.

She couldn't help but smile at the way he always asked how she was, as though it were important to him. And how had he been since she had last seen him at Ruth's? He sat down across from her and lifted a hand off the table as if to wave away any response other than that he was the same. She jumped in then, ignoring the rest of the polite preliminaries, the give-and-take of random comments meant to affirm the human connection between them before business could be discussed. The connection with this man was always there. From one meeting to the next—after weeks or months—always the same. They always picked up where they had left off.

"I understand you heard from the anonymous witness." The dining room started to fill up, chairs scraping the floor, people scrambling into booths. As many tourists as Arapahos.

"He told me he had called you."

Vicky nodded. "What do you make of it?"

"He sounded Arapaho, and he sounded scared. I think he's telling the truth. I tried to convince him to go to the fed."

The waitress appeared, a frazzled look about her, glancing from table to table as if she wasn't sure where to alight first. The buzz of conversations mixed with the noise of the kitchen door swinging back and forth. They ordered hamburgers and iced tea and, when the waitress moved away, Vicky said, "He's too frightened to come forward, even though it could be the only thing that will save him." She leaned closer, conscious of the people at the tables around them. The Arapaho lawyer and the mission priest having lunch together! The news would hit the moccasin telegraph by midafternoon. All the better if someone could report what they had been talking about.

Keeping her voice almost to a whisper, she said, "If the killer knows there was a witness, he will go after him. He's already killed once." She looked away for a split second, then went on: "The witness could explain how Robert got into the lake. What happened? Did someone hold him down in the water? Ruth thinks Robert always went treasure hunting alone, but Cutter . . ."

John O'Malley's face remained still, the face of the confessional, she thought, the counselor. And yet, she had caught the flash of light in his eyes. She knew him so well, the little ways in which he revealed himself, the thoughts he would never express. "Cutter Walking Bear, Robert's cousin," she explained. "His name used to be James. He's returned to the rez."

"I've met him. He stopped by the mission this morning. Visiting the old place, remembering when he was a kid in school."

Vicky waited while the waitress delivered plates of hamburgers with fries dangling off the edges and glasses of iced tea. An image of Cutter fluttered in her mind: tall and good-looking, brave and competent, like a warrior in the Old Time. "He's trying to reconnect with the past," she said when the waitress had moved away. "His family moved to Oklahoma when he was a kid. It must have been hard." She stopped, surprised at the compassion, the raw feeling in her own voice. Another look in John O'Malley's eyes now, a reluctant acceptance, as if something like this were bound to occur. "We're just friends," she hurried on, sensing an odd urge to explain. There was no need for explanation, and yet . . . somehow there was. "We were in school together. Reconnecting with schoolmates is a way of remembering what he lost." She opened the bun and poured a little ketchup over the hamburger, wanting to eradicate any notion of a personal relationship between her and Cutter Walking Bear—he was a friend; she had other friends. Except that she didn't. They were both adrift, searching for their pasts, she and Cutter.

She kept going: "He claims he went treasure hunting with Robert from time to time. If Robert took Cutter along, why wouldn't he have taken others? There's more." She was warming to the subject now, moving the conversation onto safer ground. She told him that someone had ransacked Ruth's house last night. "Ruth thinks it was Big Man, Bernie Walking Bear's husband, and I suspect she's right. Bernie and Ruth went barhopping in Riverton, and when Ruth got home, she found the house turned upside down."

John O'Malley finished chewing a bite of hamburger, then he said, "You think they were looking for Robert's treasure map?"

"What they didn't know is that the map was destroyed. I found a torn, singed piece at the lake." She saw by the little nod he gave and the flare of comprehension in his eyes that John O'Malley reached the same conclusion she had reached: whoever had ransacked Ruth's house didn't realize the map no longer existed. "The cousins thought the map was as much theirs as it was Robert's."

"What about Cutter?"

Vicky took a bite of her own hamburger. After a moment she said, "The treasure hunt was an excuse to go to the mountains and spend time with his cousin. He thought the map was a phony, like all the other maps around here. Even Ruth thinks that Robert's grandfather had probably bought the map at a trading post."

John O'Malley took a drink of tea. A puzzled look in his expression now, as if he had been turning something over in his mind that didn't make sense. "Let's say Robert's map was genuine, from Butch Cassidy himself. How would Robert's grandfather have gotten it?"

The same question had occurred to her. "All we know is that when he died, Robert found the map before any of the other cousins got there." She paused, a new idea inserting itself into her thoughts. "Ruth said none of the cousins had shown any interest.

No one had ransacked Robert's house looking for the map. Then Robert died, and rumors started on the moccasin telegraph that he had found something. All of a sudden, the map looked genuine, and the cousins started thinking there might be more treasure buried in the same location. Why else would the cousins show an interest?"

John O'Malley finished the last of his hamburger and came back to the same topic. "There is still the question of how Robert's grandfather acquired the map."

"What bothers you?"

"Eldon Lone Bear told me the Walking Bears didn't own their own ranches until Robert's grandfather managed to cobble together a few dozen acres in the 1950s. He didn't know of any connection between Cassidy and the Walking Bears, although Cassidy had other friends on the rez. He visited Lone Bear's grandfather from time to time. Stayed at the ranch when he was on the run from robbing banks. After the Wilcox train robbery, Cassidy hid out with Jesse and Mary Lyons. He had known Mary earlier."

"You're saying there had been something between Cassidy and Mary?"

He nodded. "If he did leave a map behind, he might have left it with her. But Mary's great-granddaughter, Charlotte Hanson, told me she had never heard any family stories about a map."

Vicky pushed her plate aside, half the hamburger left, the fries untouched. She drank some of the cold, sweet tea. "You think there might be something to the rumors? Robert might have actually found something?"

"The caller said he was murdered. If that's true, the killer could have been after the treasure."

"There's nothing he could do with it for a long while," Vicky

said. Then she told him what Gianelli had said about how difficult it would be to dispose of one-hundred-and-twenty-year-old
banknotes and gold coins. "The killer would have to wait until the
news about Robert's death faded away. He would have to take
the treasure to another state where people haven't heard stories
about Butch Cassidy's buried treasure."

"So the killer has to bide his time, unless the witness decides to
come forward or . . ." John O'Malley paused. "There is another
option."

Vicky got it then. All the mysterious phone calls, the pleas
for help in bringing a killer to justice; all of it could be a ruse to
pressure the killer. "The caller wants a share of the treasure," she
said. "Cut him in, and he'll shut up about Robert's death being a
homicide. No one will ever know who he is or what he saw. The
investigation will grind to a close, and the death will be either
unknown or an accident."

"If that's so," John O'Malley said, "he is playing a more dangerous game than we had suspected."

It was close to five o'clock when Father John pulled into Eldon
Lone Bear's yard. The breeze had gathered force through the afternoon, and now it stirred basketball-sized dust balls around the dirt
yard. He turned off the engine and waited. The air was dry and
hot, the sun inching west in the vast blue sky. *Pagliacci* soared
around him. Eldon's pickup stood against the side of the house,
which meant that most likely the elder was home. If he was up to
company, he would come out.

After he had left Vicky, Father John had spent a couple of hours
at the senior center, drinking coffee and playing checkers with Ray
Dark Horse. Watching every move because Ray was used to luring
opponents into traps that allowed him to clear off the board. Then

he had driven to Arapahoe and visited two parishioners, Lucky Nightman, recuperating from surgery, and Janice White Moccasin, left bedridden after a stroke. All the while, trying to ignore the question following him like a shadow: how had a Walking Bear come to possess Butch Cassidy's map? Because everything they had discussed, he and Vicky, was speculation. Without a genuine map, Robert couldn't have located the buried treasure. But what if the map was genuine and Robert had managed to find the treasure?

Father John had been heading back to the mission when he decided to veer west toward Lone Bear's place. Maybe it didn't matter how Robert's grandfather got the map, unless the map was genuine. Then it was the logical connection that held everything together.

The front door opened. Lone Bear leaned outside, squinted into the sun, and waved him in.

25

THE OLD MAN bustled about like a kid excited to have company. Obviously he had gotten everything ready, made coffee, carried the mugs into the living room, and set them on the little table next to the sofa before he opened the door. He urged Father John to an upholstered chair, adjusting the cushions first, offered coffee and poured milk into the mug before he handed it to Father John. Finally he sank into the sofa.

Father John sat down on the chair that rode low to the floor; his knees popped up in front of him. He placed his cowboy hat on one knee and took a sip of the coffee. Hot and fresh, with a strong, pungent odor. The polite preliminaries came first: the wind kicking up a howl this afternoon, blowing everything around, the pow-wow next weekend offering the biggest prizes yet. "Ever thought about taking up dancing?" Eldon's eyes twinkled, probably at the image of the tall white man stomping through a dance. "You seen enough dances, probably could do the grass dance in your sleep."

"And probably have, but not in broad daylight." Father John laughed.

"Sure am glad you put me onto the Cassidy movie they're making. Been out there most the day, riding Bucky around. I swear that horse took to the camera like a movie star. You should have seen him preening. Thinks he is a movie star, I guess."

"You've been out riding most of the day?" The man was at least eighty-five. A rejuvenated look about him, it was true, but still eighty-five.

Eldon took a long drink of coffee, then set the mug on the table. "The day I can't ride Bucky over the prairie is the day I'll be dead." He smiled. For a second, a distant look came into his eyes, as if he were riding through the past—on the prairie, across the pasture, up into the mountains. A lifetime of rides. "They're doing good work," he said. "Intend to tell the real story of Butch Cassidy. Everybody knows he was an outlaw, robbed banks and trains, but that wasn't all of him. Oh, he ran with a wild bunch, that's for sure, but he never killed anybody and he kept the rest of the gang from hurting people. Sheriff was killed after the Wilcox robbery, but Butch wasn't around when that happened. And if he had been, it wouldn't have happened. Naturally he got blamed, 'cause he was the supposed leader, and if he hadn't been a good one, a lot of folks would've gotten killed."

Father John finished his coffee and set the mug on the vinyl floor beyond the fringe of the woven rug that connected the chair and sofa. "How much longer will they be filming here?"

"I'm darned if I know. Today Butch, Sundance, and the others were escaping from the posses, riding hard and fast to the rez. Finally lost the posse, but more showed up, figuring Butch would be looking to hide out with friends here. That's where we got involved . . ."

"We?"

"Raps and Shoshones are showing up with their rides. Want to be in the film."

"They weren't keen on the film being made." Father John could still see the disturbance after Mass, hear some of his parishioners telling the director to go home. He had to admit a surge of tourists prowling through the mountains looking for Butch Cassidy's treasure was a disturbing idea. "I guess when you agreed to be in the film," he told the old man, "it made it okay."

Eldon leaned so far forward, Father John thought for a moment he might fall off the sofa. "People started hearing how much the movie company was paying. That's what made it okay." He settled back. "That director, Paxton, kept asking me what I remember about Cassidy. They're getting ready to shoot scenes in the 1930s when Cassidy came back. Looks like I'm the only Rap alive that remembers him."

"You believe he came back?"

"Everybody believes he came back, except the historians that get their stories from books. Paxton's been talking to people around here, and he's heard a lot of tales about Butch coming back. I remember Butch when he came to my grandfather's camp. Big white man with a loud laugh. Scared me to death at first. I must've been four years old. But he had candy in his pocket, and I sure liked candy. Wore brown trousers, rough kind of material that scratched my legs when I sat on his lap. It was like sitting on a log, his thighs were so big. Chewing on my candy. I couldn't stop looking at his face. He had more hair than I'd ever seen on a man, covered his cheeks and chin and was real stubbly. I reached up and patted his chin. He just laughed. I remember his big, bellowing laugh. And my grandfather saying, 'This here white man is a friend. He helped out the people when we needed help.'" Eldon was shaking his head, remembering. "Refill?" he said, pushing himself forward.

"Let me get it." Father John set his hat upside down on the floor, got to his feet, and picked up both his mug and Eldon's. In the kitchen he found the metal coffeepot on the counter next to a box of cereal and a can of pork and beans. He refilled the mugs, took the milk from the refrigerator, and poured a little into his mug, then went back into the living room. He handed Eldon his coffee and sat down with his own.

"Seems to me it would have been dangerous for Butch to come here. There must have been men who would have liked to claim they brought down Butch Cassidy."

Eldon took a long drink of coffee. "Butch had ties hereabouts, and he was a man that appreciated ties. Came from a Mormon family that he had to stay away from, so having an outlaw son didn't shame them. He was always looking to replace his family."

Father John took a sip of his own coffee, the idea of a genuine map and a treasure turning in his mind. "Do you think he came back hoping to find the treasure he buried?"

Eldon went still a moment, then started nodding. "Story I heard, he went camping in the Wind Rivers with some of his friends. His old girlfriend Mary went along. You talk to her people?"

Father John said he had visited Julia Marks at White Pines, but the woman's memory was gone. "Her daughter, Charlotte, told me it's possible they're descended from the daughter Mary had with Butch before he left the area. The child grew up with an Arapaho family on the rez, and Butch never knew about her."

Eldon was still nodding, as if he were nodding Father John through the story. "I heard the rumors on the telegraph a long time ago. I figure Butch wanted to check up on Mary, so he hid out with her and Jesse after he robbed a train. I heard he came back other times to see her. Last time he came, they were both old, but . . ." He drew in a quick breath that expanded his thin chest. "There's still life in us old folks. Butch and Mary went hiking into the mountains themselves and left the others at the campsite. Reckon they had a lot of reminiscing to do." He finished his coffee and set the mug on the table. "Could be Butch was looking for his old treasure. If so, Mary might've brought his map along."

Father John finished his coffee and set the mug back on the floor. "There's something I don't understand," he said. Eldon hunched forward, eyes leveled on him. "It makes sense that Butch would have left a map with Mary, but her great-granddaughter says she never heard anything about a map. As far as she knows, the idea of a Butch Cassidy treasure map was concocted by store owners for the tourists. But Robert Walking Bear believed the map he found in his grandfather's barn was the original map . . ."

Eldon held up his hand, palm outward. "Don't believe anything those Walking Bears say. They always been a loose cannon rolling around the rez, taking advantage of folks, claiming things that weren't true. Robert's grandfather, Luther, used to claim *his* grandfather was Butch Cassidy's best friend. Said he even rode with Cassidy." He shook his head. "Out-and-out lie. Wasn't anybody in the gang from around here. Butch came here to be safe, not to find other outlaws."

"If the Walking Bears weren't ranching back then, they couldn't have hidden Butch. I don't understand how the map came to be in Luther Walking Bear's barn."

"You ask me, they stole it. Maybe drew up a map themselves and said it came from Butch." Eldon lifted a fist in the air. "Oh, I've heard how Robert must've found the treasure and that's why he was killed. I don't believe any of it."

Father John spent another ten minutes with the old man, chatting about the movie and about a man with a big laugh and stubbly hair on his face. Like a shadow, Father John thought, moving across the rez, the past making itself known. Finally he got to his feet, told Eldon—shifting forward on the sofa—not to get up, and let himself out the door. The wind had died down to a warm breeze that brushed his face and flattened his shirt against his chest. He set his hat firmly on his head and got into the pickup, the cab as hot as a boiler. He had turned on the engine and rolled down the windows when the cell in his shirt pocket started buzzing. "Father John," he said, holding the cell in one hand, shifting into reverse with the other.

"Mike Denton, state patrol." An unfamiliar voice, a name he didn't recognize. "We have a fatal accident on the Loop Road. Arapaho man. We thought you would want to know. We're about to bring the body out. No ID yet."

"Where exactly are you?"

The officer gave him the mileage from the turnoff on Highway 26 as Father John backed across Eldon's yard. He shifted into forward and said that he would be there in twenty minutes.

THE ROAD TWISTED and turned, lifting itself above the reservation that lay in the distance, rooftops glinting and small tornadoes of dust blowing off the roads. An Arapaho, the officer had said. It could be anyone. A parishioner or a member of the Eagles team who had grown up and was driving in the mountains. A couple of thousand families, and tonight, one of them would be bereft.

He prayed silently as he drove, shunting the conversation with Eldon to the back of his mind and forcing himself to concentrate on the present—the dead man in a vehicle down the mountainside. Let the past take care of the past.

He glimpsed the line of vehicles ahead—SUVs, an ambulance, patrol cars with roof lights flashing—as he came around a curve that swung out over a drop-off. A little creek, icy blue in the distance, bubbled through the valley below. Ahead, the road narrowed into another curve. He could picture an oncoming vehicle veering into the uphill lane, forcing the driver to react quickly, turning the wheel to avoid a head-on crash, and shooting off the mountain. Everything could change in an instant.

He pulled in behind a state patrol vehicle and got out, a familiar uneasiness moving over him. Uniformed officers stood about the vehicles, staring down the mountainside where four men were struggling up the hill, hauling a litter with the lumpy outlines of a body beneath a tarpaulin. Farther down the slope, Father John could see a white truck that looked as if it had run itself out and crashed into a clump of pines, hood pointed downward as if it were bound for the creek. The doors hung open, the sides black with dust, suggesting the truck had rolled before coming to a stop upright. Several men were poking about the vehicle, fastening thick wire cables to the undercarriage and threading them upward to a wrecker that squatted close to the drop-off.

One of the officers broke away and came toward him. "Father O'Malley? I'm Trooper Denton."

"Thanks for notifying me," Father John said. "Any idea of who was in the truck?"

"Nothing official yet, but the truck is registered to Dallas Spotted Deer. We found a driver's license on the body in the same name. Do you know the man?"

"I've met him a few times."

"Then you can confirm the initial ID. How about family? Wife? Children?"

"I don't believe he was married." He could picture the man hovering around Ruth Walking Bear after Robert died. Round, pockmarked face, belly that hung over a silver buffalo-head belt buckle, and a lonely, gentle look about him, self-effacing with a kindness in his dark eyes. "He's a cousin of Robert Walking Bear, who died up here."

"We're going to need a family member to come to the morgue and make a positive ID."

"I can tell Robert's widow, Ruth."

There was a palpable relief in the way the officer turned toward the officers struggling over the lip of the road with the litter, as if the matter were settled, the most difficult part taken care of.

"I'd like to bless the body." Father John stepped past him.

"Sure." The officer's voice trailed behind him. "Blessings never hurt anybody."

26

DALLAS SPOTTED DEER dead. No wife or children. Closest relative, the wife of a cousin. A lonely man.

The thoughts tumbled through Father John's mind as he drove back down the mountain, across town, and onto the reservation, columned in shadow. Stars popped like diamonds in the silvery light of early evening. The image of Dallas Spotted Deer on the litter had imprinted itself in his mind: eyes staring into nothingness, face contorted with bruises and broken bones, the right side of his head smashed in. Dallas had been found half in and half out of the cab, left leg nearly severed beneath the truck. *Dear God, have mercy. Mercy. Mercy.* All time was present to God. The past, the future, all caught up in the present. *Have mercy on him.* He prayed out loud for Dallas Spotted Deer *then*, shocked, terrified, going off the edge, rolling and plummeting down the mountainside, doors flying open.

The state patrol officer assumed Dallas had been drinking. Why would he have taken the curve so close to the edge? Fast enough to go over? Well, the autopsy would show his alcohol level. Another question bothered Father John: what had taken the man up a narrow, steep mountain road in the first place?

AHEAD, OUT ON the prairie with the darkness coming down, was a small house, lights glowing in the window. Father John slowed for a left turn, then crawled over the borrow ditch, part of him thinking how terrible an accident could be, even a pickup overturning in a borrow ditch. He had seen accidents like that, passengers and drivers taken to the hospital. He stopped next to the front stoop and waited.

The door flung open immediately. Ruth stood in the opening, leaning forward, peering into the night. She let her gaze run over the pickup, leaned out farther and surveyed the yard. Then, a little wave as she drew herself back inside, gripping the edge of the door, her skirt billowing in the breeze.

Father John followed her into the house and closed the door behind him. Ruth had walked into the center of the small living room and turned to face him, shades of surprise and disappointment moving across her face. Finally, she said, "I was expecting someone else." In the kitchen at the back of the house, Father John could see the table set for two, plates and glasses neatly arranged, napkins tucked at the sides of the plates. A pair of candles stood in the middle of the table. "You being a priest," she said, "I sure hope you're not bringing bad news."

"Why don't we sit down?" He kept his voice low: the voice of the counselor, the voice of the *priest*.

"Oh my God! Oh my God, no!" She sank onto the edge of the sofa, lifting both hands into the air, as if that might keep her from falling to the floor. "Not Cutter. Please tell me nothing's happened to Cutter."

Father John pulled over an ottoman and perched in front of her. He took both of her hands into his own. They were cold and moist. He could feel the tremor erupting from somewhere deep inside. "It's Robert's cousin Dallas Spotted Deer."

"What?" Ruth looked at him as if she could pry the rest of it out of his features. "Dallas? What happened?"

"An accident. His truck went off the road in the mountains. It was a steep drop. He didn't have a chance."

She seemed to be absorbing the news one word at a time, as if she were stepping across the boulders in a rushing creek. "In the mountains? Where in the mountains?"

He told her the road and explained that it was close to Bull Lake. "Any idea of where he might have been going?"

Ruth pulled her hands free, leaned back against the sofa, and stared at the ceiling. A new thought moved behind her eyes. "How would I know what Dallas was doing? Like you say, he was Robert's family. He tried to hang around Robert, but Robert didn't have much use for him. Said he wasn't the shiniest tool in the box, if you get my drift. I expect nobody knows what Dallas was up to."

"Is there someone else I should notify? Who was closest to him?"

She reached across the table next to the sofa and picked up a cell. Tapping the face, she said, "I'm going to call Cutter. He'll know what to do." She placed the phone to her ear and listened a moment before she said, "It's me again. I need to talk to you bad. Dallas is dead." She pulled the phone away and studied it as if she expected Cutter to call back immediately. Finally she set the cell on the table. "I don't understand why he doesn't answer." There was a tightness in her voice. "When I saw him this morning, he said he'd be by later. I made his favorite dinner, fried chicken and mashed potatoes." She gestured with her head toward the kitchen. "My way of saying thank you. He's been such a good friend since Robert died. When I didn't hear from him, I got to thinking something must've happened. That's why, when you came over . . ."

"I understand."

Ruth looked at him straight on, as if to make sure he did understand. Then she said, "The rest of the Walking Bear cousins? Pretend they love you, and all the time they're figuring out how to screw you. Bernie takes me for a nice girls-night-out so Big Man can trash my house. Of course they denied everything. So the police say, 'We don't have any proof.' You ask me, Big Man left his filthy DNA all over the place, but the police don't want to be bothered. Indian family. Let 'em duke it out."

Father John gave her a moment before he said, "I'm sorry to bring this to you when you're still dealing with your husband's death."

She was patting at her hair, refastening a barrette in a clump of curls. "Yeah, I got my own problems. Coroner's taking his time deciding Robert's death was an accident, and the fed keeps poking around and asking questions. Meantime I can't get on with my plans." She stopped and drew her lips into a thin line, as if she might keep herself from saying any more. Then she reconsidered. "Does it surprise you that I have plans?"

"No," he said. "Robert's dead; you're in a different situation now. I'm sure you've been trying to figure out what you want to do."

"Yeah, that's it." She seemed to jump on the idea, as if it were new, something she hadn't considered. "I had to figure out what I want to do. Soon as I can, I'm going to L.A. Been wanting to move out there for a long time." She hesitated again. "I mean, me and Robert used to talk about leaving here, all the snow and cold in the winter. Who needs it? Sun shines all the time in L.A. Now I figure I'll go by myself. I'll rent out this place, get a little money coming in, and I'll be fine." Her voice rose with excitement, her hands leaping over her lap. "I'm going to go to beauty school, like I always wanted. I got a real talent with fixing hair. I looked up beauty schools on the internet, and there are about a thousand in L.A."

"Look, Ruth." Father John tried to bring the conversation back to the present. "Is there anyone else you can call? A friend who would come over?"

She gave a brittle laugh. "They're all Robert's people, his family, his friends. There never was much here for me. My people are scattered all over the place, or dead. I used to have a brother. I don't know if he's still alive."

"Vicky's been your friend." She would be here in a heartbeat, Father John was thinking, if she knew about Dallas's death and Ruth's loneliness. "I can call her."

She smiled. "I already called her. When Cutter didn't show up, I got worried and thought maybe she'd heard from him. She didn't know where Cutter is."

"I don't like to leave you alone."

"No, it's okay. You delivered your message. Maybe I'll call Bernie and tell her about Dallas. I mean, he's her cousin. Let her worry about it. I'm pretty sure Cutter will be here before long. When he says he's going to do something, he does it."

Mingling with the soft swish of the wind outside was the sound of tires beating the dry earth, an engine gunning and cutting back. Ruth went to the window and peeked around the edge of the curtain. "What are they doing here?" Her voice sounded muffled in the curtain. "I mention her name and poof, she arrives, like the witch she is." She stepped back, seemed to consider something, then walked over to the door, flung it open, and moved backward into the room. Father John got to his feet behind her.

There was the sharp whack of a car door shutting, followed by the rhythmic tap of boots. Bernie came through the door first and right behind, hovering over her, was Big Man. Ruth hadn't moved, and Bernie lunged toward her, throwing her arms around her shoulders. "Oh, Ruth, you've heard. We came over soon's we got the news on the moccasin telegraph. Another cousin dead! And Robert not even in his grave yet, poor soul. We're so glad you're here, Father." She glanced at Father John over Ruth's shoulder. "It would be terrible for Ruth to be alone after all she's been through."

Ruth made an effort to extricate herself, but Bernie kept holding on. Finally Ruth jerked herself free. "Dallas is your cousin, not mine. Gonna be up to you to take care of burial. I got enough on my mind." She set both hands on her hips and looked up at Big Man. "Didn't help me none that I had a real mess to clean up here. Don't know what I would've done without Cutter. He's been a true cousin to Robert and a real friend to me."

"So we heard." Big Man spoke out of the corner of his mouth. "You ask me, nobody would've bothered you if that husband of yours had thought about his cousins. They got a right to Butch Cassidy's loot, only Robert wouldn't share with anybody. You heard the rumor that he found the treasure and that's why he got killed? What I want to know is, what happened to the treasure?"

"There is no treasure!" Ruth was trembling, and Father John

placed a hand on her arm to steady her. "There was no Butch Cassidy map! Just an old map from an old trading post." She lifted both hands to her face, sobbing quietly now. "Why won't people leave it alone? Why does everybody have to put in their two cents? The investigation is never going to be closed. I'm never going to get on with my life."

"Ruth. Ruth." Bernie waved her hands between her husband and Ruth, as if she might calm a storm blowing over a lake. "No reason for you to be upset. Sooner or later the fed's going to come to his senses and quit bothering people, and the whole matter will be closed. Right now people are on their way over here. I heard them making plans on the telegraph. Kitchen's going to be filled with casseroles and cakes before you know it. Only natural people are thinking about you first, with Robert hardly dead a week. You sit down and relax. Don't worry about a thing. I'm going to make coffee." She was already halfway to the kitchen. "Looks like you were expecting company," she called. "Nice table. Sure smells good in here."

"See how they do?" Ruth wrenched herself sideways and flopped down onto a chair. "Take over, that's their way. Control everything. Drove them crazy that Robert had their grandfather's map. Well, Luther always told Robert that map was his. God, what does it matter? An old fake map. But it gave him a dream, and Robert was a dreamer. He liked going off into the mountains by himself and dreaming of finding treasure so we could get out of here. Start our new life in L.A."

From outside came the sound of other vehicles crossing the yard, then a cacophony of engines shutting off. Big Man went over, opened the door, and waved. In a moment, people began filing in, nodding to Big Man, coming over to Ruth, and leaning down to hug her. For a moment, Father John thought she might jump to her feet and flee out of the house, but she sat ramrod straight, one eye peeled on the door.

"Cutter will be here as soon as he hears."

FATHER JOHN WORKED his way through the crowd that was filling up the living room and out to the yard that had turned into a parking lot. Walking Bears, he thought, a scattered family, not very close, except in times of death. He made a U-turn around the cars and pickups and took the borrow ditch a little too fast, hitting his head on the roof. A little cloud of dust swirled in the headlights. He could feel the uneasiness taking hold. Cutter, the perfect cousin, the only Walking Bear Ruth trusted. Or was there something more? What else had come between Ruth and Cutter?

He turned onto Seventeen-Mile Road and drove east. The blue and white billboard with St. Francis Mission in large, black letters gleamed in the moonlight ahead, and he slowed for the turn into the cottonwood tunnel. The quiet of the mission closed around him, but questions kept pounding in his mind: Who was this man who called himself Cutter? Where had he come from and what did he want?

27

A PERFECT EVENING, with the last daylight falling over the mountain, and a half-moon blooming in the faded sky. A gentle, quiet breeze brushed the ground and cooled what remained of the day's heat. The pine trees all around swayed and sighed. Vicky spread the blanket Cutter had brought, smoothing out the wrinkles, as if it were the cover on a bed, while Cutter built a fire. He was quick and adept in the way he mounded the wood chips he'd collected among the trees, rolled up sheets of a newspaper and stuffed them among the chips, then held a match to the paper. The little fire sputtered and licked at the chips, and Cutter laid logs on top, propping them at an angle so as not to cut off the oxygen.

Vicky moved the picnic basket onto the blanket and sat down. She pulled her knees to her chest and clasped her hands around her legs, watching Cutter. Every movement smooth and controlled, as if he had been building campfires all his life. He was an expert. An expert at a lot of things, she was beginning to think. Today he'd accepted the offer of a job with Fowler Oil in Casper, but he would be working in the oil fields on the rez, supervising and managing. He had come home, and he planned to stay.

She had been winding up the day at the office. Annie and Roger had already left when the phone rang. Ruth, wondering where Cutter was. "I have no idea," Vicky had told her. She had just hung up when there he was, standing in the doorway between her office and Annie's, the beveled-glass doors swung back. "Ruth's trying to reach you," she had told him. Information he seemed to ignore as he strode into her office and plopped a small ice chest on her desk. "We're going on a picnic," he announced.

No, Cutter. No. No. Too much to do this evening. An important custody hearing coming up. Absolutely not.

Cutter Walking Bear had waved away each objection. She had to eat, or had she given up eating? It was beautiful in the mountains. He would have her back by nine o'clock. Promise.

She had given in. A change of scenery, change of schedule sounded good. She had been working hard lately, worrying over Robert's death and the anonymous caller, worrying over Ruth, trying to pull together compelling arguments in favor of Luke Wolf's claim that he was not a neglectful parent. "I have to go home and change," she had said.

Fine, and Cutter would come with her. She had put up one hand. "I'll meet you in the parking lot at my apartment in thirty minutes."

He had been waiting, leaning against the front of a ratty old pickup the color of mustard. His pickup was in the shop, he'd explained, a small fender bender today. He had a loaner. "I'm not sure it can make it to the mountains," he'd said. She had offered to take her Ford. It hadn't surprised her when she saw that Cutter had already stashed the cooler, a brown grocery bag, and folded blankets in the back of the Ford. It was all part of Cutter, making the world turn in his direction.

Now he sat back on his heels and admired the fire he'd built. "We're going to appreciate the heat when the sun goes down," he said. It was true, Vicky was thinking. The temperature could drop twenty degrees in what seemed like seconds after the sun disappeared behind the mountains.

"What will you have, my lady?" Cutter jumped to his feet, pulled the grocery bag over, and opened the ice chest. "Beer? I brought a bottle of chardonnay." He was extracting little plastic glasses from the bag.

"Water? Soda?" She didn't drink alcohol. In the years with Ben Holden, he had drunk enough alcohol for both of them. He had drunk her lifetime share.

Cutter laughed. "Should have spotted you for a water-soda gal. So what is it? You buy into the old stereotype that Indians can't handle alcohol? Never been a problem for me."

Vicky didn't reply. It was a problem for Luke trying to regain visitation rights with his son, a problem for clients charged with DUIs.

"Coke?" He popped the lid and handed her the can. "Hope you like fried chicken and french fries because they are on the menu tonight." He pulled two white Styrofoam boxes from the brown bag and a wad of napkins. Everything arranged, tied down before he had appeared in her office and mentioned the picnic. Before she had agreed to come with him. Vicky felt an uncomfortable prickling sensation on her skin. Was she that transparent, that lonely?

The chicken and fries were still warm, spicy and tasty. The fire crackled and spit, and Vicky scooted back a few inches. Cutter came with her, one knee leaning out, touching hers. "Heard any more from the anonymous caller?"

Vicky chewed a bite of chicken a moment. "What makes you ask?"

"The fed's questioning the cousins and anybody that knew Robert. I figure he's still investigating Robert's death because of the guy that called you." She felt the pressure of Cutter's fingers wrapping around her wrist, holding her hand suspended over a piece of chicken. "Any idea of who made the call?"

"What difference does it make?"

Cutter took his hand away. "I understand client confidentiality. If he's a client, you can't talk about it. Thing is, people are on edge, wondering when some anonymous caller might accuse them of murder. Gianelli takes the whole thing seriously. Looks like the investigation will never be finished. It's not fair to Ruth or to any of the cousins. Long as the investigation goes on, the rumors go on. Everybody thinks Robert actually found a treasure, so now people want to know what happened to it. Whole thing has gotten out of hand. I thought . . ."

Cutter paused. He finished a beer, squashed the can, and threw it into the bag. Then he pulled another beer out of the ice chest.

"You thought what?"

"You could call your client off. He's a liar, trying to cause trouble. Some kind of sociopath angling for attention now that everybody's thinking about Robert and poor Ruth."

Vicky took a long drink of Coke and another bite of chicken, aware of Cutter's eyes on her. The air was thick with anticipation. She tried to figure out what he wanted. The name of the caller? She didn't know who the caller was. Somehow even telling him that the caller was not a client seemed like a breach of confidentiality.

"Why would someone claim he saw Robert murdered if he hadn't?"

"Because he's crazy, Vicky. I'm trying to tell you he's crazy, and if you have anything to do with the guy, you should be careful. I'm worried about you."

Vicky ate the last of the chicken that she wanted and closed the box. "Who else might have gone treasure hunting with Robert? If he took you along, he could have taken someone else. Maybe several people."

"You're beginning to sound like Gianelli. I don't know the answer. I didn't know Robert all that well. Only reason I agreed to go along on those crazy hunts was to get to know him. Let me tell you, hiking around steep mountainsides, climbing over boulders was not my idea of fun."

"Maybe he took other cousins. What about Dallas Spotted Deer or Bernie and her husband?"

"I doubt it. They wanted Robert's map, and there was no way he was going to let them get close to it."

"Why you, Cutter? Why did Robert let you get close?"

"I have no idea." He squashed the second beer can, took another out of the cooler, and popped the lid. Foam and beer sloshed onto the blanket. "Could be because he knew I didn't want anything. The whole idea of buried treasure was a crock, you ask me. I didn't care about any old map." He put his head back and drained part of the can. "Old, rotten map and buried treasure that never existed! Robert was going nuts, you ask me."

"What do you think happened?"

"What?"

"At the lake."

Cutter leaned back on his elbows and stared up at the sky. A silver-gray now, stars everywhere, and the moon bright and low hanging. The crickets had worked themselves up into full throttle, and the breeze made a hushed noise in the pines. The fire had died back to a warm glow. "He liked the lake. I picture him tromping along the shore, stooping down to splash some water in his face, trying to cool off. Lost his footing and fell in. There's a steep drop-off, and he must've fallen headfirst into the deep part. Upended him, the way I see it. He couldn't regain his balance and pull himself up and out of the water. Accident, only the fed refuses to believe it so long as that crazy caller keeps stirring things up." He paused. "What did the caller say happened?"

Vicky shook her head. "You never give up, do you?" She was trying for a lighter tone that masked the uneasiness she felt. They were alone, she and Cutter, darkness falling over the mountains, the nearest campsites a mile away.

Cutter sat back up. "Why are we talking about a dead guy when we're alive and the night is ours and it's beautiful." She could feel the warmth of his arm slipping around her shoulders, drawing her to him. "From now on, let's talk about us. You and me, Vicky. We're a great pair. It's like I came home to find you. And, well . . ." He hesitated before pushing on. "You've been here all this time waiting for me."

"Oh, Cutter." She tried to pull away, but he was holding her close. She could feel his heart beating beneath his plaid shirt, strong and steady. "We don't know anything about each other." Her own voice sounded muffled against his shirt, and she managed to push herself back and face him. "We have to take things slowly."

"I don't like slowly. I see what I want, I go for it." He gave a little laugh. "It might take you a little longer, but you will come around, I promise you."

Vicky started to her feet, and he pulled her back. He was on her then, kissing her, pressing her against the hard ground. "Take a chance on us," he whispered. "Be brave, Vicky. Be brave."

She managed to scramble away and jump to her feet. She could feel her heart pounding against her ribs. What difference would it make if she and this handsome, take-charge man made love next to the campfire? Who would care? Except there was something about him—unknown and yet familiar, something reminiscent of Ben Holden, so handsome and always in control. "I'd like to leave now," she said.

"We'll leave later. When I say so." He reached up, grabbed her hand, and pulled her back onto the blanket. "You have to learn to trust me, Vicky." His lips were warm and moist against her face and neck. "Trust me. I'm the best thing for you. We'll be good together."

She tried to push away again, but his chest was hard and stationary. It was like pushing against a boulder. "What about Ruth?" The question surprised her, erupting out of nowhere, and yet, she realized it had been hovering at the edge of her mind.

Cutter drew back, taking a moment to marshal his response. "Ruth is my cousin's wife. She's family, and family means everything to us Raps. I'm not telling you anything you don't know. Why would you ask such a question?"

"She's in love with you." Vicky knew with a dead certainty it was true, the shadowy truth that had been following her around since the day at Ruth's house when Ruth kept looking for Cutter, wondering when he would show up. An ugly suspicion, Vicky had told herself. What right did she have to be suspicious of a woman who had just learned that her husband was dead? She had tried to push it aside, and still it had followed her, nagged at her. *Pay attention. Pay attention.* Grandmother's voice in her head. *You can feel when something isn't right.*

"Enough about Ruth." Cutter was on her, pushing her hard into the ground. She tried pummeling his chest, but he swept her hands away and locked them down.

"No, Cutter!" She was yelling, but there was no one around. Crickets somewhere, maybe a squirrel scampering up a tree. She was alone with a man about to rape her.

"I said, no!" She kicked at the brown bag that tumbled back into the fire. Flames swooshed into the air and licked at the blanket. Then a loud crack as the flames ignited the alcohol Cutter had spilled.

"Damn it!" Cutter jumped up and started stomping the fire.

A half second was all it took. Vicky was on her feet, scooping up her bag as she ran. Down the path and through the trees, a shortcut to the road. Cutter behind her, yelling her name. "Come back. Come back."

She was inside the Ford, the door locked, the keys in her hand. She jammed the key in the ignition and willed the engine to turn over. Cutter outside, banging his fists on her window. My God, he was going to break the window! She shifted into forward and threw her weight onto the gas pedal. The Ford jumped into life, up and over a clump of dirt and out onto the road. Cutter running alongside, shouting and banging, and then he was in the rearview mirror, hands thrown in the air, as if he could call the evil spirits down on her.

28

THE ALCOHOLICS ANONYMOUS meeting had ended thirty minutes ago, but several members remained behind. Folding up metal chairs, stacking them against the far wall of Eagle Hall, dumping coffee grounds and washing up the containers, bagging Styrofoam cups and wadded napkins. Father John had stood outside, shaking hands as members filed out—more women than men this evening—telling them to keep up the good work. Live in hope. He had been living in hope for more than ten years now. It was the best you could expect. The evening breeze had turned cool. Out on Circle Drive he could hear engines ramping up, tires skittering on gravel. When he went back inside, the place had been wiped clean, as if no one had been there for weeks. The only telltale sign, a slight whiff of coffee that lingered in the air.

Usually Father John stopped in the church for a few moments, allowing the quiet and peace to reach into his soul. But tonight he found himself heading back to the administration building. The heavy oak door creaked on the hinges as he yanked it open. A dim light burned in the corridor and cast a pattern of light and shadows over the photos of Jesuits past that lined the walls. He thought of them as mentors, these silent men, standing firm and showing the way he must go. He never wanted to let them down; it would have meant letting down the past.

His office was on the right, but he kept going. He flipped on the light in the small hallway that led to the miniature kitchen, a bathroom, an alcove that served as the storeroom and, at the far end, what passed as an archive. The room was the size of a large closet, ringed with shelves that sagged under stacks of books. A lightbulb hung over the rectangular table in the center, with a chain that dangled alongside it. He pulled the chain, then pulled it again, coaxing the bulb into life. A circle of light flowed over the table and melted against the shelves.

It took a while to find the records he was searching for. A series of books, piled against one another and double stacked, with dates from the 1970s imprinted on the spines in a faded gold tint. He pulled out the first book, 1970, and set it on the table. Then he pulled over a stool and began thumbing through the brittle pages with yellowing edges. *St. Francis Mission School Kindergarten through Twelfth Grade* appeared in black print across the top of each page. He turned back to the first page, and there, like a shepherd guarding his flock, was Father Patrick O'Connor, pastor of St. Francis Mission. In the paragraph below, he welcomed the students and the parents, "the St. Francis family," to a new year at the mission school, a new journey toward learning and growing closer to God.

Father John started with the kindergarten section, scanning

three pages of black-and-white photos of Arapaho kids, some with smiles as big as their faces. Names of students, as well as the names of parents and contact information were printed below each photo. A few kids looked familiar, but that was because the families were still on the rez, and family resemblances ran strong. No photo of Vicky, no photos of Walking Bears.

He turned to the first grade section: He found Ruth first, dark hair and lively eyes, energy bursting from the photograph. He thumbed through the next pages, and there was Vicky, staring out at the world with the familiar determined look, as if she were looking beyond her six-year-old self into a big future filled with possibilities. He would have recognized her anywhere, at any age. Through all the changes and growth, her soul was the same. Below the photo were the names of her parents: Mary and Albert Plenty Horses. After she had divorced Ben Holden and moved to Denver to become a lawyer, they had raised her children. Whenever she spoke about the fleeting weekends, the snatches of summer vacations with Susan and Lucas, it was accompanied by the sound of pain. The children grown now. Susan making a life in Los Angeles; Lucas, in Denver.

He turned to the W's. Still no Walking Bears. He moved to the next classes. In the third grade photos he spotted Dallas Spotted Deer. Round, puffy pockmarked face, the signs of scarlet fever that, from time to time, had raced across the reservation. A smiling miniature of the man he would become. In the fifth grade, Father John found Bernice Walking Bear and, next to her photo, Robert Walking Bear. The same eyes and noses, the jut of their jaws, all elements he recognized. He thumbed forward. A few other Walking Bears in high school, but no names he recognized.

Father John returned the book to the shelf and took the one

with 1975 on the spine. There was Vicky, eleven years old in the fifth grade, smiling at the camera now, more confident and self-assured. *Yes, I will be a lawyer someday. I will help my people.* He smiled back at her. He wished he had known her then, but in a strange way, he felt as if he had.

The name James Walking Bear appeared under the photo of a brown-faced kid who peered at the camera out of narrowed, deep-set eyes, a look of daring in his expression, as if there were a world to explore and take possession of, and nothing could hold him back. A lank of hair had fallen over his forehead, but at any moment he might have tossed his head and pushed the hair into place, if he chose. There was something unpredictable about him, unmanageable, and yet Father John had enjoyed teaching kids like that, enjoyed the challenge of channeling all that energy and imagination into something positive.

He slid the book toward the center of the light and studied the features, looking for something familiar. The wide-set eyes, the nose with the prominent bump, the ears that stood out at attention. The eleven-year-old boy who would become Cutter? Who had come to the mission to reminisce, who remembered a boarding school that didn't exist when he was a student? Maybe, Father John thought. The photo could be of Cutter. Dark skin, black hair, and suspicious eyes. Perhaps they were the same, changed and developed over the years. Life had a way of inscribing itself on faces. Still the photo made him uneasy, as if it were untrue, inauthentic, like an image forged from multiple pieces. With Vicky's photo, and even photos of the Walking Bear cousins, their elemental selves shone through. He slipped the small pad out of his shirt pocket, found a pencil on the shelf, and wrote down the name of James Walking Bear's parents: Agnes and Macon Walking Bear . . .

my father took us to Oklahoma. Where in Oklahoma? Cutter hadn't said.

The sound of an engine shattered the silence, followed by footsteps on the concrete stoop and the crack of the front door opening and shutting. He should have locked the door, but it was late for anyone to stop by. He hadn't expected a visitor. He left the book on the table and went down the hallway to the corridor. Vicky stood inside the door, staring into his darkened office, a dazed look about her as if the wind had deposited her in a strange place.

"Vicky!" He hurried past the photos of Jesuits past, and she fell into his arms.

"Oh, thank God you're here." She was shaking, her fingers pulling at the back of his shirt.

"What is it? What happened?"

"I'm a fool."

"You're not a fool. Are you hurt? Are you in pain?"

Vicky shook her head, but she kept her eyes down, avoiding his eyes. He waited. When she was ready, she would tell him. He guided her across his study to the upholstered chair in the corner. Then he hooked a hard-back chair with his boot and pulled it over. He sat on the edge, leaning toward her, circling her again in his arms.

They sat in silence for several minutes. Finally, she said, "I went with him on a picnic in the mountains. I shouldn't have gone. I have a court hearing in the morning; I have to get ready." She didn't say who he was, and Father John didn't ask. He understood they were talking about Cutter Walking Bear. "I never should have trusted him. He comes on so strong, so assured, like the world exists just for him. He had taken care of everything. The food, the cooler with drinks, a blanket, newspapers to start the fire with. He handled it all, and I allowed myself to think . . . God, I was so blind. I thought he was strong, confident, interesting and . . ." She hesitated a second before she said, "Respectful. I thought he really wanted to get to know me, and that maybe, just maybe, when we got to know each other, we might find something. How could I be such a fool."

"Did he hurt you?"

"He held me down. He tried to rape me, but I was able to get away. I kicked at the fire until it spread to the blanket, and I ran."

Father John could feel the heat rising inside him, like the fire spreading to the blanket. He wanted to protect her; somehow he should have protected her from this. But how? At what point should he have warned her? Warned her of what? A good-looking Arapaho who seemed to know who he was, where he was going? It had been only minutes since he found the photo, minutes since he had wondered if Cutter Walking Bear was an impostor. He felt his muscles tensing, his hands closing into fists. He wanted to smash in the impostor's face. He pulled her closer and tipped his head onto the top of hers, his lips on her hair, the warm, frightened smell of her in his nostrils. The whole scene played like a movie in front of his eyes: the mountains, the night falling, the fire crackling. Cutter and Vicky on the blanket . . . He struggled to make the scene fade out, and yet he didn't want it to fade. He wanted to share the fear and the horror. He didn't want her to carry it alone.

"He assaulted you. He tried to rape you. You have to report this."

Vicky pulled away and sat back against the chair, a sad amusement in her eyes, a smile almost of pity at the corners of her mouth. "Call the sheriff? Make a long report? I've seen cases like this,

John. Nothing will be done. He didn't succeed. There is no evidence, and it would be my word against his."

"He assaulted you."

"He didn't hit me. I don't have any bruises. I don't want the trouble. It's bad enough . . ." Her voice was cracking, tears blossoming in her eyes. "I want to put it behind me, get over it. Learn from it. Listen to my own instincts. There was always something about Cutter that wasn't, I don't know, real."

He told her then about the photo, and when she said she wanted to see it, he went to the archive and retrieved the book. On the way back, he stopped in the little kitchen and filled a glass with water. He handed her the water first, which she took in both hands and drank as if she had been wandering the parched prairie for days. After she set the glass on the floor, he found the page of smiling fifth graders and handed her the open book.

"I don't know." A long moment had passed before she spoke. "How can we know for sure? Look at me?" She tapped a finger on the photo of her eleven-year-old self. "I don't look like that anymore."

"But *you* are there."

She went back to staring at the kid named James Walking Bear. After a moment she looked up. "All the Walking Bear cousins accept him. They would know if he were a fake. Besides, why would anyone come around and claim to be someone he wasn't when there are people here who knew him as a kid?"

"There's something else." He had debated telling her about Dallas Spotted Deer. She'd been through enough tonight, but now it seemed that she should know. "Dallas Spotted Deer's truck went off the mountainside today. He was killed."

"Killed! My God. How sad for the family."

"He drove a white truck."

Vicky jolted upward, eyes wide in shock and comprehension. "The caller drove a white truck. He witnessed Robert's murder."

"Vicky, we don't know . . ."

"Oh, you know that we know. Dallas must have gone on the treasure hunt, and whoever killed Robert has now killed him. What happened? How did he go off the road?"

"It was a sharp curve. He must have taken it too fast and couldn't correct. Or another vehicle could have been in the oncoming lane and he veered to the outer edge."

"Or somebody nudged him off the road."

"Why do you say that?"

"Because, John. Because . . ." Then he was listening to the rest of the story. How Cutter had shown up at her office prepared for a picnic, how he was driving a rental pickup because he'd had a fender bender and his truck was in the shop. They had taken her Ford. Somehow she had managed to drive off, Cutter running alongside, pounding on her window, shouting and swearing. "He'll have to hitchhike out," she said. "He might have to walk."

"He knows where you live."

She nodded. "He left the rental at my apartment."

"He could be very angry when he gets back. You have to stay here tonight. The guesthouse is vacant."

She nodded again, as if she had been turning the idea over in her mind. "I'll have to leave in the morning in time to get to court for a hearing." She looked at him with such trust that after a second, he had to look away. He couldn't shake the sense that somehow he had let her down. He should have taken care. Take care. Take care. The words echoed in his head. Take care of the people you love.

"You'll be safe here," he told her. "I promise."

29

1899

A THUNDERSTORM HAD moved across the prairie, with great bolts of lightning that shook the house and left the air heavy with electricity. Mary had stayed at the kitchen table, sipping on a mug of coffee and telling herself that Jesse would be fine out in the pasture. He and Anthony had been caught in storms before. They would know what to do. Maybe head into a dry arroyo and wait. Nothing to do but wait. After the storm had passed, she turned her attention back to the chores. Always the chores. A basket of laundry to fold and put away, the kitchen floor to scrub, butter to churn, dinner to put on the table.

Jesse spent long days out in the high pasture now that Butch and Sundance had gone. Just Jesse and the hired hand left to round up the cattle and herd them down to the lower pastures where they could feed them in the winter months with the bales of hay stacked against the barn. And yet, they hardly spoke. A few nods and grunts, but mostly Anthony stayed to himself out in the bunkhouse. He even carried his meals out there now rather than sit at the table with her and Jesse. She hadn't minded. It was nice to spend time with Jesse; it eased the emptiness she felt after Butch left.

The Pinkerton agents had returned twice, and it wouldn't surprise her to see them riding up the road again. They never gave up. Sometimes she had to sit down for a moment to fight off the waves of nausea. At first she had allowed herself to hope there might be a baby coming, but all the hoping and praying did not make it true. For several years now, she and Jesse had accepted the fact there would be no child for them. Not long after they had married she had asked Jesse if she could bring Little Mary home, and he had agreed. Laughing and making plans to raise a daughter, building a small bed out of wood stashed behind the barn. But when they took the wagon to the reservation and found Mary playing with children she thought were her brothers and sisters, happy with her Arapaho family, they had understood the child was already at home. And later that year Mary had lost their child, a tiny, unformed life that had slipped out of her. No, the nausea that came over her now was from the thought of Butch running, running, always running from the stone-faced agents. They would chase him to the ends of the earth. It was only a matter of time until they caught up with him.

She hadn't told Butch about Little Mary. All the time he was here, she had argued with herself over whether she should tell him. She had tried to imagine what he might do, but she couldn't form a clear picture. An outlaw on the run? How could he claim a child? And what about Little Mary? Settled in her family. What did she need with a white man she had never heard of? She had decided not to tell him. Their child would stay settled and happy.

But there was something else—a ripple of pain that ran through her every time she allowed herself to think of those past times.

Butch, running his own ranch near Dubois. Going straight, living an ordinary life, like the other ranchers. Dancing at the get-togethers, and oh my, how he could dance. All the girls lined up to dance with him, but he had wanted to dance only with her. She, a half-breed, sneered at and looked down upon by the white cowboys, had caught his eye. Her heart fluttered even now at the thought of those days.

He would come back for her as soon as he got out of prison, he told her. Imagine Butch going to prison for stealing a horse that he hadn't stolen! Justice, she supposed, for all the bank robberies and train robberies he would later get away with. When he got out, he hightailed it out of here without even stopping by to see how she was doing. Without the courtesy of telling her he had to ride on, that some wild restlessness called him and he couldn't stay. Without even that much, and it had come to her over the years, the painful knowledge that she hadn't wanted to face: he hadn't loved her enough.

She lifted herself off the chair and went out to the back porch to churn the butter. She supposed the knowledge would always hurt, but it made no difference. She had met Jesse, another white man who had looked beyond her black eyes and black hair, the brown of her skin, and loved her. So it was for the best, all of it, wasn't it?

She had started to pour the cream into the churner when she saw Anthony galloping across the lower pasture with a large bundle behind him. She set the metal cream container down, stepped off the porch, and started for the fence, alarm spreading through her, bells clanging in her ears. Anthony dismounted and she saw the boots dangling below the tarp. She was running now, throwing open the gate. "Jesse! Jesse!" She could hear the panic in her voice.

"Best to stay calm." Anthony grabbed her and tried to pull her back, but she was already yanking at the tarp. Jesse's face, smashed and bloody, his eyes staring out as if he were examining the haunches of the horse. "Nothing we can do."

She fought him with all her strength, punching at his iron-hard arms, flinging herself sideways and bucking like a wild horse to get free. "He's my husband!" she shouted. "Let me go!"

Gradually he let her go. She would not be restrained. "My husband!" she was screaming, and the wild, frantic screams filled her ears.

"It's too late. Nothing to be done," he said as she cradled Jesse's head in her arms, pulled him close against her body.

"Don't go!" Screaming again. "Don't leave me."

"Let's take him inside." Anthony started lifting Jesse's body off the horse. "You take his feet; I can handle the rest."

And there they were, carrying Jesse through the gate, across the yard and onto the porch, past the butter churner, across the kitchen floor still wet from the scrubbing and into the living room. They laid him on the sofa, his eyes now staring at the ceiling.

Mary knelt down beside him. She had no idea of when she had dropped down. All she could focus on was Jesse, stretched in front of her, one arm dangling over the sofa, fingers touching the floor. She had the sense she was looking at a tintype, an image of someone else. How could this be Jesse? She laid her head against his chest and listened for the familiar heartbeat that had sustained her through the long, dark nights when the sense of loss had pressed down over her.

She was barely aware of Anthony, a blurred image standing at the foot of the sofa, starring down at Jesse. "How could this have happened?" she said.

"The storm came on out of nowhere. Lightning flash spooked

the horses, and Jesse's mount bolted and threw him off. Hard, rocky place."

"I don't believe it." Jesse was an expert rider; he had ridden horses all his life, through all kinds of storms. There wasn't a horse he couldn't handle. So what if the horse had bolted? Jesse would have kept control. No horse would throw him.

"You better believe what's real."

"He would've known what to do."

"Didn't have time. It was an accident."

Mary turned back to Jesse and sank down into her skirts. She picked up his hand, warm but still and lifeless, little smudges of dirt in the creases around the nails. Pieces of the ranch he had built for her. She pressed her lips to his palm. Then she rose on her knees and placed a finger on the top of his right eye and closed the lid. Then the left eye, the way Grandmother had done when Grandfather died.

She waited a long while before she spoke again, conscious of the man stationed like a guard a few feet away. Eventually she said, "We have to notify the sheriff."

"It was an accident," Anthony said again. "Sheriff will stir up trouble, ask a lot of questions, want to go out to the pasture where Jesse got bucked. Won't none of it bring him back. Best thing's to bury him on the ranch. Sooner better than later."

Mary felt his eyes sweeping her face. She mopped at the moisture on her cheeks and kept her own gaze on Jesse. The red and black bruises on his face, the black-shadowed eyes, and what was this? A small crater on the right side of his head. It sank in on her then, like an iron pressed against her skin, that, rather than allow her to ride into town and notify the sheriff, the man at the end of the sofa would kill her.

What she couldn't know, couldn't work out in her mind was why. What had happened between Jesse and the hired hand? The nervousness she had felt lately, the nausea that came over her out of nowhere—worry over Butch, she knew, but now she understood there had also been something else nagging at her, something as hard to grasp as the electricity after the storm. Jesse and Anthony had seemed to get along well enough—for a man who owned a ranch and a hired hand with no hope of ever owning a spread himself. Anthony did his chores, but now and then, yes, now and then she had caught him staring out over the pasture and, sometimes, even staring at her with such envy in his eyes that it had made her look away. As if the world should make up to him for all the ways in which it had failed.

"I want my family to know," she managed. "They will help me . . ." Help me grieve, help me find a way to hold this man accountable for Jesse's death. "Help me bury my husband."

"I say we bury him now out behind the barn."

Mary rose to her feet. "My husband is not an animal." She tried to keep her anger down. A small nerve had started to twitch at the side of Anthony's face. His hand rode on the holster on his belt. She was aware of being alone, surrounded by nothing but land and air and sky, twenty miles from town, fifteen miles from her family. "Besides, if we buried Jesse like that, the sheriff would hear about it and come out here asking more questions."

She could see by the way he flinched that she had struck home. He did not want the sheriff coming around; that was her trump card. "I'm asking you to ride over to the rez and tell my people about Jesse. I want to stay here with my husband." For a moment, she didn't know if he would agree. Then something in him, perhaps the desire to appear normal and innocent, overrode whatever objections rose in his head.

"You'll stay here?"

"I just told you." The man was so easy to read, she felt a chill run through her. A simple man capable of grasping one thought at a time, and that thought was to save himself. "My family will help me bury him," she said, hoping to dispel any lingering thought of the sheriff.

Anthony took a few steps into the living room, then stopped and glanced about as if he had forgotten something. Finally he strode into the kitchen and out the back door. Mary waited until she heard his footsteps in the yard before she ran to the back door and threw the bolt. Then back to the living room to throw the bolt on the front door. She took the rifle down from the rack, cocked the hammer, and went into the kitchen. Out of the side of the window she watched Anthony head into the barn. He was there for a long time. And doing what? The sorrel stood in the yard, still saddled. He had only to mount the horse and ride away.

She slid the bolt back and stepped outside, the rifle trained on the open barn door. Slowly she made her way across the yard. Afternoon sun, clean and hot after the storm, flooded the barn and outbuildings; thick shadows fell over the ground. Inside, the barn was in half darkness. She had to squint in the sunlight to make out the figure moving about. She moved closer to the door. "What are you doing?" she called, but she could see what he was doing. Packing up his gear, rolling everything he had brought with him into a knapsack that he flung over one shoulder. She kept the gun steady as he came toward her.

"You fixing to shoot me?"

"Not if you ride out of here and don't ever come back." She waited a moment before backing outside into the sunshine to give him room.

"Why the hell I'd ever want to come back here." He fixed the knapsack behind the saddle and, in one smooth move, mounted the sorrel and yanked the reins to the side. The horse trotted toward the house, and Anthony yanked the reins again, directing the horse down the side of the house and out to the ranch road. Mary kept the gun trained on him until he was nothing more than a dark speck in the middle of a dust cloud out on the main road.

She went inside and rebolted the door. Then she sank down on the floor again, next to Jesse, the rifle beside her. She wasn't sure how long she had stayed with her husband; she would have stayed forever. Time collapsed in her mind, the present and the past all bunched together. The time when Jesse had come courting in such a fancy surrey that she'd had to stifle a laugh. A fancy surrey for the likes of them, a cowboy and a half-breed. He had big plans. He had been saving money for years, he said, and he had enough to get them a stake. A little spread just over the line from the reservation, where she would be close to family. Close to her child, and she had loved him the more for understanding. Working hard on the ranch, hiring hands from time to time, whenever money allowed. But there was never enough money until Butch had come back and insisted she and Jesse take some of his.

She understood everything then. Jesse going to the bank to pay the mortgage, and where did he get all that money? And Anthony going into town and seeing the reward for eight thousand dollars, all for turning in outlaws nobody cared about anyway. The Pinkerton agents riding down the road a few days later. All of it making sense now. Anthony had been set to collect his reward, but Butch and Sundance had gotten away, and he was left with nothing.

She made herself get to her feet and, still cradling the rifle, went outside, taking her time to affirm what she knew was the truth. In the barn she pushed through the dimness to the large chest under the tackle wall and lifted the heavy cover. "Nobody'll ever think of looking in here," Jesse had told her when he stuffed the small envelope into the folds of a saddle blanket. She pulled the blanket apart and ran her fingers over the folds until she touched the crisp edges of the envelope. She pulled it out, went back outside, and leaned the rifle against the barn. She opened the envelope and turned it in the sunlight. The map was gone.

30

FATHER JOHN WOKE early, the sun spreading orange and vermilion through the eastern sky. He felt as if he hadn't slept at all. All the long night, tossing and turning and listening for the sound of a vehicle on Circle Drive, heading down the alley to the guesthouse. And Vicky alone in the little house, the door nothing more than plywood. A sturdy boot could kick it open. Dear Lord. He never wanted her to be hurt, and yet a man who called himself Cutter had tried to rape her. Would have raped her if she hadn't kicked at the fire. Distracted him, the flames blowing up on the blanket.

At some point in the middle of the night, in the midst of the fear and anger that gripped him, had come the rational, logical, unemotional truth. He could not protect her from the world. She lived in the world, and the world was dangerous. Still, the thought of her alone in the mountains, fighting off an attacker, had sent him back to tossing, getting up again to look out the window and make sure he hadn't missed the sound of a pickup or car, that no headlights flared in the alley. Thinking that he could go to the house and stay with her. Knowing that if he did, he would never return.

He showered, shaved, and pulled on his blue jeans and red plaid shirt and boots. The house was quiet. It was the bishop's morning to say Mass, and the old man would be in the sacristy putting on his robes. Father John hurried down the stairs, grabbed his cowboy hat off the peg in the front hall, and set off on the path across the field. Walks-On trailed alongside, bounding through the grass. A couple of pickups pulled into Circle Drive and parked close to the church. The door was open. He could see a few figures bent in the pews. He waved to the elders getting out of the pickups and kept going. Across the drive and down the alley that separated the church from the administration building. The mission grounds quiet, expectant, cottonwood branches crackling in the soft morning breeze, Walks-On running ahead and doubling back.

He stopped. The Ford was gone. Vicky had parked close to the house last night while he had run ahead to open the front door. Now he rapped on the door, not sure what he expected, but wanting to make sure Vicky wasn't inside, that nothing had happened, that no one had come and taken her car. The knob turned in his hand and he pushed the door open. "Vicky?"

He knew by the vacant atmosphere that she was gone. Still he looked into the kitchen alcove, the bedroom in back. The bed neatly made and only the faintest sage-tinted smell of her remaining. Walks-On sniffed around as if he were surprised Vicky wasn't here. Father John checked his watch as he walked back to the residence. Six thirty. Mass about to start. He wondered when she had driven away. He hadn't heard her car leave, but the sound had probably mingled with the stutter of the old pickups heading to the church. It made sense she would want to get home and get ready for the court hearing this morning. He retraced his steps down the alley.

The dog leapt ahead of him into the residence, and Father John followed him to the kitchen. The air was thick with the smells of hot oatmeal and fresh coffee. He shook food into Walks-On's dish and filled his water bowl, aware of footsteps coming up the basement stairs. The soft roar of the washing machine sounded through the floor. Elena pushed the door open. "You sit down," she ordered. "I'll get your breakfast."

"Why don't you sit down and have breakfast with me?"

"I already ate." She brushed at the white apron tied at her waist. "I don't need two breakfasts and I got my work to do."

There was no arguing with Elena. This was her house, her mission, her work, and he had learned it was best not to interfere. He sat down while she spooned the steaming oatmeal into a bowl, poured a mug of coffee, and set them in front of him. "You need a hearty breakfast." The same pronouncement he had heard every morning since coming to St. Francis.

He poured milk over the oatmeal, sprinkled on some sugar, and dug in. It was tasty and familiar. Not a bad way to start the day, he had decided. When he finished eating, he poured milk into his coffee, sat back, and took a long sip, his mind still racing over last night. Vicky in his office, scared and angry and triumphant all at once, and the photos of the long-ago fifth graders at St. Francis Mission School, with James Walking Bear smiling out from the past, a mixture of confidence and sadness in the dark eyes. Cutter's voice jabbed at his thoughts. *My father took us to Oklahoma.*

He took another sip of coffee, then he said, "Elena, do you remember when Macon Walking Bear moved his family to Oklahoma?"

Elena took her time swishing dishes back and forth in the sink, stacking them in the drainer. Of course she remembered. She remembered everything.

Finally she turned around. "Good riddance, I'd say. Never fit in on the rez, those Walking Bears. Pushy, trying to get more than everybody else."

"Where in Oklahoma did they go?"

"Concho, that's where Arapahos go. Knowing that bunch, they liked to be different, so they might've gone to El Reno or Geary. Why are you asking?"

"I met his son, Cutter. There are a few questions I'd like to ask his father."

Elena nodded, as if it made sense. The son shows up on the rez. Only natural folks wanting to know about him, make sure he didn't come here to hide out from trouble.

Father John thanked her for another delicious breakfast and, leaving Walks-On snoring on his rug in the corner, walked back down the hall and out the front door. Most of the pickups had left, but a few were still righting themselves on Circle Drive before heading into the cottonwood tunnel and out onto Seventeen-Mile Road. The bishop was coming along the path. "An amazing morning." The old man lifted both hands into a sky that had settled into a crystalline blue with billowy white clouds blowing across. The bishop stopped and faced him. "Trouble last night?"

"Vicky had some trouble." Lord, the old man was prescient; nothing eluded him. "She spent the night in the guesthouse."

"I trust she will be safe and well."

"I hope so," Father John said. He assured the bishop that the oatmeal was as tasty as ever and hurried on. He took the steps in front of the administration building two at a time, unlocked the oak door, and stepped into the corridor, dim and cool with the faint musty odor of a building that had settled into a stately old age. He flipped on the light as he entered his office, sat down at his desk, and opened the laptop. It took a moment for the old computer to blink into life, but eventually icons scattered about the monitor. Another moment he was in the telephone white pages, typing in the name *Macon Walking Bear*. A number of Walking Bears appeared in a number of cities, including Arapahoe and Ethete on the rez. At least ten people by the last name in Oklahoma, but no one named Macon. He maneuvered to another site and eventually found his way to cities in Oklahoma. When he tapped on Concho, a new Walking Bear listing appeared. Still no Macon. Next he tried El Reno. Finally, Geary, and there was the name, followed by the number.

Father John grabbed the phone and dialed the number. Voice mail. *Can't take your call at the moment. Call back later.* No directions about leaving your number, but the beep sounded and Father John gave the inert plastic phone his name and said he was calling about Macon's son. He left his cell number.

He hung up and dialed Vicky's number. Voice mail again, but this time followed by instructions to leave his name and number. She would get back as soon as possible. "I wanted to make sure you got home okay and everything was all right." He hesitated, then plunged on: "Call me. I want to hear your voice; I want to know you are safe."

Why wouldn't she be safe? Cutter would have cooled off by morning. But what if he hadn't? What if being left in the mountains had fired his anger? Father John could feel his muscles tense. "Call me, call me," he said out loud.

It was midmorning when the phone finally rang. Father John

was refilling his coffee mug over at the metal table in the corner, and he nearly tripped lunging back to his desk. "Father John," he said, every muscle taut with expectation.

"Charlotte Hanson, Julia's daughter. Remember me?"

"Yes, of course." Another call buzzed. He could hear the bishop answering in the back office.

"Thought you might like to know Mom is having her most lucid day in months. That film director showed up a couple of days ago and wanted to talk to her, but she couldn't remember anything. You ask me, something about him being a film director got through to her and she brightened up yesterday and said she wanted to do an interview. She's always been crazy about the movies. I think that somewhere deep inside she saw this as her last chance to be in the movies. Well, Todd Paxton is bringing his crew over this morning, and I thought you might like to hear what she has to say."

Father John walked down the corridor and stuck his head into the office. The bishop was bent over a book that lay open on his desk. "Mind holding down the fort for a while?"

"It can be managed." The bishop lifted his eyes and gave him a thumbs-up. "By the way, Maris Reynolds called. Wanted to thank you for recommending her to that film director. She said she was able to tell her family stories and set the record straight."

Father John thanked the old man and was about to start back down the corridor when the bishop said, "Something else. She said to tell you she expects you to use the Central City Opera tickets this summer. She called them a special gift for you. Not to use them would be pertinacious, which she said is a very useful word that she hopes you will pass on."

Father John laughed. "Pertinacious! We should all pass it on."

"Go to the opera, John," the bishop said. "Even pastors deserve a few days off. I will hold down the fort."

"HOW DID YOU get in?" Vicky stood in the doorway to her apartment, the door open, one hand on the knob.

Not five feet away, Cutter lounged against the counter that divided the small space into the kitchen and the living room. "Don't insult my intelligence," he said, a settled look in his expression, as if he had come to a new understanding and reached a reluctant decision. "Shut the door!"

Vicky flung herself around and started running all out down the corridor, the sound of her own screams filling the space around her. In an instant he had hold of her, the strength in his arms hauling her backward, one hand clamped over her mouth. A door at the end of the corridor opened, and the elderly Mrs. Williams in flannel nightgown and fuzzy slippers, gray hair rolled into curlers, looked out. "You all right?"

"Everything's fine," Cutter called, but by then he had pushed Vicky back into her apartment. "Lovers' quarrel is all. You know how that goes."

"Oh my." Vicky could hear the uncertainty in the old woman's voice. "Is that nice Indian lawyer okay?"

"She's fine." Cutter's most soothing and reassuring voice. A man in control. "Please don't worry. I'm her fiancé, and I'll take care of her."

"Fiancé? My goodness, I hadn't heard."

"Thank you for your concern." Cutter slammed the door and turned toward Vicky. All the time, she realized, he had not taken his eyes off her. "We should have a heart-to-heart." The hard pressure of his hand propelled her across the living room and down onto the sofa. "Don't you agree?"

"What do you want?" Vicky struggled to keep her voice steady, to camouflage the terror rising inside her.

Cutter straddled a stool at the counter and observed her for a long moment, as if she were a wild animal that had wandered too close to his campsite. Her cell had started ringing in her bag. "Leave it," he said. "I want to know what lies your client told you."

"Client? I don't know who you're talking about, and it doesn't matter. Anything a client tells me is confidential. You know that."

"Your client's dead. So your precious attorney-client relationship doesn't mean squat. Besides . . ." His voice took on a low, soothing quality. "Don't be alarmed. Nobody else will ever know. I need to know what lies he told about me. I'm a stranger in these parts, and I have to know what people think."

"If you're talking about Dallas Spotted Deer . . ." She stopped herself from saying that Dallas wasn't her client. What excuse would she have not to tell Cutter what he wanted to know? "Anything he may have told me is none of your business."

"You told Gianelli." Cutter got up and strolled over to the window, and Vicky glimpsed the grip of the small pistol tucked in the back of his belt. She thought about bolting through the door again, screaming down the corridor. He would be on her before she could throw back the bolt. "Which sent him all over the rez causing a lot of problems. Keeping the investigation open when it makes sense to call it an accident. End of story." He looked sideways at her. "Ruth can't bury her husband and get on with her life, thanks to you. None of us can move forward. Never know when the fed will show up with more questions." He went quiet, his gaze fastened on something outside the window. "That old bat! She called the police. We have to get out of here."

Vicky got to her feet. "I'm not going anywhere with you." The police were here. This was her chance. All she had to do was stall.

"We're leaving now." The pistol was in his hand, nearly hidden by the large fingers, the popping white knuckles. The muzzle pointed at her, urging her to the door.

Stall, she told herself. *Keep stalling*, but the muzzle came closer until she was staring down a black hole that went on forever. Slowly she fastened her bag on her shoulder, turned, and walked to the door. As she passed the counter, she made a point of reaching for the keys in a bowl, praying he wouldn't remember she hadn't dropped any keys in the bowl. These were extras she kept in case—in case she couldn't locate her keys in her purse and was in a hurry.

She felt the sharp edge scrape her fingers as Cutter yanked the keys out of her hand. "I'm in charge of the keys this time."

31

THE RED VAN with Cable TV emblazoned on the side stood in front of the retirement home. The rear doors hung open and two crew members in dark shirts and red vests were lifting out cameras and tripods. Like a relay team, others in identical vests carried the equipment down the sidewalk and through the front door. Father John pulled in next to the van and followed the second team inside. The reception desk was vacant. It looked as though everyone had migrated into the community room, where residents, leaning on walkers and sitting in wheelchairs, bunched around the wide doorway. The crew dodged past them.

Charlotte came through the opening the crew had made, hands in front as if she were bearing a gift. "Father John! Mother will be so pleased. She is having the time of her life." A wide smile creased the woman's face. "It's like she's gone back to when she was young. It's wonderful, but . . ." He felt her fingertips digging past his shirtsleeve into his arm. "We know it won't last. Todd Paxton's here." She tossed her head toward the community room. "I've explained that she should tell the most important stories first because, well, you never know how long she can stay in the past. Come with me." She propelled him forward. "Mother's waiting for you."

The room was packed. At least fifty people, mostly residents, seated in rows of folding chairs or on the sofas and chairs pushed in a U shape against the walls. Aides in green scrubs moved among them, leaning down and patting arms, placing walkers and canes in a vacant corner. In the aisle between the folding chairs, Todd Paxton and two crew members were aiming large, rectangular lights toward the front of the room, where Julia Marks sat in a cushioned, wing-backed chair, shoulders straight, head high. She lifted her face into the light and surveyed the audience—her audience. All the folks in the nursing home were her neighbors, whose names she probably couldn't remember. But this morning, Charlotte said, she remembered the past.

Father John realized the old woman was waving at him. A royal wave, hand barely moving. Beside him, Charlotte was nodding him forward. He waited for a crew member to set up a large tripod, then walked over. Julia's eyes were so bright that for a moment he thought she had been crying. She reached out and took one of his hands, then the other. "Oh, isn't this lovely? All these film people wanting to hear about my grandmother and George Cassidy. She always called him George, you know." She twisted around and stared up at him for a long moment. "My, it's been such a long time since you've stopped by. You must come more often."

He smiled. He was here a couple of days ago. Memory was a strange thing, the way it focused on different events at different times. So many times with the grandmothers and elders, he had seen the way past memories washed over those of the present. He promised her he would come again soon and told her he was looking forward to hearing her family stories. Her hands were like cool leaves wrapped around his. After a moment she let go and started dabbing at her hair. "Oh my, I do hope I look presentable for the camera," she said.

"You look fine," Charlotte said.

"Good to see you, Father." Father John turned around. Todd Paxton, a little frazzled-looking, long, black curly hair springing about his ears, and the faintest stubble on his cheeks, stood behind him. "We're ready to start filming. Charlotte's mentioned that we should get right on it, if you know what I mean," he said, dropping his voice to a whisper. He nodded toward chairs that had been pulled into the aisle. "What I would like is for you and Charlotte to sit next to the camera and prompt Julia with questions. Keep her on track."

With that, the director stepped past Father John and leaned over Julia. "Are you ready, Mrs. Marks?"

"Certainly." Julia lifted her face and gave him the coquettish smile she had probably given suitors a half century ago. "You want to know about my grandmother and George. Well, I can tell you everything."

"What I want is for you to look at either Father John or your daughter when you speak. Don't worry about looking into the camera. The camera will find you." He nodded in emphasis, stepped back, and clapped. "We're going to need your cooperation. Silence your cell phones and please, no talking, coughing, or laughing."

Heads bobbed, and several people started shuffling through bags in search of cell phones. Father John took his own phone out of his shirt pocket and put the ringer on vibrate. Then he walked over and sat down in the chair Paxton had indicated. Charlotte had already taken the other chair. The cameraman hunched next to the camera, and Todd Paxton stationed himself right behind. As if on cue, the ceiling lights dimmed, and Julia pulled herself up even straighter, gripped the armrests, and smiled and blinked into the bright light.

Then Julia began speaking, her voice strong and energetic. "My grandmother, Mary Boyd, was a very tough woman. If she hadn't been tough, she wouldn't have survived. I remember her well, although I was still a kid when she died. She lived in Riverton, and we went to her house every Sunday for dinner. Mom and Dad and me, but I have to say that Dad would've just as soon stayed home. Every Sunday the same fried chicken, potatoes, and gravy, but every time Dad tried to make an excuse about not coming back next Sunday, Mary reared up—oh my, she didn't take to excuses— and told him she would expect us as usual . . ."

Out of the corner of his eye, Father John saw Charlotte glance back at the director. Then she interrupted: "Mom, tell us about Mary and Butch Cassidy. How did they meet?"

Julia's gaze seemed to go inward for a moment. Finally she said, "George. George Cassidy was his name then. Oh yes, my grandmother was in love with the man. Didn't matter to her what he might've done in the past, rustling horses or robbing banks. None of that mattered because he was ranching on the border of the reservation. Living a good, straight life when they met. George came to the barn dances and carry-in suppers, made himself real popular the way he danced with all the ladies. Wasn't a lady in the area, Indian or white, that didn't fancy George Cassidy with his big smile and gentlemanly way. But George took a fancy to Mary.

She was a half-breed. I heard stories she was part Shoshone, other stories she was Arapaho. She had their good looks. She was tall and straight as a cottonwood with black hair and eyes that shone like black diamonds. Even when she got old, she stayed pretty."

"What happened between her and George?" Charlotte said.

"Oh, lots happened. They fell in love when Mary was nineteen years old, and George promised to marry her. It was plain bad luck that he got sent to the state prison. Mary said she knew he'd taken to rustling again, and he got away with a lot of horses, but he never stole the horse he went to prison for. Ranching bored him. She understood George couldn't stay in one place long. Always had plans and dreams and schemes. Didn't matter to Mary. She would've gone anywhere with him, but she couldn't follow him to the state prison. He'd come for her, he promised, soon as he got out. But when he got out, he disappeared. So he never knew . . ."

The room went quiet with expectancy; the words hung in the air. "What didn't he know?" Charlotte said.

"She had a little girl that she gave to an Arapaho family to raise because she was alone and she had no way to bring up the child. Little Mary, they called her. My grandmother worked on different ranches, cooking and scrubbing, and lots of times tending to the horses and killing rattlesnakes. She could shoot a snake between the eyes. When she knew George wasn't coming back for her, she married Jesse Lyons. They ran a spread south of Lander."

Charlotte broke in again: "Tell us about when George stayed at the ranch."

"He never forgot Mary. When he needed a safe place to stay, he headed back here where he had friends. Arapahos, whites, all kinds of friends. Worst time was after his gang held up the train down near Wilcox and made off with a lot of money. Posses and sheriffs and all kinds of do-gooders came after him, so George and one of the gang called the Sundance Kid headed to Mary's place. Sure enough Jesse welcomed them, just like they figured. They hid out on the ranch for some weeks and helped with the work. They were sure welcome because the work was hard for just Mary and Jesse and the one hired hand they could afford. Barely afforded him. Matter of fact, they were having a hard time making it, and the bank was threatening to foreclose. George wasn't about to see Mary thrown off the place she and Jesse had worked so hard to keep, so he gave them the money to pay off a loan. That's the kind of man he was, always helping out people. Would've kept on helping out folks, except the railroad sicced the Pinkertons on him and Sundance, and they had to light out again. George was always leaving, my grandmother told me. The way she put is was, 'He didn't like good-byes, so he just left.'"

Father John leaned forward. "Rumors are that he buried treasure in the mountains and left behind a map. Did Mary say anything about a map?"

"Oh, he buried the loot, all right." Julia bent forward as if she were about to jump out of the chair. Her features froze with anxiety. "But if George had left a map, don't you think Mary would've used it during all the troubles?"

"Tell us about the troubles, Mom."

The room was quiet. Father John could feel his cell phone vibrating against his chest. Vicky, he thought. He pulled the phone out of his shirt pocket and glanced at the ID. An Oklahoma number; Macon Walking Bear returning his call. Vicky was in court, Father John told himself. She was okay.

He replaced the phone and forced himself to concentrate on the elderly woman framed in the bright light. She seemed to be turning the answer over in her mind. Finally, she said, "Jesse got killed; fell off his horse, which Mary said was no accident because Jesse was the best rider in the county. He could tame a wild horse, saddle, and ride it before the horse knew what was going on. In his rodeo days, he could stay on a bronco longer than any other cowboy. But one day the hired hand came galloping across the pasture with Jesse's body slung behind him and said the horse got scared by lightning and Jesse got thrown. Mary had hard times after that, real hard times. The hired hand took off and left her alone to run the ranch. If she'd had a map to hidden treasure, don't you figure she would've used it? There was no map. There was nothing."

Charlotte seemed to take a minute to see if her mother intended to go on before she said, "How do you think the rumor of a map got started?"

"Everybody wants to find treasure. It's exciting to think of buried treasure up in the mountains. You can go up there and dream you're standing on it, thousands and thousands of gold coins."

"So Mary denied there was ever a map," Charlotte said, clearing up something for herself.

"Denied? I didn't say that. She never mentioned it, that's all, and us kids sure didn't ask her even though we'd heard the rumors and seen the treasure maps in the tourist stores. She would've called it hokum, and she didn't like hokum. She was real practical, down-to-earth. Accepted what came and made the best of it. Married a rancher near Rawlins after a couple years, but she always stayed in touch with her daughter. I never met Mary's second husband; he died before I was born. That was when she moved to Riverton to be closer to her daughter. Little Mary was my mother." Julia was quiet a long moment, as if she were pulling a reluctant memory from the back of her mind. "We were a small family, just

Mom and Dad, me, and Grandmother. When Mother died, it about killed Grandmother, but she went on. Like I say, she was a tough woman."

"What about George Cassidy," Father John said. "Did she ever see him again?"

"Oh, more than once. Like I say, he never forgot her. I heard he came to visit old friends in the 1920s before I was born. Came again in the 1930s, and every time he came, he visited Mary. I remember her talking about how all of them went on a camping trip in the mountains in the summer of 1934. She told stories about how they left the others at the campsite and hiked around the mountains together, just her and George. He told her all about himself, how he'd gone straight, got married and had a son, and built a business in Washington. It made her happy to know he hadn't been run to the ground and shot like an animal, and all those stories about him and Sundance getting killed in Bolivia was just hogwash."

"Were they looking for the treasure?" Father John said.

"They were looking, all right, but they never found it. I figure George must've told Mary where he'd buried it, and he was counting on her to help him find it. But she said she didn't know anything about it." Julia put up a hand and waved at the light, as if she might turn it off. "Where are we now?" she said. "The sun is awful bright."

"It's okay, Mom," Charlotte said. "You're still telling stories about your grandmother Mary."

"Mary." Julia spoke the name softly, and her gaze took that inward look again. "She was a fine woman. Very tough, or she wouldn't have survived. I remember how she always wore a red gingham dress with a big white apron she'd lift to wipe her face. She worked hard . . ."

"Mom, do you remember any other stories about George Cassidy?"

"He gave Mary this ring with a real opal." She raised her hand again and turned it in the light. A gold ring with a round stone sparkled on her finger. "Sent it to her after he went back to Washington. Look here, inside." She slid the ring off her finger and held it out.

Charlotte got up, took the ring, and peered at the inner circle. Then she handed the ring to her mother and sat back down. "Tell us what the inscription says."

"Geo C. to Mary B." Julia slipped the ring back on her finger and patted it, as if she wanted to protect it. "Grandmother wore this ring until the day she died."

THE RESIDENTS HAD settled into a steady line that shuffled out the double doors when Todd Paxton slid in beside Father John. "That wraps things up," he said. "We've got other folks that claim Butch Cassidy came back here. Lone Bear remembers seeing him. Historians aren't going to like it, but people hereabouts say they know what they know. I appreciate your help." Father John shook the man's hand. The film crew was about finished packing up.

Father John went over to Julia and thanked her for her stories. The old woman looked up, blinking him back into memory. "My stories, yes, my stories," she said, and he realized that she was about to sink again into the space that she occupied most of the time. He leaned in closer. "One other thing, Julia. Did your grandmother ever mention the name of the hired hand?"

She started shaking her head before he had finished the question. "She said, 'Let it be. What's done is done.' But one time I heard her talking to my mother. She said Walking Bear seen Jesse get thrown from his horse."

One of the Walking Bears. Never owned a spread of their own. Hired out on ranches. It made sense. Father John thanked the old woman again.

Charlotte stood by her mother, an arm around her shoulders. She smiled at Father John as she said, "You did great, Mom."

"Did I?" Julia said.

OUTSIDE FATHER JOHN checked his cell. A voice mail from Macon Walking Bear. He got into the pickup, pressed the callback button, and listened to the ringing of a phone somewhere in Oklahoma.

32

"THIS IS MACON Walking Bear. You called me."

Father John thanked the man for returning his call. A hot, dry breeze whipped around the pickup. The air tasted of the West, of dust and dried sage and pine trees and asphalt leaking heat. He had parked in the shade of a tree, but arrows of sun lay across the passenger seat and the heat rose toward him. He left the driver's door open and sat crosswise behind the wheel, one boot on the pavement, explaining to the man on the other end that he was the pastor at St. Francis Mission on the Wind River Reservation.

"I remember the place. Sent my son to school there."

"I'm calling about James."

The line went silent, and for a moment Father John thought the connection had been cut off. Then the voice said, "What about him?"

"I understand he graduated from college and worked in the oil fields."

"Yeah, that's true. Always was smarter than the cousins. Accounts for why I moved the family to Oklahoma to be close to my wife's people. They were a smart bunch, real good educations, not like that bunch of Walking Bears on the rez. I didn't want James to be like them. After he got out of school, he got real good jobs, made a lot of money."

"Did he ever . . ." Father John took a moment to parse the words and arrange the question. "Show an interest in the treasure Butch Cassidy supposedly buried in the mountains here?"

"That old myth!" Macon Walking Bear chuckled, or perhaps he was coughing up phlegm. "Swore up and down from the time he was a kid that one day he'd find that treasure. Had a collection of maps when we moved off the rez. Always sure one of them was genuine." Another gravelly noise came down the line. "I never took much notice of those old stories myself. Folks got to believe in something. I figured if James wanted to believe in a treasure, it was all right with me."

Father John leaned his shoulder against the seat. He was thinking that Cutter could have come here to find a treasure he had always believed existed. Which meant he had left a good job, moved away from family. Which meant he was serious. How serious was he? Enough to murder a cousin and perhaps cause the death of another?

And something not quite right here, something off. He could sense it. The logic made sense: local boy grows up with rumors of a treasure, moves away, but never forgets and one day, he returns. He could still see the brown-faced boy smiling out of the photo, and he tried again to fit the image into the features of the man who had come to the mission. Looking for his roots. And remembering a boarding school he had never known.

"You still there?"

"Sorry," Father John said. "Do you think your son came back here to look for the treasure?"

"He always talked about going back, but he was too busy working, never got to go anywhere. Hardly ever came home. I guess that's what happens. You get your kids up and educated, and they leave you."

"What do you mean?" Cutter's father didn't know his son had moved here? "He seems to be settling in here just fine."

The line went silent again. Then, a strangled sob, like the sound of a branch breaking. "Who are you?" The words were shaky and uncertain.

"I'm the pastor . . ."

"You're an impostor. What do you want? What are you trying to sell me?"

"I don't understand," Father John said, but he was beginning to understand. He pushed on: "Tell me about James."

"My son is dead. You call me with some fool story about him being on the rez! What do you want?"

"Mr. Walking Bear," Father John said, taking his time. "There is a man here who claims to be your son. I'm sorry."

"Who? Who would claim such a thing?"

"I was hoping you could help. I know this is painful . . ."

"You don't know anything."

"Do you mind telling me how your son died?"

"Yeah, I mind." Silence again, but this time it came with a heaviness, as though the man's grief and thoughts had moved ahead of his words. "It was an accident, they said. They said James was up on an oil rig inspecting some equipment when he slipped and fell. James had crawled all over oil rigs for years. He was sure-footed as a mountain goat. They said he hit his head and it killed him. Now you tell me there's somebody there . . ."

"I am so sorry about your son," Father John said. He waited a moment before he went on. "The man here calls himself Cutter. The Walking Bear cousins said they recognized him."

"They're fools. I thought about sending word up there that James had been killed, but I never got around to it. We left that bunch of Walking Bears behind. The family we belonged to was here in Oklahoma."

"Did James ever mention anyone named Cutter?"

"James was Cutter! He was the best at cutting out the cattle that needed branding. He was the best . . ." Another sob broke in. "The best at everything he did. Sure he used to talk about taking a vacation and going to the rez to look for treasure. Uncle of mine named Luther Walking Bear always claimed he had Butch Cassidy's map, which was a lie, but it got the kids excited. He was going to ask my uncle if he could see the map. When my uncle died, James figured one of the cousins took the map. He thought he could make a deal. The cousin would let him see the map, and he'd share whatever he found. A dream was all it was."

A dream he could have passed on to someone else, Father John was thinking. "Did he ever mention anyone he worked with?"

"James had a lot of friends. Everybody liked him."

"Anyone he might have told about the treasure?"

"Didn't talk about it to strangers. Didn't want people thinking he was nuts. But there was one guy—give me a minute, I'll come up with the name. This guy was a treasure hunter. Used to take off from time to time to hunt for gold the Spanish buried in Colorado. James said he never found anything, but he liked the hunt." Another pause before the man went on. "He showed up here after

James got killed, said he was real sorry. Big, good-looking fellow, reminded me of James. His name just came to me, Mike Nighthorse. He was with James when he fell."

Father John told the man again how sorry he was. Then he asked if he had heard that two of the cousins, Robert Walking Bear and Dallas Spotted Dear, had died. Mysteriously, he said.

Macon Walking Bear said nothing, but the sound of his breathing rushed over the line like the wind. "That impostor around when they died?"

"It's possible," Father John said.

"You got to root him out. You hear me? You got to root out evil."

ROOT OUT EVIL. Dear Lord! Is that what the man who had made himself into Cutter Walking Bear was? Evil. Father John stared at the cell in his hand for a long moment after the line went dead. He had told the dead man's father that he would take the information to the FBI agent. The wind had picked up and was whipping through the pickup and banging the door against his leg. He slid inside, closed the door, and called Gianelli's office.

"Sorry, Father." A polite voice on the other end, a new recruit, maybe, anxious to please. "Agent Gianelli isn't in, but I can try to reach him and give him a message."

"Ask him to call me," Father John said. "It's urgent."

He put the pickup into reverse, then shifted into forward and followed a sedan onto the street. The light at the intersection ahead was green, and he sped up, close behind the sedan, making a left as the light switched to red. He made another left onto Highway 789 and called Vicky's office, the cell tight against his ear, waiting for Annie's voice. The phone rang several times before the robotic voice told him to leave a message, and that was strange. Annie was in the office every weekday, nine to five.

He had slowed down for the right turn into the reservation. Ahead, the steeple of St. Francis Church poked through the cottonwoods and rose against the clear, blue sky. He pressed hard on the gas pedal and drove on. A left onto Rendezvous Road. He was close to Lander when he tried Vicky's office again. The same message; no one in the office. He realized he was weaving across the lanes and tried to concentrate on holding the pickup steady as he called Gianelli again. The same polite voice assured him he would pass on the message the minute the agent called in.

Vicky was in court. He kept reminding himself. In court. In court. She was safe.

"WHERE ARE WE going?" Vicky gripped the steering wheel; her knuckles rose into small white peaks. A part of her knew exactly where Cutter would take her. He had forced her down the back stairs and out into the parking lot. Her car, he'd said, not that old wreck of a rental. Besides he had left it six blocks away and walked to her apartment. No sense in alerting her he was here, now was there? He had handed her the keys she had taken from the bowl.

He was laughing to himself. Congratulating himself. He ignored her question, and she asked it again.

"Let's say you were so distraught over the death of your client . . ."

"What are you talking about?" The two-lane road ahead lifted itself into the foothills, the same road she and Ruth had taken to Bull Lake. The same road she had driven alone when she had found the piece of map at the campsite.

"I'm through playing games with you." A new menace in his voice, as if he were no longer engaged, as if whatever happened next would happen on its own. "We could have been a great couple, you and me. I know you saw it. What is it about you? So suspicious, asking questions that were none of your business, pushing all the time. I never liked pushy women. I wanted you to trust me. Stop asking questions and trust me."

"You killed Robert." The words surprised her, welling up from someplace deep inside.

"Dallas told you that?"

"It's true, isn't it?" The road started to wind upward. Around each bend she could see the roofs of the reservation shimmering in the sun, an ordinary day, people going about their lives. The red and blue lights of police cars flashed in the distance. She pushed on: "Dallas told me how you killed Robert." It was a lie, but it was all she had. "He told Gianelli, too."

"Really?" Cutter laughed to himself again, and the sound was like the gurgling of water deep inside a pipe. "Too bad Dallas is dead. That leaves only you. I doubt any judge would allow that kind of hearsay, but you're the lawyer. Maybe you know some way to get around it. Can't take any chances, can we?"

"You dragged Robert to the lake and threw him in." She was making it up now, imagining how it must have happened. She waited for Cutter to object, but he stayed quiet, and she went on. "There's a steep drop-off. You made sure Robert was in the deep water, while you stayed where it was shallow and kicked him under."

"Kicked?" Cutter flinched forward. He lifted the gun and pushed the muzzle into her neck. Show him nothing, she told herself. Not the tremors running through her body, not the fear thumping inside her. A lifetime passed, as she maneuvered the Ford around another bend. He would not kill her here. A plunge off the side of the road, and he would die as well.

She felt the pressure release, the cold, hard muzzle move away. "The fool couldn't swim. All I had to do was watch him flail around trying to keep his face out of the water and put a boot on his back. God, he took a long time to die, and that fool cousin of his shouting how we had to help him, get him out before he drowned. Well, that was the point. I told Dallas to shut up or he'd be in the lake with him. That Indian turned white, so I knew he couldn't swim, either. That was my mistake, my only mistake besides being taken in by you. What a shame. You and me could've made a great team."

"Your mistake?"

"Not killing that sonofabitch right then. Not throwing him into the lake. I got to thinking, it might look strange. Two men, both drowning? Of course, it would've made perfect sense. Robert got himself in too deep and his cousin went after him. Yeah, that was my mistake, leaving Dallas around to shoot off his mouth, drag you into it. Soon as I realized he was talking to you, there was nothing else I could do."

"You killed him."

"It was an accident. Just like Robert drowning. Accidents, both of them. I admit I helped a little. Got Dallas to agree to meet me up here where nobody would overhear us making plans. Oh, he was greedy. Kept thinking he was going to get some of the treasure, so he drove up here. All I had to do was bash him in the head with a rock, stuff him back into the cab of his truck, and push it over the edge. Damaged the front of my truck, was the only problem."

An awkward silence stretched into minutes. He had told her everything, but what difference did it make? He intended to kill her. They would go to the lake, where he would force her out of the car and march her into the water, and she would go. Because otherwise he would shoot her. In the water, she would have a chance. She could swim, but how far would she make it? To the far side of the lake? She swallowed the laugh that bubbled up inside her, crazy and wild. The water was freezing; she would go under in minutes.

She drove around another curve. They were high up the mountain now, in the area where Dallas's truck had gone off the edge. She could see the lake below in the distance, silent and glistening.

"Take it easy, my love." The menacing voice again. "We're going to take that dirt road down to the lake nice and slow so you can enjoy the view."

33

FATHER JOHN TURNED into the driveway past the sign that said, Vicky Holden, Attorney-at-Law. Vicky's Ford was usually here. Annie's car. Roger's car. All stacked up, one after the other. The driveway was empty.

He jumped out, ran across the grass, and tried the front door. The doorknob was rigid. A door that was never locked during business hours. Anyone could walk in.

He felt a chill shoot down his spine. The man who called himself Cutter could have walked in and . . .

Dear Lord. He went to the front window and peered inside. The screen glowed on Annie's computer. The ceiling lights shone on the tabletop and the beveled-glass doors that stood open. He could see Vicky's vacant desk. There was no sign of anyone.

There were more rooms, bedrooms that had been turned into Roger's office and a conference room, and he made his way around the side of the house, looking into the windows. Roger's computer was also on. It was as if they had all vanished.

He went back to the pickup and tried Gianelli's office again. The same assurances from the same voice, a little testier now. "As I explained, Father . . ."

A thousand images ran through his head. Cutter bursting into the office, rounding up Annie, Roger, Vicky. He would have a gun—how else could he control them? Order them out into a truck or SUV? Maybe Vicky's Ford, Cutter in the back, the gun on Vicky. *Drive where I say or she dies.*

But that didn't make sense. The other vehicles would still be here if Cutter had forced them all into Vicky's SUV. He had to think logically. Vicky had a court hearing this morning, which meant she wasn't in the office. Did Cutter manage somehow to force Annie and Roger to go somewhere? It was Vicky he was after. Vicky, he would suspect of having worked things out. Maybe Dallas Spotted Deer had told her more about what happened to Robert—more details than he had relayed to Father John—and Cutter had to make sure she didn't pass on those details to Gianelli. But what if she had?

Nothing made sense. If that were the case, she would have told him, he was certain. He knew her so well, how she thought and felt about so many things. He would know if she had been holding something back. The wind knocked at the sides of the pickup, sending the cab into a swaying motion like that of a boat on a windy lake.

Another thought hit him then, like a fist to his stomach. Suppose Vicky hadn't gone to court? Cutter could have waylaid her before she got there. He could have gone to her apartment. The court clerk would have called the office and Annie and Roger—

dependable Annie and Roger, looking out for Vicky as if she were family—had gone in search of her. They would start at the apartment.

He rammed the gear into reverse, sped backward, squealed onto the street, and drove forward. Taking the corners fast, rolling through the stop signs, all senses alert. He took in everything at once, the street ahead, the cross streets, the other cars lumbering along as he drove past. He saw the lights flashing a block away, the congestion, the gawkers coming down the sidewalk. Oh God. Please, no. Please, no.

He spotted Annie huddled with a bunch of people outside the apartment building as he swung into the parking lot. She had seen the pickup, because she was running toward him when he jumped out. He left the door open behind him. "Where's Vicky? Where is she?" The sound of his own voice clanging around him, frantic, angry.

"Oh, Father!" Annie burst into sobs. Beyond her was a blur of officers at the entrance to the apartment building, Roger gesturing with both hands. "She's gone."

She told him the rest of it, sobbing and trying not to sob, struggling to make sense out of the senseless, fit the pieces into an order that kept dissolving into the chaos of reality. How an elderly woman on Vicky's floor had heard a loud argument, how a man told her everything was fine, just a quarrel with his fiancée, and how she knew that wasn't right because that nice Indian lawyer didn't have a fiancé. She had called the police, but by the time an officer arrived, they were gone, Vicky and the man. A tall, dark man, looked Arapaho, and she didn't know how they had left, because she had been watching through her peephole and they hadn't taken the elevator.

"Cutter took her," Annie went on. "He was always around.

Everywhere you looked, there he was. Wanted to be helpful, he said, but there was something wrong. Oh, I see it now. Something wrong, and now he's got her." She started sobbing hard, mopping at her cheeks. "I don't know where he could have taken her."

"I do," Father John said. A policeman had walked over, and he told him to get ahold of Agent Gianelli. "The man who killed Robert Walking Bear and Dallas Spotted Deer has Vicky. Tell him he has taken her to Bull Lake to kill her."

He swung around, ran back to the pickup, and drove out of the lot, past the officers milling about, the cars slowing along the street, the gawkers and neighbors standing on the sidewalk, the blue and red flashing lights, and nothing clear except the road ahead, the strip of asphalt leading through the reservation and into the mountains.

"WHO ARE YOU?" They were parked on the dirt path that ran between the campsite and the lakeshore. Keep him talking, Vicky thought. Cutter, or whatever his name was, liked to talk about himself and, in some strange way, she understood that he wanted to tell his story. He was proud of what he had done. Gotten away with killing two men, making the deaths look like accidents. All that careful planning, and no one would ever know. He had to brag to someone, and she would not live to tell anyone else.

"Who do you want me to be? Your brave warrior taking care of you, walking ahead to make sure the path is clear for you, keeping you safe?" He paused, and for a moment his features dissolved into a sad, wistful look. "That was all I wanted, to be your warrior." He let out a deep sigh, as if an impossible future had somehow melted away.

"You are an impostor."

"Please." He turned toward her and smiled. "Tell me, Vicky Holden, attorney-at-law, who isn't an impostor? We all remake ourselves, don't we? Become different people as we go along. It is necessary, you know. We put on a certain face, depending upon where we are and what we want to accomplish. What's that quote from Shakespeare? A man can smile and smile and still be a villain?"

"You came here pretending to be James Walking Bear. You are an impostor with a made-up story. Fowler Oil Company has never heard of you, right? All of it was part of your story."

"And I have lived it very well, I must say. The cousins fell all over themselves to welcome James home. James would've been pleased." He pointed the gun at her head; his other hand worked the door handle behind him. "It's time to complete my mission."

Vicky felt her mouth go dry, and that was odd because tears were blurring her vision. She fought to keep herself from breaking down and crying. She would not go to her death crying! "Mission?" she said, grabbing for a lifeline, anything to keep him talking. He was a madman, a chameleon, two people, three people—who knew how many—at the same time. Dimly, as if she were already underwater, vision blurred, gasping for breath, she saw that this was her only hope. "What mission? An old map to a treasure that doesn't exist?"

"Doesn't exist?" He tossed his head back and laughed. The gun waved in his hand. "A smart lawyer like you, and you don't get it. Well, that means nobody else is going to get it, either. No matter how many rumors might float around on your moccasin telegraph that Robert found the treasure, I can just sit tight for a year or two until everybody forgets. Then I can cash in."

"I don't believe you."

"Let me help you. A wooden box, twice the size of a cigar box, dirt lodged in the wood, the hinges rusted, and a lock that looked pretty solid, I have to admit. Robert wanted to break the box open with a rock, and I had to stop him. We weren't sure what was inside. I took the rock and struck the lock, and it fell off."

"You're lying," Vicky said, but part of her wasn't sure. A part of her had never been sure about this man.

"Stacks of gold coins, beautiful as the day they were minted. They shone in the sun like—well, like treasure. Real treasure. We started shouting and laughing. We danced around the campfire and threw the coins in the air, and you should've seen us scrambling to get them all. In the bottom of the box were stacks of banknotes and old bills. Who knows what they're worth? A fortune, a fortune, and for that I can only say, 'Thank you, Butch Cassidy.'"

Vicky stared at the man. A treasure people had been hunting for more than a century, that most people—sane people—had never taken seriously, had never believed. Something for the tourists. Keep them amused.

"You're telling me that Robert found the treasure?" True, he had been looking for years. He had taken the matter seriously; for him, the treasure had been real. And he had gotten the map from his grandfather's barn, a map that could have been genuine after all.

"He never would have found the treasure without me." Cutter had moved the gun back into his lap. He stared out the windshield as if the scenes of a movie were unfolding in the lake ahead. "The man couldn't read a map, that was his problem. He had it oriented all wrong. Mountains on the west so everything else was supposed to fall into place. But Butch had oriented the map from that strip of land over there." He nodded toward the shoreline where a finger of land jutted into the lake. "From over there, the mountains look like they are south, not west. Once I figured that out, I knew we had to look in a different place. We started at the strip and walked forward. According to the map, there was a tree with a horseshoe nailed on it, but that tree was gone. We kept walking until we found the four ponderosas that Butch had drawn, and twenty paces off—just like the map said—there was another clump of ponderosas. They were still there, and that's where we started digging, on the spot Butch had marked with a big X. We weren't three feet down when we hit the box."

"You wanted it all to yourself, so you killed Robert."

"I've been looking for treasure for a long time. I'm an expert at reading old maps." He spoke like a ventriloquist, lips clamped together. Vicky could almost smell the determination and outrage. "Robert would have spent the rest of his life looking, but he never would have found it. I wasn't greedy. I told him I wanted half, my fair share. I figured Robert could give Dallas a little out of his share—the cousinly thing to do. We would've all been happy. Sit on our treasure box for a while and then live like kings. But Robert . . ." He tossed his head back and studied the roof. "He was greedy. Claimed it was all his, that he got the map from his grandfather, and the treasure was his inheritance. So . . ." He let the rest of it hang between them.

"You killed him."

"I tried to make him understand. He wouldn't listen to reason."

"So you dragged him to the lake and threw him in. Why didn't Dallas try to stop you?"

Cutter grinned at whatever images were flashing in his mind. "It's a lot of gold. He figured he'd get a bigger share."

She understood now; the whole sordid account lay between them like the carcass of a buffalo. This man had strung Dallas along, letting him think he would get half of the treasure, and when Dallas realized Cutter had no intention of giving him more than a few coins—and maybe not that—he had started making anonymous phone calls, and for what reason? Blackmail a killer? Give me half or I'll go to the police?

My God. Vicky dipped her face into her hands. Her cheeks felt hot and moist. The man beside her had already killed twice for the treasure. And no one was coming to the lake. They had been talking for at least thirty minutes, and no one was coming.

The man who called himself Cutter must have sensed the same thing because he leaned over, yanked the keys out of the ignition, and swung them in front of her. "Like I said, I keep the keys this time. Get out."

She stopped herself from saying, *You'll have to shoot me here*, because she understood that he would. And he would concoct another story, make it look like somehow she had shot herself. She pushed the door open and made as if she were about to turn sideways to get out, her mind racing with the possibilities. The freezing lake loomed ahead; she would never survive. Cutter got out, slammed the door, and started around the SUV, waving her out with the gun. She was on automatic now, no longer thinking, a robot going through the motions. She kept her eyes on him and dug into her bag on the seat next to her, past her wallet, her glasses case, a package of tissues. Then she had them, the cold, sharp edges of her keys in her fingers. Cutter still waving the gun, starting down her side of the SUV. She opened the door not more than an inch and jammed the key into the ignition. He was close, half a foot from her side mirror. Grinning. Grinning. She took hold of the handle, threw her weight against the door and slammed it against the man with everything she had. He staggered backward, a startled look replacing the grin. She pulled the door in as he lunged toward her, then slammed him again, and this time he went down.

She turned the key, stomped down on the gas pedal and drove off, the door still open, banging back and forth. She kept driving. In the rearview mirror, she saw Cutter getting to his feet and racing after her. Then he stopped and went into a crouch, the gun steady in both hands.

She swung the SUV off the road to the left, and the bullet blew out a rear window. Driving like a crazy woman now, weaving back and forth, on and off the road, gunshots crashing around her, until she was tearing along the highway, barely slowing for the sharp turns, rocking back and forth. Finally the lake and Cutter and the gun lay far below, out of sight, and she slowed down a little and drove on.

She was halfway down the mountain when she saw the red pickup coming toward her. She pulled over and rocked to a stop, and in the next moment, she was in John O'Malley's arms, no longer able to hold back the sobs.

Everything moved in slow motion now. Pulling herself back, choking out the words: Cutter at the lake. Cutter had a gun. John O'Malley held a cell to his ear, shouting to someone on the line to get officers to the lake. The man calling himself Cutter had abducted Vicky Holden, but she had escaped. She was safe. Then repeating her own words: *He had a gun.*

John O'Malley put the cell back into his pocket and guided her toward the pickup, his arm firm about her waist. And she was safe, she was thinking. She was safe now. "Let's get you home," he said.

The panic rose again, stopping her breath, as he drove up the mountain—back toward Cutter and the gun. A wide spot on the road, a deep shoulder, materialized. John O'Malley turned around and headed downhill. The panic began to lift, like a fever that came and went. She willed her heart to stop racing, her hands to stop shaking, and started to tell him what Cutter had told her, then stopped herself. A dim realization moving like a shadow through her thoughts. She was the only one who knew, and she should be dead. If Cutter evaded whomever John O'Malley had called, he would come for her. And he would come for the man beside her.

"Tell me," John O'Malley said, as if he had read her thoughts, and the words burst forth, a dam breaking. She told him how Cutter had helped Robert find the treasure, how they had quarreled, how Cutter had thrown the man into the lake and pushed him down, how Dallas had seen it happen and hadn't done anything to help Robert. The treasure was all that mattered, and Dallas had started making anonymous calls to force Cutter to give him half.

"Do you think he was telling the truth? That they really found the treasure?"

Vicky shook her head, coming back to herself now, acutely aware of John O'Malley beside her. "Dallas thought so."

The reservation was rising toward them when she saw the flashing blue and red lights on the vehicles racing up the mountain. John pulled over and got out. The lead car stopped, two officers in the front seat. She caught a part of the conversation: John O'Malley saying that Vicky had left Cutter at the lake and that he had a gun, and the officer saying something about a SWAT team.

THE APARTMENT WAS hot and stuffy, even though someone had opened a window and the curtains were blowing in a hot wind. They sat around the coffee table, Vicky on the sofa, John and Roger across from her. Annie bustled about the kitchen and from time to time brought the coffeepot over and refilled their mugs. They weren't leaving, they had told her at least a dozen times. Not until Cutter was in custody. She watched the way their eyes kept sliding toward the door, as if they half expected Cutter to burst in.

She had told them everything she had told John O'Malley. They all knew what had happened; she had come to the conclusion that everyone should know that Cutter was an impostor. He was a killer. The news would spread over the moccasin telegraph, and he wouldn't be able to stop it. He couldn't kill everyone on the rez.

They had gone over and over it, trying to find a logical sequence that would explain what had happened. The more they talked, the more she felt like herself. A lawyer, examining the evidence, the anonymous voice on the phone saying he had witnessed a murder, the killer's own account of the murder.

A cell phone rang. "Yes?" John had put the cell phone on speaker, and Annie hurried over and perched on the armrest of Roger's chair. All of them, Vicky thought, hypnotized by the small rectangular object in John's hand. Gianelli's voice echoed around them, as if he were speaking from inside a metal chamber. "Cutter Walking Bear is dead. We found his body near the shore of the lake with a bullet wound to the head. Looks like he shot himself." There was a pause before he said, "I'm going to need statements from both you and Vicky."

Father John told him they were at her apartment, then ended the call and set the cell on the table. Still staring at it, all of them. Vicky felt a deep sense of relief wash over her, and something else, harder to grasp: a sense of sadness at the madness of it all.

She held John O'Malley's eyes for a long moment. "It's over," he said.

34

A SMALL GROUP of people had gathered in the far corner of St. Francis cemetery when Vicky turned onto the dirt road and parked behind a line of vehicles. It was eleven o'clock in the morning, the sun stationary in a glass-blue sky. On the graves, yellow, red, and white plastic flowers swayed and bent in the breeze. She made her way down a path of trampled grass to the open grave with the wooden casket suspended above it and took a place in the back, behind the other mourners. John O'Malley walked along the edge of the grave and sprinkled holy water from the pottery bowl he held in one hand.

She had meant to come to the funeral Mass for Robert, but Luke had stopped by the office with his son, Sam. The hearing had been rescheduled for last Monday, and the judge had agreed that there was not enough evidence to support a petition of neglect and dependency. He had reestablished the visitation orders that had been issued at the time of the divorce. An energetic child, Sam, smiling and scampering about while Luke talked about the plans he had made. Camping trips, powwows, rodeos. Every other weekend would be their weekend, he and Sam, and he intended to show his son the world. At least his part of the world. By the time they had left, she knew Mass would be over. It looked as if the burial was almost over.

Ruth stood in front, not far from the opening. Bernie on one side of her and Big Man on the other, holding her upright as if she might topple into the grave herself. The red hair had been pushed and prodded into place, except for a few curls that sprang loose on each side; the back of her neck looked pink in the sun. She wore a blue dress that pulled across her hips. Sobs and gasps of air mixed with the sound of the wind.

The uneasy feeling that Vicky had struggled with since the day at the lake still gripped her. It was over, John O'Malley had said, and yet something continued to nag at her. She had lain awake nights trying to assemble the pieces, but the picture eluded her. She tried to shrug away the unsatisfied feeling. Not all the truth could be known. It was enough to focus on the facts: an Arapaho from Oklahoma named Mike Nighthorse had assumed another man's identity, ingratiated himself with the Walking Bear cousins, located a treasure, and killed two men before he had killed himself. It made sense. And yet, the sense of a missing piece rankled like a burr under her skin.

John O'Malley had stepped back now, and Eldon Lone Bear moved toward the grave. Lifting both hands toward the sky, he began to pray: *Ha, hedenieaunin nenetejenuu nau neja vedawune. Hevedathuwin nenaidenu jethaujene. Hethete hevedathuwin neha-the Ichjevaneatha haeain ichjeva.*

The words floated into her mind—so many funerals, so many elders beseeching the Creator to remember his creature who was returning to his true home. She wasn't sure if she understood the words or if the meaning had been imprinted on her heart over the years. *Our bodies die and return into dust. Our souls live forever. Good souls go to God, to our home on high.*

The mourners remained still, heads bowed. Even John O'Malley, bowing, in respect for other ways. *There is only one God*, Grandfather said, *and many ways to pray*. Vicky bowed her own head and tried to put away the image of Robert Walking Bear going underwater, struggling to come up, and being pushed back. He was at peace now with the Creator and the ancestors. And the man who said he was Cutter? Where was his soul? She squeezed her eyes shut against the glare of the sun and the dark figures around the grave. Let the elders and John O'Malley's theologians grapple with the answer. The man's body lay in the morgue in the basement of the courthouse in Lander while Gianelli tried to locate a near relative. Even James Walking Bear's father had offered to look through his son's things on the off chance there was a mention of Nighthorse's family. It was the humane thing to do, he had told John O'Malley, even if the man had killed his own son. There must be someone who would want to know what happened to him.

The prayer ended, and two musicians seated at the foot of the grave began pounding the drum. The thuds reverberated around the cemetery, rising into the heavens, beseeching the Creator himself. Someone had begun turning the wheel that lowered the coffin into the grave, and the squealing noise mingled with the drumbeats.

"No! No!" Ruth twisted and pulled against the efforts of Bernie and Big Man. "Robert! Come back. Come back." Then John

O'Malley was beside her, bent close, saying something that Vicky knew would be comforting. He was a priest; he understood grief.

Finally the little crowd started to break up. One by one walking up to Ruth, taking her hand, giving her a hug, kissing her cheek, then walking back to the road, grass blowing about their ankles. Lone Bear stopped to talk for a moment before he nodded and moved on. Pickups belched into life and started toward Seventeen-Mile Road. Ruth's hands rested in John O'Malley's. She should feel free to come to the mission any time she needed to talk, he was saying as Vicky walked up.

Ruth yanked herself free and pulled herself to her full height, like a drunk trying to pretend she was sober. Her face was strained and tear-smudged. "I didn't expect to see you here."

"I'm sorry I was late."

"You had better tell me, Vicky. I have a right to the truth."

Vicky sensed the uneasiness falling over her again, pinning her to the ground. "I don't understand."

"If you think you're going to get away with it, you couldn't be more wrong. I will follow you to the ends of the earth. I will have what belongs to me."

John O'Malley stepped closer to Vicky, as if he might shield her from a breaking storm. "What are you talking about?"

"You know where he hid the treasure, don't you?" For a moment Vicky thought the woman was referring to Butch Cassidy. "He told you how he killed Robert and that traitor, Dallas, so I figure he told you the rest of it."

"What makes you so sure he found the treasure?" Vicky was beginning to understand, as if a shadow had moved past, leaving her in the sunlight.

"Cutter told me he found the treasure. Oh, Robert was close, but it was Cutter who could read the map." She tossed her head sideways and laughed, and in that instant, Vicky understood. The pieces fell into place, the picture now as clear as if she were staring at a photograph. She exchanged a quick glance with John O'Malley, and in his eyes she saw a new understanding take shape.

Vicky kept her gaze on the redheaded woman, anger flashing in her dark eyes. "Is that what you told Cutter? Robert was close to finding the treasure? Did you encourage him to find a way to go with Robert? Convince Robert they'd have a better chance of success together? And what about Dallas? Did Robert ask Dallas to come along in case they found the treasure and a cousin they hadn't seen in years tried anything? Was that how it went?"

Ruth took a step backward, as if she could escape the questions. Her features were like stone, not a muscle flinching, a nerve pulsing. Her eyes as dark as the color of dead leaves. "Twenty years listening to how Robert was going to dig up a treasure box and make us rich. One day he told me he was getting close to where it was buried. The next time he came back from the mountains, he said he was getting closer. It was by Bull Lake, he said. All he had to do was get the right orientation. I believed him. I started making plans to go to L.A. and start beauty school and get me a new life. Robert told me to forget it. He said the treasure was going to buy him a big ranch; he had his eye on a spread in the red hills. There wasn't going to be any share for me. I could move onto his fancy new ranch or not, it didn't matter to him. Then Cutter came around, and I fell for him, just like he fell for me. He said he'd see I got my share of the treasure. Funny, isn't it?" She tilted her head back, looked up at the sky, and laughed. "Now the treasure is mine. All I have to do is find it. Where did he hide it, Vicky?"

"Cutter lied about a lot of things."

"He told me he loved me, and he didn't lie about that. He took care of me. Came over to the house, fixed things. Looked out for me."

And bided his time, Vicky was thinking. Waiting until he could leave with a box of gold coins and old banknotes, disappear and become someone else in a faraway place where nobody had heard of Cutter Walking Bear or Butch Cassidy's buried treasure. Vicky swallowed back the acid rising in her throat. She had to turn away. Ruth had believed in the man, and so had she. Missing all the signs, the phony, helpful, on-the-spot man trying to reconnect with his roots because she had wanted to believe. My God, what a fool she had been.

"You won't get away with it." Ruth's voice was low, infused with contempt. "The fed's looking everywhere. Safety deposit boxes, the house Cutter was renting. The cops tore out the walls, lifted the floorboards. But Cutter was too smart to leave the treasure in any obvious place. He buried it, didn't he? The way I figure, he buried it in the same place where he'd found it and destroyed the map. He was the only one who knew where the treasure was."

"If he had told me," Vicky said, "I would have told Gianelli."

Ruth shook her head. "You're biding your time, like Cutter did. Waiting to go up there and dig it up yourself. Well, you won't find it. I looked at that map enough times to memorize it. I know where he hid that treasure, and I will find it." She pivoted about and started off, arms pumping in the wind, the blue dress wrapping around her legs. She reached a pickup, flung herself inside, and drove off, clouds of dust rising around the wheels.

They were alone, she and John O'Malley, the empty space and sky, the whole reservation and open plains stretching around them. Vicky turned toward him, but before she could say anything—as if he could read her thoughts—he said, "The man was good at what he did, Vicky."

She started walking, aware of John O'Malley beside her. Two vehicles parked at the side of the road now, the Ford and the old red pickup. They were almost to the road when she said, "Do you believe Ruth is right? Cutter reburied the treasure and burned the map?"

"It's possible." John O'Malley was quiet a moment. Finally he said, "It would have given Cutter another reason to kill Dallas Spotted Deer, if he thought Dallas might remember the location."

All of it making sense now, Vicky thought. "Even if Dallas had never made the phone calls," she said, "he was a dead man. Cutter had been waiting for the right time, but that's what he did best. Lure people in, wait for the right time to do what he wanted."

John O'Malley didn't say anything, but she could feel the warmth of his hand on her back. Then he stopped and turned her toward him. "I have something for you," he said, holding out a ticket. "It's for *Rigoletto* at the Central City Opera House outside Denver in August."

"Opera?" Vicky took the ticket and stared at it. She had never attended an opera, and the thought of all that music and story unfolding on a stage made her feel like a kid about to open a package.

"Maris Reynolds gave me two tickets," John O'Malley was saying. "I think you'd enjoy seeing an opera."

Vicky looked up at him, then went back to staring at the ticket in her hand. "Denver." So far away, a different world. She lifted her eyes to his again. "I've promised Lucas I would spend a week with him this summer. I'll schedule my visit around the opera. How wonderful."

"You should take this," he said, holding out the other ticket. "For Lucas."

Vicky laughed and shook her head. "Oh no, John. No one will enjoy the opera as much as you. And I'll need you to explain it to me. Thank you."

They started walking, and she said: "There's something else I want to thank you for. Coming to Bull Lake after me."

"You already thanked me."

"If you had gotten to the lake, Cutter would have killed us both."

"Don't think about it, Vicky." They reached her Ford. John O'Malley took her hand and reined her to a stop beside him. "We're here, aren't we? We're still here."

AUTHOR'S NOTE

This is a work of fiction, although I have endeavored to convey a sense of Butch Cassidy from the research I did into his life and times. With few exceptions, Butch's story conveyed here is drawn from historical sources. For the purposes of the plot, I have taken the following detours from the historical record:

Butch is believed to have buried a part of his stolen treasure near South Pass City in the Wind River range, southeast of Lander. For the purposes of the plot, I had him bury the treasure near Bull Lake on the Wind River Reservation. In my story, he left behind a map, but there is no record that he may have done so.

Mary Boyd is a historical figure who had an ongoing relationship with Butch Cassidy in the early 1890s. At one point she referred to herself as Butch's "commons-law-wife" [sic]. She was half white and half Indian, from the Wind River Reservation, although the historical record is not clear whether she was Shoshone or Arapaho. She may have been both. She gave birth to a daughter in 1892 and gave the child to an Arapaho family to raise. Since she was involved with Butch at the time the child was conceived, Butch may have been the father. But he never recognized the child, and it is possible that Mary never told him about the child. Instead, she named an anonymous man in Lander as the father. Mary married a rancher by the name of Ol. E. Rhodes (a name that would fit in a Western cartoon.) Again, for the purposes of the story, I have given Mary a fictitious first husband—Jesse Lyons, who exists only in my imagination. Which is also the case for Charlotte Hanson and Julia Marks.

As far as I know, no one has ever found Butch's buried treasure, which doesn't keep people from looking.

Whether Butch Cassidy and the Sundance Kid were gunned down in Bolivia has been argued by historians since 1908 when the shoot-out occurred in the small town of San Vicente. The Pinkerton Agency, which prided itself on always getting their man, had followed Butch and Sundance all the way to Bolivia. The agency did not believe the outlaws died there, and they never closed the case. People who knew Butch well during his sojourn in the area of the Wind River Reservation believed that he returned several times in the 1920s and 1930s to visit old friends. In 1934 he took a camping trip into the mountains with several close friends, including Mary Boyd, then a widow. It is hard to imagine that folks who had been close to Butch—and in Mary's case, had had an intimate relationship with him—over a period of years could have been taken in by an impostor.

On the other hand, it is hard to let go of our legends. We want them to live on. And Butch Cassidy was a legend.

* * *

THERE ARE DOZENS of books and hundreds of articles on Butch Cassidy. I read as many as possible. The books I found most helpful were: *The Last Outlaws,* by Thom Hatch; *In Search of Butch Cassidy,* by Larry Pointer; *Butch Cassidy, My Uncle,* by Bill Betenson; *Butch Cassidy, A Biography,* by Richard Patterson; *Butch Cassidy in Fremont County,* by A. F. C. Greene; and the especially helpful *Butch Cassidy: Beyond the Grave,* by W. C. Jameson.